W9-BWT-203

Just a Girl

Look for these titles by
CARRIE MESROBIAN

Sex & Violence
Perfectly Good White Boy
Cut Both Ways

CARRIE MESROBIAN

HARPER
An Imprint of HarperCollinsPublishers

Library of Congress Control Number: 2016957936
ISBN 978-0-06-234991-0

Typography by Ray Shappell
17 18 19 20 21   CG/LSCH   10 9 8 7 6 5 4 3 2 1

First Edition

For Matilda, the girl of my world

SOPHOMORE YEAR

LONG, LONG AGO, before everything, before Rianne Hettrick-Wynne became the Hat Trick Girl thanks to Gabby, before Kaj had sex with Kip in the back of his mom's minivan, before Mercy and Caleb became the unbearably sweet pair that no one could stand to look at, there was the night of the first football game of the year, Rochester versus Wereford, when Eli came back.

Rianne hadn't drunk anything that night, though Kaj had helpfully made a mix of Sprite and Penny Drop that she and Gabby shared. Rianne hadn't liked it, so instead, she and Mercy smoked a ton of weed they'd gotten from Mercy's sister's gross ex-boyfriend, Jeff Melk, who'd been arrested with a meth lab in his mother's Oldsmobile's trunk, right in front of Jimmy John's.

From the time they'd all met behind the boarded-up Gas & Grub a few blocks from school to the moment they arrived at the football field, all four girls were somewhat fucked-up, but the walk had helped them get it together. They were still in volleyball season, still accountable to their coach and school rules. Lots of people got wasted during their sports season; the trick was knowing how to be sneaky, appear normal.

But after paying for admission, stopping at the concession stand for Kaj's popcorn and Mercy's Diet Coke, and weaving through the bleachers, Rianne realized she was a little *too* fucked-up. She hadn't eaten much dinner and she'd been up super late creeping on Aidan Golden online. Now everything was noisy and enlarged and slow. She watched Kaj wave at Kip and his hockey-player friends, watched Gabby rush over to Aidan Golden, and she immediately froze. She was sure everyone was looking at her, everyone would know she was wasted, everyone would know she thought Aidan Golden was cute.

But then Mercy was beside her, steadying her.

"Are you okay?"

"No."

"It's fine, you're fine, no one can tell, sit down," Mercy said. She took Rianne's hand and led her to an open spot on the bleachers. They were near the band, so it was too loud to talk. Mercy held Rianne's hand and nodded at her, smiling. Patted her shoulder. Rianne nodded back, though she couldn't talk. She barely wanted to move.

She was working on keeping her back straight and tight, fighting the dizziness, when Mercy said, "That's that chess nerd in my Spanish class," and pointed to the field. "Caleb Coyle," she added.

Caleb Coyle, in addition to chess nerdiness, was also a kicker for Wereford's football team.

Rianne nodded stiffly. Just nodding at her friend was a big deal, because she thought many other things. Like, *why don't you admit you like that kid, he's a cute guy, who cares if he's a freshman.* Mercy talked about Caleb the chess nerd way too much; Rianne knew Mercy liked him, but she didn't know why. She wanted to ask why, now, but she couldn't be sure she hadn't already. It was hard to tell what was actually happening in her mind and with her actual words.

This is when the words started tumbling in, of course. They tumbled in, whether she was sober or drunk or high. Whether she was awake or asleep.

CLAMOR. TURMOIL. COMMOTION. HAVOC.

And then she started to feel better. She wanted to laugh.

Rianne's brain was a pile of words. In any subject, she aced vocabulary tests. Even if she hated the rest of the class, even if she didn't keep up otherwise in a subject, even if her grades were a sad column of C+ and B−, and the classes she was put in were never Honors or AP—"So . . . what? We're stuck taking *Dishonorable Math*?" Mercy liked to say—words always came to her. She could spell anything. She could remember any definition. She only had to see the word, and ask what it meant, look at the definition, and it was there, marching across the screen of her mind. Then the words would break up into chunks. New words.

TUMULTUOUS: *out, molt, slum, slut, stout* . . .

Her grandma Hettrick had a game that did the same thing.

Boggle, it was called. You shook up cubes of letters and made as many words as possible. She played it for the first time as a little girl at her grandma's house. Before Grandma Hettrick's mind went into the shitter with Alzheimer's, at least. After that, Rianne got her own game of Boggle and played at the YMCA girls' sports camp on Gullwing Lake, with Kaj and Gabby and Mercy.

She slowly put on some lip balm, the honey-plum flavor spreading in a way that felt delicious. Her mouth was so dry.

PARCHED. DESICCATED. ARID.

She stared at the sweating cup of pop Mercy held. It wasn't hot, it was mid-September, but the cup was full of ice and Diet Coke and it looked absolutely delicious. After a while of contemplating how much she'd like to drink it, she worked out the sentence to ask. Put the words in the right order, slow and steady, across her brain.

"Mercy. Can I have some of your pop?"

Mercy laughed at her, handed it over. Like she'd been expecting this all along. They looked at each other and then Rianne laughed. Laughed and laughed and laughed.

"What are you laughing about?" Mercy asked.

But Rianne didn't know. So she sipped Mercy's Diet Coke until her cheeks hurt. Until the ice cubes squeaked. Until Mercy glanced at her and laughed again.

"Jesus, Ri," Mercy said, taking the cup and rolling her eyes.

Rianne watched the game flash in front of her. Piles of blue

Wereford players, piles of red Rochester players. Suddenly, she stood up, wobbling so bad that people in front of them freaked out and hollered at her.

"Whatever, assholes," Rianne said.

"Shh! Rianne! You are so fucked-up," Mercy whispered, grabbing her elbow. "Just chill."

"But I need to pee," she said. "Do you want me to pee right here? There's little kids playing under the bleachers! Do you want them covered in pee? Think of the children, Mercy." Rianne laughed at her own dumb words.

"Fine, go pee!" Mercy said. Laughing again.

People were laughing at her, but Rianne didn't care. Finally, the fun part of being high was happening. She wove her way down the bleachers, past the parents, past the cheerleaders doing basket tosses, past the field toward the bathrooms by the concession stand.

A guy in a red hoodie standing outside the girls' bathroom looked familiar. She squinted at him. He looked at her, like he knew her. Like he was waiting for her? Why? Rianne didn't trust it. Probably he was waiting for someone to come out; his girlfriend. She ran into the bathroom to pee. Then she washed her hands, put on fresh lip balm, fluffed out her hair. Checked her phone, which was almost dead. The battery had been draining quickly lately; she needed to ask her mom for a new one but had been avoiding it. All conversations with her mom lately ended up in a lecture about Rianne's lack of responsibility.

When she came out again, there was red hoodie guy. She looked away, feeling weird. But then he stopped her and said, "Hey, Rianne. Having fun?"

Because, yes: she knew him. Eli. Eli, one of the coach assistants at the YMCA girls' camp the summer after eighth grade. Eli, who wasn't the cutest of all the coach assistants, but he was okay. Eli liked playing Boggle too.

"I could be," she said back.

"Good answer," he said.

Then—she couldn't explain how or why, later—she was walking with him, through the parking lot. Then they were in his car. He was driving and he was talking, telling her how weird it was that she was here. He asked if she wanted to smoke out and she said yes, though she didn't need to. They were parked outside of Pizza Palace. The smell of pizza grease was so delicious and she wanted to go get a slice, but he said, *no, no. Let's go up and listen to music.*

"I thought you were going to college in Colorado?"

"I am," he said. "I'm just in town visiting some friends. Come on."

She followed him out of the car to a door beside Pizza Palace, up a set of steep stairs where he unlocked another door and sort of pushed her inside.

"Get comfortable," he said, and disappeared. She sank into a sofa across from a dusty television. Then he was back. He took off his red sweatshirt and he was wearing a tie-dyed shirt that said "FURTHER" in wavy letters and then he put on some live jazz thing and she didn't like it much. But it wasn't like she wanted to move. Or tell him that. The sofa they were sitting on was a dull yellow, the color of morning pee, but it had a velvety upholstery that her fingers kept sweeping over in no apparent rhythm.

Then he was in her face, his mouth over her mouth, full of the taste of pot and pizza sauce. The same Eli that stood behind her the last bonfire the last night of camp. She had accidentally touched his hand while they stood there, and then she'd grabbed it. He had looked at her for a minute, before sliding his hand around her waist, just above her shorts, to the material of one of the two sports bras she wore, and lightly brushed over her left boob. Eli held her boob while she stood in the dark and listened to the ghost story one of the girl coaches was telling, and she felt her nipple get hard under both sports bras. Later, she kissed him behind a tree before she went back to her cabin. The next day, camp was over and she was in the back of Mercy's mom's car with Gabby and Kaj and their sleeping bags and sports duffels, talking about everything except what Eli did.

Now Eli backed up for a second, repositioning himself over her. She watched him do it, her fingers clutching the material of the sofa. She smiled up at him, and asked him the one thing she could summon into her brain: "Is that why you didn't want to eat any pizza?"

"What?"

"Because you already ate it?"

"Can you just let me touch you?" he asked.

Except, he already was. Rubbing himself on her chest, her

boobs, his hands under her sweatshirt, pushing her bra and sweat-shirt up under her neck in a way that made her feel even heavier.

She tried to lie back so he could reach better but he kept press-ing and pushing like it didn't matter. Like he didn't care if she made it easier or not. Then he stuck his hand down her pants—they were just black elastic leggings beneath her blue Wereford volleyball sweatshirt—at least that was easy. But it didn't *feel* any easier. It was like he didn't know what he was grabbing for, because his hand smeared all over the place. Then he started rub-bing her in a way that made her feel like she had to pee and that was when reality returned. How much time had passed since leaving the football game. How heavy he was on top of her. How her hands remained by her sides. How they hadn't even talked about anything.

And it was as if her head was a hundred pounds and she was beneath him, sinking into the soft sofa, inch by inch. He lifted up and she wanted lift herself up but the sofa felt like it was suck-ing her lower. He unzipped his jeans and then there was his dick. Naked and hairy in the full light of this apartment.

She looked up then, past his head, at the curtain rod above the window behind the sofa, at the rust-colored draperies. Was that an iguana clutching the drapes? Was she hallucinating? The iguana didn't move. It was the color of overcooked peas.

Eli's dick was still out. He was squeezing it, for some reason. She looked at his face but he wasn't looking at her; he was looking down at his dick. She thought, *why? How did we get here so quick?*

His fingers flicked inside her in a way that hurt. She wished it didn't hurt, but wondered if that was because it had to hurt, when you were a virgin. Maybe it would hurt less with his dick than his fingers?

She looked back up. The iguana blinked at her. At least she thought it did. Maybe it was the bead on Eli's necklace blinking? The bead was shiny, and when the lamp behind them on the side table hit it just right, it made a spray of rainbow light. She wiggled her underwear out of the way, pushed them down, opened her knees, and then he was inside her. And weirdly enough, that didn't hurt.

Rianne wondered what he was thinking. His eyes were wide open. Now the bead on his necklace was a weird color. Bluish, then greenish. She wanted to touch it, ask him what it was made of. That was probably weird during sex, though. Still she reached up and touched it. He flinched and jerked back like she'd hurt him.

Then he was not inside her. She opened her mouth to ask what was wrong, and the blinking bead necklace disappeared down the collar of his shirt. Then he came all over her stomach. It felt warm, then instantly cold.

For a minute, neither of them moved at all. His eyes were closed tight.

"Whoa," he said finally. Then he moved off the couch and she listened to him walk away and she was completely still. She was afraid to touch the cum on her belly. Her stomach was round and full and she imagined his cum like the frosting on a cinnamon roll.

He came back with a roll of paper towels, nodded toward her belly, ripped off a few sheets to dab at her. She was embarrassed that he saw her stomach like that; it was her least favorite part of her body. She grabbed the paper towels, covered the sticky part of her belly with them. Asked if she could use the bathroom. He said, *yes, of course, it's right down the hall, on the left.* As if he was a stranger she'd just asked for directions.

The bathroom had a cat box in it full of twisted shits and the tile was speckled with bits of litter gravel. The shower curtain was tinged with rust and the toilet lid was already flipped up, gross and piss-stained. She wiped her belly off, catching bits of paper fluff on her skin. Her belly was too white to be a cinnamon roll; she should go tanning, just to make it look better. Not so sad and pillowy. Mercy said tanning was *batshit*, which was Mercy's word for everything she didn't like.

She tried to pee but couldn't. Her *cha*—again, Mercy and her sister's word for girl junk—burned and twitched, which made her feel sick. She straightened out her bra and then looked around. In the medicine chest, just toothpaste, toothbrushes, a crappy disposable razor. The toilet tank had a box of Q-tips and a bottle of generic lotion and, glinting beside it, Eli's weird necklace with the blue-green blinking bead. The clasp on the black cord was broken. Had she broken it? She thought she'd only touched it? Did it mean something to Eli? Maybe another girl gave it to him and now he was upset it was ruined. She slipped it into the pouch of her sweatshirt.

When she came back, there were other people coming in.

Carrying cases of beer, taking off their coats. She said to Eli, to these other people filling in around him, that she had to go. He just said, *okay*.

She took the stairs instead of the elevator. Then walked away from Pizza Palace, away from his car. Walked past the strip mall, counted the stores. Liquor Barrel. Planet Tan. Tobacco World. The Jimmy John's where Jeff Melk got busted, surrounded by six cop cars. The empty place that used to be a Kinko's. She was freezing cold and her head ached and her cha felt squishy and bruised. Her stomach, in her mind, was now branded in a coil of cinnamon roll icing. Why she thought of food, especially cinnamon rolls, which she liked, rattled her. The fact that he had come on her, like he was the only one thinking about getting her pregnant, made her feel dumb. She hoped it worked. She could not think about it. She had smoked too much weed.

The noise of the band and the football game was faint. The lights from the field glowed through the dark as she walked. She walked behind the out-of-business Gas & Grub and sat down on the pile of pallets where they'd met earlier. All of her friends knew who Eli was but she had never told them about what had happened at camp two summers ago. Two summers ago, Rianne was the tallest of all of them, with the biggest boobs and the longest hair and at that time, none of them had kissed anyone, unless you believed Gabby about her cousin Hector's friend at her aunt's wedding, which no one did.

But this was sophomore year and most of that had all changed. Now Mercy was the tallest, Kaj's hair was the longest, and Gabby had made out with Aidan Golden during the fireworks at Cattail Park on the Fourth of July. Only Rianne's boobs were still the biggest, a trophy that didn't seem to matter. Aidan Golden didn't like her; nobody had ever wanted anything to do with Rianne Hettrick-Wynne.

Which was why she had already decided not to tell them. The story wasn't a good one, either. What would she say? There was an iguana and a pee-colored couch and a blinking necklace and it didn't hurt, but now my cha feels irritated? Like your nose when you have a cold and keep wiping it with Kleenex. And he didn't say anything when she left. Just, *okay.* You couldn't tell that story to anyone and expect laughs. You couldn't explain how your belly was a cinnamon roll. Not when you weren't really sure you'd want to see Eli again, anyway.

"Where the fuck have you been?" Gabby shouted.

She blinked up at Gabby, at the rest of them. Told them she went to get food. That she was hungry. She was the hungry one. It was a joke. Rianne, the one who was always eating. Mercy, the picky one. Kaj, the only one who could cook. Gabby, the one who didn't ever give a shit about food. Gabby, the one who used to only eat orange foods for a while back in middle school. Not an eating disorder, but something weird like it.

And then they walked, shivering, to Perkins, to get coffee and pancakes before Kaj's dad came to pick them up. Nobody noticed that Rianne ordered pancakes even if she'd been off getting food. They talked about Kip Jelinek and Aidan Golden and Luke Pinsky having a party at his cabin on Gullwing Lake tomorrow and

Mercy was getting her license in a few weeks and it was another Friday night, like so many others they'd go on to have.

Rianne ate her pancakes and didn't say anything. She looked at her friends like they were a kind of foreign tribe. Observed Kaj's golden hoop earrings with the little bells on them, Gabby's short nails she painted dark bloody red, Mercy's blond hair in silly braided pigtails. Life was like that sometimes, even if you weren't fucked-up. It didn't make sense, how things ended up. How time went fast or slow. How things were heavy or light. Gabby was the rich one, Kaj the smart one, Mercy the athletic one. Rianne was a little of all those things, but not enough of anything to make her distinct. The hungry one. Not really the thing you wanted to be known for.

That night, she whizzed past her mother, who was reading in her chaise lounge in the new TV-room addition, said she had a headache and was going to bed. Her mother murmured, "good night" or something like it and Rianne, thankful to avoid her mom's usual scrutiny, sprinted up the stairs to take off her clothes and get in bed, pulling out Eli's broken necklace and putting it in the red lacquered jewelry box her dad had sent her from the Philippines.

It wasn't fair, that your friend's hair was longer or her legs were thinner and skinnier or that she got to kiss a boy you thought was cute. There was a weight of knowing things, Rianne decided, and it wasn't fair that everyone could see the numbers on the scale. She could skip the strange parts, tell them what Eli had done with his fingers and his mouth and dick. But telling them even that felt like losing to Rianne. You couldn't compete all the time, even if Coach Paula said that all of life was a game, a sport, unfolding on the court, a mass of defense and offense. The minute you said anything, offered it up, you were going to lose. That was why the red lacquered jewelry box on her dresser would come to fill up with many more things, not all of them secret. But most of them.

ONE

SENIOR YEAR

THE WORD CROSSING the screen of her mind: EXHIL-ARATE. An English vocabulary word, long past. But it fit right now, and the other words she could chip off from it were endless: *hex, ate, eat, hat, trial* . . .

It was eleven o'clock on New Year's Eve of her senior year of high school and Rianne smacked her hockey stick on the ice.

"Come on already!" she shouted. "Let's play!"

The word wasn't important. She knew the definition. She understood the feeling all too well. But her mind stuck on things sometimes. Broke them into little interesting bits, long after the class moved on from the word or the topic itself.

EXHILARATION was even better: *not, tone, next, lion* . . .

Buzzing from several cups of beer, she was feeling good. Punchy, though. Impatient. Because Luke Pinsky was dicking around on the sidelines, brushing up a bank of snow that marked the boundary lines of the rink. His friend Kip had crashed into it going ass over teakettle for the puck. Not the first boot hockey victim, not the last either, as long as the Pinsky brothers maintained their homemade rink by their cabin on Gullwing Lake.

"You gotta have order in the game, Rianne," Luke hollered back. "Lines are lines."

"It's boot hockey. Who cares!" Rianne's voice echoed across the dark of the lake.

"Lance does," Luke replied. Of course Lance would care. Of the Pinsky brothers, Lance was the typical buzzkill older brother. Since Rianne and Luke were the only ones left playing, the lines mattered even less.

But she didn't want to go in yet. She liked Luke Pinsky. And she liked the crack of the stick on the pale blue ice, liked shouting so her voice echoed across the dead frozen lake, out into the dark where everyone else's fishing cabins and fancy cottages had been closed up for the season. Everyone but the Pinskys, who ice fished and skated all winter long. Mercy's family had a cabin on Gullwing Lake but they didn't winterize it.

None of her friends were out on the ice tonight. Kaj was inside celebrating with Kip, because she had gotten into St. Thomas in December. Kaj didn't do anything athletic unless it was serious, an actual game situation. Mercy had left because she and Caleb were in a fight, which was unusual. Caleb was usually pretty quiet, but tonight he'd been yelling about Mercy graduating this year and what was the point, since she was leaving.

And Gabby hadn't even come. Gabby hadn't really been talking to any of them since Rianne first hooked up with Luke.

Gabby said she wasn't mad or anything, but she hadn't done anything social since she found out. Gabby was mad at Rianne solely because Gabby had hooked up with Luke in the summer, but she took it out on everyone else. Gabby'd told her, one day when they were all leaving school in Mercy's car, "You always copy me, Rianne. I get with a guy, then you have to. It's so obvious of you. What are you trying to even prove? Like, what are you going to do after graduation? You can't keep copying me."

After graduation, Gabby was going to college. She'd applied to six different schools, including St. Thomas. She hadn't heard back from all of them yet.

After Graduation. Rianne was so sick of hearing that fucking phrase.

Luke Pinsky never talked about After Graduation. Another reason she liked hanging out with him.

Luke stabbed the shovel into the snowbank and started toward Rianne. He didn't wear his hockey skates, but being a real hockey player, he was fast. She was, unfortunately, wearing a pair of Sorels that were too old to have much grip. So she was in no way able to keep him from slicing ahead of her and flicking the black disk into her goal.

"Ha, got you," he said. "That's two–zip. Still wanna play?"

"Until I win."

"That Russian guy's coming with his vodka in a little bit."

"You've been saying that shit all night," Rianne said, blowing a cloud of frosty air at him. "I'm starting to think he doesn't exist. 'Hi, I'm Luke, and I have an imaginary Russian friend!'"

He collected the puck from the netting and skidded over to her, slid it into the pocket of her coat. All in the space of like two seconds. She loved the quickness he had.

"I can say some other shit, if you want," he said, leaning closer. "Like, hey, what if we get naked? How's that shit?"

Rianne smiled. She wasn't surprised he said it, because they'd been hooking up since Thanksgiving break. But it still was nice to hear. You didn't get a lot of clarity in hooking up with guys sometimes. Sometimes that was the point, though she liked the stuff with Luke. His hair was the color of beer and it curled long out of his blue Wereford hockey knit cap. His eyes were blue and he had a billion-dollar grin. After hooking up with him, Gabby had dismissed him as hype. Gabby said Luke was like "a Ken doll mixed with a yellow Lab." Rianne didn't see the downside of that. He had this way of ducking his head down and looking up at her from under the fringe of his hair that was textbook adorable.

"So?" he pressed, his frost-breath on her face.

"Maybe," she said, sliding away toward the other goal, enjoying the feeling of the ice and the cold. Of the chase. Of the general fun of just acting like a little kid. That was the best part about getting drunk: you could do dumb things you weren't allowed to do anymore. Dance. Slide around on ice. Sing cheesy songs on the radio at the top of your lungs. Eat cookie dough straight from the tube in the middle of the night.

Of course, Luke chased her, caught her. Then they were kissing. Of course. She was expecting that too. Was happy about it. She dropped the hockey stick and grabbed his crotch. He laughed like he was surprised. Though why would he be? She'd given him head last weekend in the bathroom at Cuddy's house; the next day they'd met up at the movies and had sex in his truck afterward, and neither of them was even drunk. But that wasn't weird. He was Luke Pinsky. He hooked up all the time. Just like she did.

"You're so fucking crazy," he said, between kisses. "I fucking love it."

Rianne wondered if this was turning into something besides a good time. She didn't see why it had to stop, but she'd have gotten over it if it did. Because now they were seniors; they'd partied and gotten easy with almost everyone in their school. It wasn't hard; there were less than two hundred people in their graduating class. All people they'd known since elementary school. And now it was almost over, their last year and none of it mattered. Rianne had never had a boyfriend the entire time and that was fine. She was Hat Trick Girl; she wasn't someone you took to prom.

Plus there was Jeff Melk, the lesson Mercy's sister, Faith, had taught them all. Faith had moved in with Jeff Melk right after graduation, setting up the place with secondhand furniture and posters and his Miller High Life dartboard over the couch. It had been sweet and a little dorky, like they were husband and wife in a school play. But then it all went to shit. Jeff Melk kept losing his job and his side business of selling pot became full-time meth dealing. People Faith didn't know were coming over all the time and they never had any privacy. Someone vomited on the sofa Faith's mother had given them. Jeff got into a fight with this asshole guy who pushed him against the wall and knocked the dartboard on the floor. The neighbors kept calling the cops about all the noise. Then Jeff Melk got arrested right in front of Jimmy John's, and Erica, Anika, Channa, and Ana took pictures with their phones of the whole thing. They even were on the local news that night, telling the whole fucking world what they saw.

Stuck in jail, Jeff Melk also stuck Faith with the bills. Then he went to prison. Faith owed so much money from the collect calls Jeff Melk made from jail, from the broken lease, from the car payments Jeff had flaked on in both of their names. Faith had suffered so much. Mercy had told them all about it.

The whole relationship thing was basically a hassle, if you really thought about it. Sure, Caleb was fully in love with Mercy, but he was such a shy weirdo about it sometimes. Like tonight, acting all dramatic and freaky. And Kip was good to Kaj, but he was like a hockey player knucklehead cartoon, knocking into everything, driving his mom's old crappy minivan. Rianne looked at Kip and didn't see romance but the kid who threw up milk all over his desk during fourth-grade nutrition break. Plus he had that weird lump on his face. It wasn't a zit or a tumor. A big strange knot on his left cheek.

"It's just an extra piece of skin," Kaj always said when anyone brought it up. Which made them all wonder, away from Kaj, why the hell Kip didn't go to the doctor and get it taken off. Who needed to store "extra skin" on their goddamn face?

At least Luke Pinsky, since elementary school, had always been cool. Funny. Cute. Strong. Everything people liked and wanted. Which was why Rianne had never considered he'd go for her in a million years, even as a hookup. He didn't stay with any girl, for one thing. It was like he knew that he was too good for any girl from Wereford.

"What if we did it right here," Rianne whispered, her hands digging under his coat.

"What if," he said, trying to kiss her again.

"No, seriously," she said, sliding backward. "Would you?"

"You're so crazy."

Sharp yellow headlights blasted out over them from the shore. A big black sedan with a smoky exhaust pipe rumbled and parked.

"The Russians are here," Luke said.

"There's more than one Russian?" She squinted toward the car. She thought she'd seen it before in the parking lot of the strip mall where she worked at Planet Tan. Now four guys slammed the heavy black doors in a huff of frozen air and laughing and words she couldn't make out, until they walked into the Pinskys' cabin, where they walked into welcome shouting.

"I only know Sergei," Luke said. "He speaks the best English. And he's the one who makes the vodka, anyhow."

"Who *makes* fucking vodka?"

"Rianne, come on," he said, teasing. "Someone has to *make* the vodka. It doesn't just fall from the goddamn sky."

"But how does he . . . ?"

"Come on!" He grabbed her hand and pulled her until she went flying ahead on the ice. She laughed and hung on.

Once off the lake, they could hear the noise inside the cabin, everyone going batshit about the Russians. Or their vodka. Probably both.

For a moment, Rianne thought about not going in. What if they were to just get in Luke's truck and . . . go somewhere? Just leave. Leave all these people and the vodka and the Russians. Wereford, too. Stupid, sad, boring Wereford. She often had thoughts like this, though she knew they didn't make any sense. *What if. What would happen next. Why not.* There was a part of her brain that never stopped wondering. A part of her brain that didn't care about facts.

Facts like she and Luke were drunk.

Facts like Rianne had to be home from Kaj's by eleven tomorrow morning because she had to go with her mom for a New Year's Day brunch at her grandmother's nursing home.

Facts like she and Kaj wouldn't be going back there, because they were going to stay out all night. Kaj was staying at Rianne's, Rianne was staying at Kaj's. That was the official story told to their parents, anyway.

Normally, when they wanted to stay out and lie about it, everyone just said they were going to Gabby's, because Gabby's dad was never home and Mrs. Vaccaro was always busy with Gabby's siblings. But Gabby wasn't an option tonight. Maybe not anymore at all. Still, the old classic move worked. Kaj was dependable, on the honor roll, on the volleyball team. All things Lucy Hettrick accepted as valuable and trustworthy.

Luke had taken off his gloves and now held her cold hands in his. His hands were chapped and calloused. Being the man-whore of Wereford High School didn't interfere with him being a guy who got shit done. He didn't just play hockey. He worked summers and winters with his family's business, shoveling snow and mowing lawns. Tools rattled in the back of his truck along-side his hockey bag and a cooler. She loved his truck, the model, the make, the way it looked. The way it made it possible for a person to throw whatever in the back and just *go*.

Probably because she didn't even have her own car. She bummed rides from Gabby and Kaj and Mercy all the time. Rianne was the queen of the C+ grade point average so her mom wouldn't pay for her insurance, much less her own car, because she didn't warrant the good-grades discount or whatever the fuck it was. She was going to change that soon. Once she turned eigh-teen, she was going to buy her own insurance. Her own car too. And then, After Graduation, she and Mercy would get the fuck out of Wereford.

"Hop on, I'll give you a ride back up there," he said.

"What? I'll crush you."

"Fuck that," he said. He acted like it was a dare. She almost wanted to knock him over, make him fail. But he carried her all the way to the cabin, up the deck steps, and to the sliding glass door.

"Nothing to it," he said.

When the sliding glass door opened, the party separated them and the countdown to midnight started. She was with Kaj and Kip, drinking shots of vodka that the Russians had brought to the party. There were four Russians total, and Kip was pointing them out to Rianne.

First there was Rink, a short, greasy-looking dude in a cheesy Chicago Bulls leather jacket. Rink was smoking an awful-smelling cigarette and talking to Luke's older brother, Lance, who hadn't been out to the cabin in a while, since he'd knocked up and then married his girlfriend.

The next two were a package deal, Kip explained. Yuri and Larry were their names, but Kip said that Larry's name was really Volodomir. These two wore soccer jerseys from some World Cup team no one knew and were sort of ugly, both the jerseys and the guys. Which was probably why they looked sort of blown away to be talking to a group of volleyball players who had always traveled in a group of four: Channa, Ana, Anika, and Erica. They all wore matching tiaras and sashes that said "Happy New Year." Which was another funny thing: Luke had hooked up with all four of them. During volleyball season, Channa, Ana, Erica, and Anika were sweet and nice to Rianne and her friends and the rest of the varsity volleyball team. Doing French braids, giving little speeches at senior night for the parents, organizing pancake breakfast runs to Perkins, leaving candy in the captains' lockers. But now that goodwill was clearly over. In between flirting with the ugly Russians, the four kept giving Rianne shitty looks while glancing at Luke as if they deserved him more.

The last Russian was Sergei. He was very tall, taller than Luke, and had the kind of white-blond hair that seemed impossible without dye. Platinum white, with bits of gold-yellow, but not one dark hairline at the root that Rianne could see. And unlike his sloppy friends, he was wearing a pressed white shirt with a collar, tucked into Levi's, and shiny black shoes, like something a mom would make her son wear to church. On his left wrist, a big thick silver watch glinted while he poured vodka. Her dad wore the same kind of watch. But when she got closer to Sergei, she saw his was different. It looked more expensive. She tried to see the brand but then he caught her.

"You have some, yes?" he asked. He said it very strange and polite. Not cute like Luke. More of a wolf than a dog. Like if Luke was the sweaty guy come to mow the yard, Sergei would be the mean butler answering the door.

"Yes," she said. She held up her empty shot glass. "I mean, no. But yes. I had one before." She suddenly felt shy, or scared. Like she was doing something wrong.

"You will have another," he said, and filled her up. It was one of those long double-shot glasses with the Minnesota Wild logo on it. She didn't want any more—she was drunk enough—but she didn't want to be rude. When he finished filling it, he stared at her, and she felt so nervous, she looked away at the blank bottle. Dark bits floated around in the bottom of it.

"What is that?" she asked.

"Cinnamon," he said. "Spices. Is used in Ukraine vodka."

"You're Ukrainian?"

"No, no," he said. He looked stern. A little regal and snobby. "I am one hundred percent Russian."

IMPERIOUS: *imp, rip, pier, sour, sire . . .*

"So, but. What are you even *doing* here?"

"Here?" He looked confused.

"In Wereford? Why would anyone ever come here? To Wereford?"

He scratched along his jaw for a moment.

"Is not your home?" he asked. "Why do you say this?"

"I wasn't born here," she said, feeling like a dumbass. She wasn't sure how much further to explain. She'd been born in Germany when her parents were stationed there in the army. But she was American. Had lived in Wereford since they divorced in kindergarten.

"But, after graduation, I'm moving," she continued. "To Saint Paul. With my friend Mercy, after we . . ." Did he know what "graduation" meant, though? And did he know that Saint Paul was the capital of Minnesota? Should she explain the whole damn thing, how Kaj (and maybe Gabby, if she stopped being such an asshole to everyone) was going to college in Saint Paul, and Mercy and Rianne would get their own place nearby so they could all keep hanging out? Mercy was thinking of going to vet tech school. Rianne wasn't sure if she could ever settle on a major. But she might do college. Eventually. Maybe. Did he even actually care?

But Sergei was waiting for her to finish her sentence. His face as still and blank as his vodka bottle.

"It's a long story," she said, speaking slow and clear. "But, anyway. Why did you decide to come to Wereford?"

"I am here to study," he said. "Many people come to US to study, yes?"

"Well, okay," she said. "But Wereford? Minnesota? It is so cold here! You could have gone anywhere else!"

"Russia is cold, also, yes? But to study agriculture is why I come. You have University of Minnesota. They have here the extension at the smaller college. You understand?"

"Wereford Community College?"

"Yes. You know it?"

"My mother teaches there."

He looked impressed. "I start in Minneapolis first. Now I have researching in Wereford for the wheats I have to study. There are not so many places for this. Minnesota. Chicago. Iowa. I do not like Iowa."

"Are you, like, going to be a farmer?"

"No. Not farmer," he said. He shook his head, dismissing the whole question. "Where do you say I should go instead, hmm? Where is a better place?"

Rianne considered how to answer. When someone spoke another language, you had to simplify. You had to be clear. You couldn't count on them knowing slang. She'd seen this, first-hand, in Spanish class, when they'd watched films from Mexico that were full of words never seen in any textbooks.

"Not Wereford," she said. "Nothing around here. Maybe Chicago? If you have to be in the Midwest."

"Chicago." He nodded. "To Chicago I have been," he said. He gestured with his blank bottle in a way that said he didn't think much of that city.

"Have you been to New York City?"

"No."

"Los Angeles?"

"No."

"Where have you been?"

"Where . . . in the United States? Or the complete globe?"

"Yes." She laughed. *The complete globe.* The way he said things was weird. But funny.

"Moscow, Reykjavik, Oslo, Gstaad, Venice, Bangkok, Berlin, London, Paris. And Houston, Texas."

"Why Texas?"

"I go with my father. He has his work there. But I am very young when I visit there."

"Which was your favorite?"

"Sorry?"

"I mean, which city. Which one did you like the best?" She spoke a little slower.

"Of those I say? None of those. I like the most Istanbul. The Black Sea. Have you been?"

She shook her head.

He leaned a little closer. "I like a place that has a surprise," he said.

"What do you mean?"

She swore he almost smiled. Almost. And he almost told her

what he meant, but Luke was at her elbow, interrupting. "This is Sergei, Rianne," he said. "And he's very real, as you can see."

"I am very pleased to meet you, Rianne," Sergei said, nodding, like this was the 1800s and she was supposed to curtsy and wave a fucking fan or something.

"Nice to meet you too," she said.

"Another toast, Sergei?" Luke asked.

Sergei nodded. He filled up Luke's Minnesota Lottery loon shot glass and then started speaking in Russian. The room turned toward him when he did. Not a lot of people came to Wereford speaking other languages beyond Mexican workers at the Murtch-Hutchinson chicken processing plant over in Dalby. Just realizing this now made Rianne feel even more embarrassed for living here.

The other Russian guys laughed at parts of Sergei's long speech while everyone else just listened dumbly. She saw Kip was standing behind Kaj, his big hockey paws around her waist, the gold necklace he gave her for their one-year glittering around her neck. Gabby had talked so much shit about that cheesy necklace behind Kaj's back. Rianne felt bad for making fun of it, but it *was* horrible. A golden heart with tiny fake diamonds, bought at Piercing Pagoda in the mall. Kip was such a dope.

Finally Sergei said, in English, "And last is for Rianne, and all her questions." He looked directly at her and raised his shot glass.

Then everyone drank and there was yelling and Luke said in her ear, "Holy shit, all of that was for you!" Like he couldn't believe it. Like it turned him on. It kind of turned her on too, but she would never admit it. She knew the words people called her were true. She was not a good girl. She had tried to be, but it never really worked.

Which was why, after everyone screamed at midnight and hugged and shouted and kissed, when Luke pulled her back to the bedroom, she went automatically. She wanted to have sex with him. Of course. On the lumpy bed that smelled like fabric softener, in the back room with the knotty pine ceiling, where the Pinskys stored their cross-country skis and old sleds and stacks of Huber Bock returnable bottles that Luke claimed were going to be valuable someday. Who would ever buy empty beer bottles, she'd asked, but he hadn't answered. He just took off all her clothes. All of his too. Even though just beyond the door, an entire party continued loudly.

"No one will come in here, I promise," he said. When they were done, he pulled the quilt over them both. Curled around her, his hands crossing over her belly. She sucked in her breath, feeling nervous about him gripping that part of her. He liked to touch it, though. He had no idea, she thought. No idea what he was touching in the dark.

"You can stay out all night, right?" he asked.

"Can *you*?" she teased.

"My mom doesn't care," Luke said. "She trusts me."

"God! Guys suck," Rianne said. "No one ever trusts girls like that."

"What do you want me to do about that?" Luke said, kissing around her shoulder.

"Overthrow the world, maybe? Make new rules? Elect me queen?"

She was teasing and he was laughing, but she still struggled with his hands over her stomach; she was even more soft there now, with volleyball season done for over a month. There was no reason she couldn't stay over. As far as she knew, Kip and Kaj would too. Kaj's lies were always believed. Her parents knew she was a good kid.

"Can you stay?" he asked again, turning her toward him. Speaking to her sternum, where his face was pressed between her boobs. Her boobs normally drove her crazy, mainly because of playing sports. But times like this, with a guy between them, she felt they were almost worth the hassle of the expensive sports bras, the chest acne ("ch-acne" Gabby called it), the bouncing while running warm-ups, the backaches, the hassle finding a decent swimsuit. Too bad a guy enjoying her boobs couldn't make all that bullshit go away.

"Rianne?" he said again, his voice against her skin making everything shiver. His voice was sleepy and deep, but a little desperate underneath.

SATIETY: *to be in a state of fullness, satisfaction . . .*

"I don't want to move," he continued. "I don't want *you* to move. Let's just stay right here. All night."

. . . ties, sat, state, site, seat . . .

She didn't say anything. She closed her eyes, pawed a hand through his hair. His mouth speaking against her body gave her a feeling that sex never did and she wanted nothing else but to be still and to feel his voice. Try to feel as complete as he sounded.

The complete globe. The weird phrase rocketed through her head. She could see the blue ball of the earth shooting like a star through black space in a way a planet never would. She could hear the party in the other room. Probably more homemade vodka plunging down people's throats, but here in this room, under a quilt that smelled odd and sweet, with a boy who smelled perfect, she decided for once, with absolute certainty, that staying in one place was the best thing to do.

She was so hungover the next morning she didn't even notice that Luke had gotten up. It was only when she felt him whisper, right into her face, his stubble on her cheek.

"I've gotta go," he said. "My dog's super sick."

"What?"

"I don't know exactly. My grandma called and said to come to the clinic right away."

Luke's grandma was a veterinarian. She worked at the animal hospital over by the self-serve car wash on Memorial Drive.

"Lance is waiting on me. Text you later?"

She wanted to nod but her head felt like it was a thousand pounds. The sun was barely up; the light coming through the window was bluish and slanted by snowfall.

"Just go back to sleep," he said. "No one will bug you. I promise." He kissed her forehead and pulled up the covers. If she'd had a brain, she would have asked him what time it was. Maybe even gotten out of bed and asked where Kaj was.

INCOHERENT: *rent, rich, tree, trench, her* . . .

But instead she let him pull the heavy quilt over her and down she sank. Her head swelling and seizing, her mouth tasting like dirt, her stomach sizzling and threatening. Her eyes shut tight, she waited for sleep again. But it didn't come. She would have killed for an aspirin. Or some water. Something.

She heard Luke's truck outside whoosh to life, gravel spitting under the tires. She wished she was in the truck with him. Because . . . fuck! She had to get to Kaj's house! She was sweating now, actually, even without another person under the quilt. She lay there for several minutes, hurting and panicked and sick, willing herself to sit up. There had been worse situations, worse problems after partying and she'd figured those out. Most of the time. It wasn't like her mom hadn't gotten mad at her before. It wasn't a shock.

She sat up. The door was open and standing in it was Sergei the Russian. Still in his jeans, his pressed white shirt untucked. His black shoes still shiny. He stared at her, tilting his head.

"Hello," he said. Startled, she flopped back. Pulled the quilt over her more. *Fuck.* She was naked and this Russian dude was staring at her.

"You do not feel well today, Rianne?" He pronounced her name slightly off—REE-inn. She didn't mind it, though; it occurred to her that her name in Russian could be something different, like John was "Juan" in Spanish. Esteban = Steven. What was Luke? Lucas? Lucario?

"I'm . . . no. My head is killing me."

33

He paused, as if it was taking a minute for him to translate what she meant. She stared up at the knotty-pine-paneled ceiling.

"I mean, I'm hungover. You know? Sick? From drinking too much?" She was trying to simplify everything. Language was so fucking weird if you thought about all the expressions for the most basic things. How they didn't mean exactly what you were saying. "My head. It hurts." She hunched the quilt up and tried to sit up more to see him.

From his pocket, he pulled out a small metal tin a little bigger than a quarter. Like his vodka, it wasn't labeled either. He sat down on the bed, right in the crumpled spot where Luke had been.

She didn't know what to do. Would moving away be rude? Sitting up more meant showing off how naked she was.

"You drink only my vodka?" he asked.

"What? No. I mean, I drank beer too."

He made a *tsk* sound that reminded her of how old he was. Old enough to wear a dad watch. Old enough to iron his shirts. Old enough to go to cities all over the world.

Paris. London. Reykjavik. Istanbul.

"With only my vodka, you don't get the hangover."

"Is my friend Kaj here still?"

"No one is here but me and Yuri."

"Is your car still here?" she asked. "The black one?"

"Is not my car," he said. "Rink drives it home."

"Oh."

She pulled the quilt over her face, hoped he would leave. She knew it was childish; acting like if she shut her eyes, she'd become invisible. But she wanted to cry. Her head ached and she was so, so sorry for being so bad last night. Sorry even for the good, fun parts with Luke. Especially because of those.

Finally, when she realized he wasn't going to leave, she peeked out from the covers. He had unscrewed the metal tin and was rubbing what was in it between his thumb and forefinger.

"What is that?"

"Close your eyes," he said.

"Tell me what it is first."

"Medicine for hangover. The woman who cleans my father's house makes it."

"Can I touch it?" She sat up, careful to pull the quilt with her. She noticed him glancing down toward her chest and clamped the quilt tighter. He held out the tin. The paste inside was silvery white and soft like lip balm. She rubbed it between her fingers just the slightest bit.

"Permit me for it," he said, and he rubbed the soft paste on her temples, circling around her cheeks and nose. Automatically, her eyes shut, and a menthol-laced fragrance enclosed her, full of mint and woody herbs. It smelled green, and somehow burnt, and had the consistency of butter left out on a hot day.

"Breathe now, please," he said.

She did and the scent rushed into her, all at once, sparkling through her nose and mouth and eyes. When he gently pushed her shoulders down toward the bed again, she let him. Maybe it was out of fear, maybe out of wonder, but she let him. He dabbed a bit at the base of her throat, lifting up her chin, lining each side of her jaw.

But when he slid closer, and rolled her to her side, her eyes flew open.

"Wait, what are you . . . ?"

"Is not sex," he said. "Shhh. Do not worry." He began rubbing her shoulders. "You drink beer last night." It wasn't a question, but with his accent, she wasn't sure. His hands pushed a long sigh out of her and then he *tsked* again. "You cannot mix. Is not good, a mix of drink. With only my vodka, never you are sick."

"I don't like vodka." She closed her eyes, brain fluttering. "I'm sorry," she added.

"*Tsk*. It is fine," he said. "I will make vodka you will like. One day you will like it. I am studying many things." He kept churning her shoulder blades.

"But . . . you study vodka? I thought you said you were studying agriculture."

"This is connected. All the agriculture. Grains have many problems. This is the science. There are many things to learn."

"You're learning about *grains* . . . ?" It was difficult to speak. His fingers pressed her scalp with such force that she couldn't decide if it hurt or felt good.

"My father has a distribution company, several distilleries. It is our business."

"Your father wants you to work in his business?"

"Yes. But it is not my choice. I am here because I am sent away. My father marries a new woman."

36

Rianne felt the tightness gripping her skull subside. Every constricted passageway in her body seemed to dilate.

"Does she not like you?" She felt somewhat high. Silly. "Is she an evil stepmother or something?"

"You sleep now." His palm held the back of her head and for a moment, Rianne thought, *here is the trap. Again, I've gone too far. Again. I am always bad. I must like being bad. Because here is where it always ends up....*

But then her head sank down into the pillow as he rose from the bed. The ghost magic of the hangover remedy whisked through her skin. Her muscles shivered.

SOMNOLENT: *lent, moot, no, loose, moon, lost ...*

She heard the door shut quietly. His footsteps. She could picture his shiny black shoes. *Clip, step, clip, step, clip, step.* And then she fell asleep.

When she woke again, Sergei coming to her with his remedy for hangovers seemed like a dream. But she knew it wasn't. She could still smell the herbal paste on the pillow, on her hair. Where he had rubbed it on her, the skin was noticeably softer. And she felt better. Not good, not perfect. But absolutely better.

She sat up. The door was still closed. It was snowing harder. She scrambled for her clothes and quickly dressed, finding her phone in the pocket of her jeans. It was 10:29. She had missed several texts from Kaj. *Fuck.*

She ran to the bathroom, calling Kaj, calling Mercy. Even Gabby. No one picked up. She splashed water on her face, smudged a bit of toothpaste she found in the drawer across her teeth with her finger. Her hair was a disaster of flatness and frizz; she looked like she'd slept in the trunk of a car, not under heavy quilts with a cute boy. She stared at the mirror over the sink, feeling hellish. Then she wiped her smeary eyeliner off with some wet toilet paper and tried her friends again.

Nothing.

She stared at the bathroom. The toilet had a pink fuzzy seat cover, with a matching rug on the floor around the base. The shower curtain had flamingos on it and the countertop was the color of SPAM, the spreadable meat crap her dad used to make them put on crackers when they went on camping vacations. Above the toilet was a little green sign that said—in pink letters—*If you sprinkle when you tinkle, be a sweetie & wipe the seatie.*

She wanted to laugh. And then her phone rang. Her mom.

She picked it up and before she could say hello her mother shouted, "If you're inside there, just know I'm here at some godforsaken cabin on goddamn Gullwing Lake and you've got two minutes before I come in there and scream at you personally."

TWO

RIANNE'S MOM'S CAR was small. So was her mom. Lucy Hettrick was a petite woman who'd been wearing the same clothes since forever. Faded flannels and men's Levi's and Birkenstocks that she'd resoled four times.

Rianne was taller than her mother by a good five inches, and built like her father. Her wrists were thick and her fingers blunt, unlike her older sister Renata's elegant piano-playing hands. Unlike Renata, who was dainty and twig-legged like their mother, Rianne's legs were long and strong. Her knees weren't pretty round circles, but big and knobby and covered in old scars from wiping out on her bike and sliding headfirst playing summer softball and every other fucked-up thing she'd done as a kid.

Now she sat in the passenger seat, her knees against the glove box, because the seat recliner lever was broken and her mother was too cheap to get it fixed. Or didn't care to get it fixed.

Rianne crossed her arms over her chest and tried to make

herself smaller as she stared at the top of her mother's head, the dark brown hair, smooth and shiny, the crown crisscrossed with gray streaks. Renata had the same exact hair, minus the gray. Rianne felt like killing her mother. Her hangover was mostly gone (*how? why?*), replaced by rage at her mother's total silence. It was like she could only speak angrily to her at a distance, over the phone, via text, from all the way across the house in another room. But once Rianne got near her, Lucy Hettrick would control the boards, turning every knob to silent.

Her mother barreled around the roundabout that had been put in this summer by the JCPenney, honking at someone who hadn't figured out how the damn thing worked. Typical.

If she followed the normal routine, her mother would now simmer in silence until the next fuck-up. Because there always was another one. There had been groundings and punishments and phones taken away and allowances cut and limits set. Whatever the price, Rianne broke the rules. Her father, always deployed somewhere on the other side of the globe, would call to "talk sense" to his daughter. Her sister had basically disappeared from caring about anyone outside her music school world, but occasionally Renata would message Rianne with a lecture that repeated Lucy Hettrick's viewpoint. Because Renata had always done whatever their mom said. Renata got good grades, Renata practiced her instruments, Renata played tennis, the only sport where you could wear a skirt and look graceful while you sweated. Unlike Rianne, Renata did everything logically, sensibly. Which was why Renata was applying to graduate schools before she even finished college and why Rianne was heading into the second half of her senior year without even taking any tests, filling out any forms. Didn't matter that she had the same ACT score as Renata; Rianne didn't have the grades, or the will to focus on what the teacher thought was important. In Rianne's experience, teachers never thought anything interesting was important. They'd introduce something cool, like how suffragettes chained themselves to the White House for the vote, and then move on two seconds later to Taft-Hartley or the atomic bomb, letting those ladies in their old-school dresses sit there screaming for equal rights in Rianne's mind.

It was snowing harder and her mother turned up the wipers. Rianne hated going to the nursing home. She hated anything to do with her grandma Hettrick. Grandma Hettrick's idea of fun was to make her grandchildren set up her eternal rummage sale every Saturday in the summer, bossing them around a hot garage filled with card tables covered in junk marked with masking tape price tags. When she was feeling affectionate, she'd brush her granddaughters' hair into a headache-inducing style, full of braids and flourishes until Rianne and Renata looked like girls from another century. Grandma Hettrick had been in this nursing home since last February, when she fell and broke her ribs, and the hospital wouldn't discharge her to live on her own. Before that, though, her brain had been gone a long time with Alzheimer's.

"Does Grandma know we're coming this time?"

Her mother sighed. Shrugged. "I told her when I called," she said. "We'll see."

We'll see. Lucy Hettrick's favorite phrase. It never meant anything good.

Mom, can Mercy and me bike to the YMCA for open swim?

We'll see.

Mom, can me and Renata make cupcakes tonight?

We'll see.

Mom, it's after seven in Bahrain. Can we Skype Daddy yet?

We'll see.

At times like this, when she'd fucked up once again, talking was the only way she could make up for her mistakes. Whether they talked about what she'd done wasn't the point. She felt like she must say something to show her mother she was human, that she had feelings, and, most important, that she had intelligent thoughts. Her mother was convinced that Rianne never thought about anything but the present moment, the current situation. Which was true in some ways, and completely false in others.

"Does she still think you're Aunt Emma when you call?"

"Not the last time we spoke," her mom answered. "I don't think she knows Emma's living in Australia right now. I tell her. But she forgets."

Once they passed through the nursing home's sliding security doors—you had to wait in between them and type in a pass code, which was designed to prevent residents from escaping—Rianne felt hungover again. Was it the stale breath smell, like air that had been breathed in and out a million times? Or was it the vague gravy scent that seemed to be present at all times, no matter the time of day or the meal being served?

TORPID: *rot, dip, prod, trip, pod . . .*

BILIOUS: *is, us, sob, slob . . .*

She wanted to hit the bathroom to see if throwing up might help. Sometimes that did the trick. But she knew her mother would side-eye that move too. Lucy Hettrick hated visiting this place as much as her children did. But everyone had to suffer equally when it came to Grandma Hettrick.

"Mom, are we eating here today?" Rianne asked softly. She wanted to be prepared in case she had to get close-up with the gaggy gravy smell. Also, they had milk in cardboard cartons, another thing that she couldn't stand, even when she wasn't hungover. It reminded her of Kip's barf in fourth grade. That, when combined with pizza in the school cafeteria, always meant she skipped lunch those days. Rianne swore she was the only teenager in the world who hated pizza.

"Maybe," her mom said. "It depends. I didn't tell the nurse we would, but they usually don't mind."

Then she stopped. Put her hand on Rianne's shoulder. Rianne held in her breath, hoping not to leak out alcohol fumes.

"This isn't a regular visit," her mother said. "And I didn't keep anything from you. He just . . . he came to town without letting me know. So please don't put this on me. Though obviously last night's circumstances might warrant his involvement." She made her wrinkled-up face. "And maybe he can talk to you about your

so-called *plans* for after graduation. God knows I've failed at figuring out how to get through to you."

"What are you talking about?" Rianne said, fighting the urge
not to throw her mom's hand off her shoulder for the snotty
way she said "plans." But then Rianne looked up and saw Dean
Wynne standing in the hallway. His hair fresh-shaved army-style,
wearing his camis and boots as if this was a field exercise.

"Daddy? What are you doing here . . . ?"

"Was wondering if I'd gone to the wrong glue factory," her dad
said, curling his hands over each other in fists like he didn't know
what to do with them. Her mother made another wrinkled-up
face at his words. Dean Wynne could be pretty crude when it
came to word choice.

"Rianne. Sweetheart. Look at you! Are you taller?"

He went in for a hug and Rianne let it happen, the whole time
feeling nervous about the sins of the previous night still cling-
ing to her. She loved her father, mainly because he was more like
her than her mother, but whether he was deployed in Qatar or
Switzerland or Guam, like his ex-wife, he was also concerned
about her in the same dumb annoying way. He'd call her or get
on Skype and not let up, saying stuff like, "What are your goals,
honey? You need to consider life after graduation. Make some
goals so you can achieve your dreams."

Goals. Dreams. Basically, Dean Wynne's version of *We'll see.*

Finally, he let go. He always smelled a little minty, her father.
She had always liked his physical, professional self: his minty
cool smell, the bristly haircut, the stiff creases of his uniform.

Usually when he showed up to take her and Renata on vacation somewhere, he had on stupid clothes: ugly board shorts, a Harley T-shirt, those gross Oakley sunglasses with the rainbow-y mirror lenses, hiking boots. He took them to lots of places that were cool, but always in the United States, never all the places he was stationed for work: Saudi Arabia, Malaysia, Bahrain, Germany, the Philippines. She could imagine him in those places in his uniform, but on vacation at Yosemite or the Everglades, he was just another dorky dad. She preferred him like this: structured, fit, tidy. It gave her weird pride about what he did, even though he'd only done one combat tour. The last ten years Dean Wynne worked in intelligence, so where he'd been on the map was really the only part of his job they knew about specifically.

"God, you're pretty," Dean said. "Isn't she, Lu? You're just such a pretty girl, honey." He looked over at his ex-wife, who was staring at her unpolished fingernails and tapping her shoe on the nursing home carpet.

"Dean, let's just get this finished with, okay?"

"Something wrong, ladies?" he asked, looking at both of them.

Ladies. Another dorky thing her dad liked to say. She knew her mother hated it when he called women *ladies.* It was better than *gals,* though. He was always saying stuff like, "I once worked with a gal in the marines who ran marathons."

"We'll discuss it later," her mother said. Rianne looked down, embarrassed. She recalled the whole night of drinking beer and downing shots. Sex with Luke. And Sergei's hands all over her skin, rubbing her down with the hangover remedy. Which her

45

dad smelled a little bit like, in a distant way. *God.*

The three of them walked to her grandmother's room, Lucy Hettrick leading the way. Rianne stared at her mom's back. Lucy Hettrick wore a "dress-up" outfit: fitted blue sweater over her knee-length denim skirt, her gray tights and sensible flat shoes with the Velcro Mary Jane straps. Her mother had been in the army once too—that's how she had met her dad—but even after being discharged, Lucy Hettrick still retained her no-bullshit look. Sensible everything, lots of plaid, nothing too tight or too trendy. No makeup beyond sunscreen, no jewelry except little diamond studs in her ears, which had been a present from her ex. It wasn't like Rianne was the girliest of girls, but her mom's frumpy-ass style was just another thing that separated them.

Her grandmother was asleep when they came in the room, slumped in a navy blue vinyl recliner with the shopper ads for Walgreens and JCPenney in her lap. Rianne could feel sweat pooling around her armpits, and everything smelled vomit-y again, not like gravy but like a dirty public bathroom. Like shit and piss and spit-up. A lot of the old people in this place had little bowls on their bed trays where they hocked up nastiness when they were sick. Rianne didn't know if the bowl was there because of a specific medical reason or if old people just were allowed to be gross and hork up their spit and snot instead of putting it into a Kleenex like everyone else. How was it any cleaner to have a bowl of phlegmy crud sitting out, really? She looked for a place to sit. There was either the unmade bed or nothing. Which was probably the main reason visits with her grandma were so uncomfortable. You just stood there, waiting to flee the scene.

Her grandmother woke up. Or started to wake up. It took her a while to open her eyes, register what was in front of her, reach for her glasses around her neck, straighten up until she was a body and not a shapeless pile in a zip-up nightgown.

"Yes?" she asked, her voice sounding clogged and sticky. "Can I help you?"

Her father had a truck with Kansas plates, but otherwise it was new, tricked out with every possible feature, and rode as smooth as a dream on the crappy potholed streets of Wereford. She sat in the passenger seat; she and her dad were headed to the grocery store. Her mother had gone home to "take care of some things" but Rianne guessed she was probably in no mood to be around her wayward daughter and her ex who'd suddenly dropped in. Which was the thing Rianne was most eager to find out.

After the visit with Grandma Hettrick where she was confused about the soldier in her room and looked at them like invading strangers, her mother had told her father about Rianne's lying. Dean Wynne had not dropped it. He kept talking about how she was such a smart girl, but she kept "losing trust." How she didn't understand that "parents worry." How she was going back on "the tight leash" now.

Yeah, yeah, Rianne thought. The tight leash was a recurring theme. Her mother got sick of holding it, Rianne got sneakier about slipping loose from it. It never lasted.

"I thought you were in Germany for another year," she said.

"Yeah," her dad said, guiding the car into a spot near the back of the lot, far from other cars. As if he didn't want any idiots crashing their stray carts into it. He was wearing his rainbow-lens Oakley sunglasses now and a cami coat and cap. She hopped down from the truck and admired its bright red paint job, its sturdy running boards. Luke's truck didn't have running boards—it was practically a swan dive getting out of his truck, but the night they'd hung out after the movies, he sped around to her side to help her out. She hadn't thought about that until jumping out of her dad's truck. Luke was weird like that. He'd chugged through Channa, Ana, Erica, and Anika in a series of weeks this fall. Rianne had heard all about it all volleyball season. He'd been such a pig, never calling any of them, just smiling and acting like plowing through two-thirds of the entire starting junior varsity volleyball lineup was no big thing. But yet he still had manners about Rianne getting out of his truck.

"You got the list?" her father asked. And just like that, she knew the whole discussion of what he was doing here wouldn't happen. He wouldn't allow it. He'd make a joke out of it. It made her want to scream, but she was too exhausted to scream.

They spun through the grocery store, and her father filled the cart with what was on her mom's list and then some. He was cheerful and upbeat. His usual self like when they were on vacation.

"Goddamn, I forgot how they don't sell beer here on Sundays."

"Mom probably has beer."

Her father didn't look too excited about that so she bagged up everything as quick as she could and then insisted on carrying stuff instead of having him use the cart. That was an old move; Renata was uninterested in anything physical unless it was a piano or a violin. She was built small, like Lucy Hettrick. But Rianne liked showing off to her dad that she had muscles. Strength.

Instead of asking him what had brought him to Wereford—and especially what had him staying at their house, his duffel and a suitcase in Renata's old room, which he had never, ever done before—she told him about her friends. Kaj made all-conference again for her setting and had been recruited to play for St. Thomas. Mercy broke team records for ace serves and kills. Gabby had won an academic athlete achievement award from the school district. They all played on an intramural league through Wereford Community College that Coach Paula recommended them for; they were 1 and 0. Her father nodded the whole time in approval. Because he couldn't talk about his work, Dean Wynne constantly referred to his own accomplished collection of friends. Pals he went skiing with, had jumped out of airplanes with. Guys that kayaked and fixed tanks and ran marathons and spoke Arabic fluently. Sometimes Rianne felt like she only knew him from the stories he told about these phantom people she had never met.

But unlike him, there was no classified top secret status she could claim for herself. So when he asked, "And what about you, sweetheart?" it was harder to summarize the good parts.

Rianne wasn't all-conference anything. And she hadn't been captain—that was Kaj and Gabby's honor. But she'd had the best jump serve of the entire team, even Mercy, and no one could handle the block she and Gabby set up. They had been, to use Coach Paula's term, a solid wall. Nothing came through while they were at the net. And though she wasn't smashing it like Mercy, being a lefty meant she could whoop ass when Kaj set her up with something good. Even if Kaj didn't. Even if Gabby had to set in a pinch, Rianne could make a decent play out of it. Coach Paula always called Rianne her secret weapon, her scrapper. She didn't tell her father this, but it was one of the reasons she loved playing sports. Coach Paula appreciated how she went in and handled the situation, no matter how shitty or demoralized the team got. That, and sports involved all her friends. Clinics in the Cities, camps at colleges, summer tournaments, road trips. She loved it all. And now, besides the once-a-week intramural game, it was all over.

"You thinking about maybe playing in college then?" her dad asked. "I know your mother said . . ."

"No," she said.

"Why not, honey?"

"You didn't go to college, Dad."

"I did too. I went while I was stationed in Norfolk. Remember that?"

She shrugged. How was she supposed to remember some place

she hadn't lived or even visited?

"You didn't go right away," she said. "Not right after high school."

"No, I enlisted, like a dumbass," he said.

"Mom enlisted too."

He ignored that point. "Don't tell me you're thinking about enlisting." He raised an eyebrow above his Oakley rainbow-lens sunglasses and she rolled her eyes.

"God, no," she said. "Give me some credit."

"Good," he said. "At least that's sunk in."

"Are you here just to yell at me about college or what? Is that why you're here?"

Her father laughed. He turned on the radio and punched buttons until he got a song he liked. "Runnin' with the Devil" by Van Halen. Rianne knew it because Gabby had been a freak about metalhead rock from the olden days all season. She did their team warm-up list: Scorpions, Bad Company, Whitesnake, Mötley Crüe, Poison. Even the band names were gross-sounding.

"I could be," her father said. "I could be here to help your mom sell your grandma's house. Or to see what in the hell's changed in this pissant town since I saw it last. But maybe I'm really here to light a fire under your ass so you'll find something else to do with your time besides getting drunk and giving your mother gray hair." He winked at her. His hair was graying just as bad, but it was harder to tell; he had the same blond as she did.

"So which is it?" she asked. Smiling. She couldn't help it; he always teased her in a way her mother never did.

"Wouldn't you like to know," he finished. Then he turned up the radio and smiled. Though she didn't want to, she found herself shouting the song along with him the rest of the way home.

THREE

MERCY CAME OVER as Rianne was helping clear the dinner dishes. She got introduced to Rianne's dad and made some bullshit small talk to her mom before Rianne shoved her up the stairs to her bedroom. Mercy liked talking to people's parents, sucking up to them, charming them. It drove her crazy that Caleb's parents didn't like her.

"Didn't you hear what happened? My mom came out to the Pinskys' cabin. I got totally busted. Why didn't you pick up this morning?"

"My phone was dead. I was texting with Caleb until three a.m. How'd she know you weren't at Kaj's?"

"Because she went over to the Vangs' and I wasn't there! Kaj had no choice but to tell her where I was!"

"Didn't Kaj and Kip stay over with you guys?"

"She was going to, but Kip got sick or something? They got a ride home from Channa. Or Ana. One of them."

She expected Mercy to say something shitty about Kip. They were all always saying something shitty about Kip. It wasn't that Kip was a jerk but there was always something with him. Some damn dumb problem. Plantar warts. Heatstroke. Getting pulled over for driving without his lights on. Having to babysit his stupid younger siblings. Flunking Dishonorable Math two times. Buying dumb necklaces at Piercing Pagoda. Kaj was always having to fix something for him.

Mercy plunked down on Rianne's bed and put her head in her hands. All sadness now. No charm and smile like a minute ago in the kitchen with Dean and Lucy.

Rianne hoped this wasn't about Caleb. But she knew, seeing her friend bent over, her blond curls in a pile on her knees, that it couldn't be anything else. Mercy was generally a happy person with a normal family, everything regular and decent. So of course she'd pick for a boyfriend a weird guy with a super religious family.

"I think something's wrong with Caleb. He's, like, crazy."

Rianne sat next to her. The mirror over her desk framed them: the two blondes of their foursome. Gabby said that she and Kaj were the dark side, but that was only on the surface. Only their hair color, skin tone. There was nothing dark about any of them, really. Even being Hat Trick Girl was only a joke, nothing tragic.

"He's just high too much. He's got to lay off the weed."

"No," Mercy said. "He's saying weird shit. And the weed makes him less shy and nervous. But it's the weird shit that freaks me out."

"Like what weird shit?" To Rianne, Caleb had always been a little off. He was shy, but could dance amazingly. Skinny as hell, but he played football. Athletic, but he loved comic books and tabletop Dungeons & Dragons. On top of all that, his family had homeschooled him until seventh grade, and while he believed in God and told Mercy that premarital sex was definitely a sin, they still had sex all the time. He wasn't even a virgin when they first had sex—he'd done it with two other girls in his church youth group. He didn't make any sense, really.

"He's got this thing about cards and messages," she said. "He's got cards in his wallet and he takes them out and flips them around and tells me that he's getting lucky or unlucky or whatever."

"Like, credit cards?"

"No, playing cards."

"God," Rianne said. *What a fucking nerd.*

"Once I was annoyed with the cards thing and was like, 'Easy, Gambit,' and he got so pissed."

"Well, that's totally fucking dorky," Rianne said. "He should feel dumb."

"And he's always kind of nodding to himself. And smiling. And when I ask him what he's doing he's like, 'Never mind, I'm taking care of it.' But he never says what 'it' is."

"Have you ever asked him?" Rianne was also a big believer in just opening your mouth and putting the questions out there. If you really wanted to know, you'd ask. Or Google it. She did that kind of shit all the time. Most of her job at Planet Tan was her sitting at the reception desk avoiding her homework while Googling shit she wondered about.

"No," Mercy said. "Plus the smoking! Jesus! It's making me crazy. He's going to get suspended again. He comes into the hallways reeking of smoke."

"Weed or cigarettes?"

"Sometimes both."

"Don't his parents notice?"

"Yeah, so they're making him talk to their pastor twice a week. And he can't have me over anymore."

"Well, that's no loss." Mercy couldn't stand Caleb's uptight family, anyway.

"But . . . he won't . . ." She started to cry.

"What?" Mercy wasn't much of a crier. None of them were, really. But especially not Mercy. Her family was so nice. You could tell her parents gave a shit about her, listened to her. Her mom was a nurse, her father was a police officer. The Kovashes would have been boring if not for the fact that they were pretty funny people. They had met standing in the returns line of Walmart right after Mrs. Kovash had finished nursing school. Officer Kovash was returning an ugly shirt he'd gotten for Christmas; Mrs. Kovash had bought a coffeepot with a broken carafe. Their life was as sweet and dorky as how they met.

"He won't kiss me anymore," Mercy said, tears all over her cheeks and fingers. "Or really, anything else. He says . . . God, I can't stand this."

"What?"

"You're gonna think he's a freak."

Too late, thought Rianne. "What is it?"

Mercy swallowed, wiped her tears in a hurried way, like she was impatient with herself for having them. "He says that we need to be careful. That God knows we've had sex."

"Oh, *gross*."

"And that God knows it and there are consequences. So he won't . . . we can't . . ."

Rianne waited. "Can't what? Can't have sex?"

"Yeah," Mercy said. "He acts really afraid of me about it. Like, we did it last week and he got out of the car and walked home. Without his coat. We were all the way down behind where the old Hy-Vee was. You know how far that is to his house?"

"He walked to his *house*?"

"I assume he did," Mercy said. "But I don't really know. Basically, he just disappeared. I drove all around looking for him but never found him. He wouldn't talk to me. Then he got in trouble at school during gym and his mother thinks it's all my bad influence."

"Why the hell would you get him in trouble in gym? He's in eleventh-grade PE and you're not!"

"Not because of PE. Because he told his parents we had sex! And he's got to do this pledge to his pastor now! It's so fucked-up. It's like, I thought being Catholic was kinda weird. But all this hanging around the pastor and telling him everything? You don't do that in my church. You just go there, feel guilty and pray, then leave. I mean, who actually *pledges* shit to their pastor?"

"Don't ask me," Rianne said. "Neither of my parents ever gave two shits about church."

Mercy laughed. "I don't mind church. But Caleb's whole family is making me see why people avoid it."

"Did you eat dinner?" Rianne asked.

Mercy shook her head.

"Stay here," Rianne said. "My dad made sausage pasta. I'll bring you some. And some ice cream too."

Mercy nodded, slipped under the quilt on Rianne's bed. "What in the hell is your dad here for, anyway?"

"No idea."

Mercy propped another pillow under her head and sighed as Rianne ran to get the food.

Mercy ate the entire plate of sausage pasta Rianne gave her. Then they both tucked into a half gallon of cookies and cream.

"Do you ever think of maybe, you know? Breaking up?" Rianne asked.

Mercy looked up from the ice cream container. "Why?"

Why. This was what she didn't get about Mercy. Had she not seen the parallels with Faith's boyfriend Jeff Melk? Faith had her car repossessed because of Jeff Melk, her credit destroyed by Jeff Melk. The sweet, quirky Kovashes had pretty much lost their minds about their oldest daughter and that shitty guy. Faith was finally getting herself together again. Bartending, putting herself through classes at Wereford Community College, living in a new apartment. And here was Mercy, getting all invested in another loser guy who could give her nothing but a pain in the ass.

"I mean, you're graduating, anyway. And what? You're going to keep going out with him, while he's in high school and we're up in the Cities?"

Mercy looked away, licked her spoon. Stabbed it into the ice cream. "Fuck, I can't eat anymore. Your dad's a good cook, Rianne. Wouldn't be horrible if he stayed."

"Yes, it would," Rianne said.

"Why is he here, anyway?"

"He's . . . I don't know. He's never, ever come to stay like this. It's so weird. And just now, I'm down there and he's sitting on the couch in his goddamn sweatpants watching TV with my mother. I want to call my sister."

Rianne lay back on the carpet with a thump. "I mean, I don't really *want* to call her but I want to tell her what's going on. She would freak."

Mercy stood up, stretched, checked herself out in Rianne's mirror.

"Your sister's clueless," she said, fluffing out her hair. "She's so up her own ass. Don't bother."

Mercy didn't have much time for Renata. Probably because Faith was a kickass, good sister. Someone who bought booze for her and took her to movies and let her stay over at her apartment to have sex with Caleb. Someone who always, always looked out for her little sister. Sometimes Rianne wished she could be sisters with Mercy too.

Appearance-wise, she could have been. Both girls were blond, tall, blue-eyed. But Mercy was a much slighter version of Rianne.

Instead of a stomach pooch, Mercy had a concave bowl sur-rounded by ribs. Her legs were thin and stork-like. And she had no boobs, really. Also, her hair was a curly blond while Rianne's was straight. Rianne had always thought Mercy was prettier. Delicate face, small nose, lips that were naturally pink. Rianne thought her own face was decent; it wasn't like she was jealous. But Mercy had that little doll quality about her. Sweet and fragile and nice, while Rianne was exactly how she looked: tall, strong, able to outrace you, outdrink you, outeat you.

"Maybe you should break up with him," Rianne said. "Just until things get settled?"

"I don't want to break up with him," Mercy said. She exhaled, turned away from Rianne.

"Faith said I can move in with her," she said, her voice casual. So casual it couldn't be real.

"What about our plan? Saint Paul in the Fall?" A stupid rhyme that had become their shortcut label for it.

Mercy slumped back down on the bed.

"Faith's roommate might move to Seattle."

"Allie's been saying that forever. Like she'll ever actually do it."

"I just . . ." Mercy stopped, felt along her forehead, where she always struggled with zits.

Rianne waited. Watched Mercy's fingers feel around her skin. There was peeling light blue polish on her pointer finger.

The word PALPATE popped up: *pal, eat, lap, teal, tape . . .*

"I can't leave him like this," Mercy said. "I mean, maybe we'll break up. But I feel like, other than me, Caleb's got no one."

Rianne said nothing. Caleb didn't have *no one*. He had his group of gamer friends. His parents were religious and weird, but they were there. His pastor was there. He was far from alone.

Plus they'd decided to move to Saint Paul together since Kaj and Gabby had applied to St. Thomas. Even if Gabby wasn't decided yet, they just assumed she'd pick where Kaj went. Because then Kaj and her would know where all the parties were and they'd all be there, together. Out of Wereford. Somewhere cool, all four of them. It had been an easy decision. *Rational*, her mother would have called it. And now Mercy wanted to chuck it because of Caleb? Rianne felt almost shaky with anger. She held it down, like a breath going backward. She started emptying her backpack, stacking folders and books on her desk, in the order she had loaded them back before Christmas break. She had zero intention of studying. On her desk were lists of apartments by St. Thomas. A map of the campus. She'd even researched tanning places that might be hiring.

"Kaj said those Russian guys were at the Pinskys'," Mercy said, yawning, trying for casual again.

Rianne instantly felt the hangover remedy on her skin again. The smell of it returned, like magic. She wanted to tell Mercy the whole thing so bad! She would have, if the canceling of Saint Paul in the Fall hadn't just happened.

"Yeah, one of them makes vodka, I guess?" Rianne said, sounding casual herself now. She looked away from Mercy, up at the corkboard above her bed. Originally, she asked her mom to put it up when they moved to Wereford, so she could keep track of where her father was on a big map that came as an insert from *National Geographic*. Since then, her little blue thumbtacks tracking where Dean Wynne was stationed had been overtaken with photos of her and her friends, along with pictures sliced from *National Geographic*, which her father gave her every year for her birthday as a subscription.

Beneath the faded map was a giant blue waterfall, right next to Gabby holding a giant chicken wing from that time they went to Applebee's on her birthday and her eyes were crossed and crazy. A pride of lions with bloody mouths eating an antelope next to Mercy curled up in Caleb's lap at Cuddy's while Kaj raised a Windex-blue Jell-O shot. The Golden Gate Bridge above all four of them in their blue-and-white volleyball uniforms: Mercy, Gabby, Rianne, Kaj; four alternating ponytails; blond, brown, blond, black; four big smiles fresh from winning their first JV match.

"That's Sergei. He works at the Pumphouse with my sister," Mercy said.

"Don't you have to be a citizen to work a job like that?"

"The owner pays him under the table, Faith said. I guess he's kind of a badass. Faith told me that the night before Thanksgiving, this customer was hassling all the female waitstaff and he had to be thrown out and it ended up with Sergei knocking the guy out. Blood and teeth all over the sidewalk out front."

"Jesus. They didn't arrest him?"

"He's a bouncer," Mercy said.

"But how can you just hit someone like that? Even for a job?"

Mercy shrugged, like she didn't care. Rianne looked at the picture of a giant golden spruce tree, a genetic mutant that some crazy guy had hacked down in British Columbia. It was one of a kind, a unique biological specimen, but the crazy man had thought it was evil or something. She felt creeped out by Sergei now, when it was too late. But she also couldn't get the scent of the hangover remedy out of her memory.

"Does Faith like him or something?"

"No. He was fucking Allie for a while. Then Faith asked why he wasn't coming around to see Allie anymore and he said to her, 'With Allie, I am done with the fucking.' Isn't that funny? He's a crazy motherfucker."

They both laughed, but she didn't think any of it was funny. She didn't like the idea of teeth and blood on the sidewalk, especially when his hands had been on her own body earlier this morning. It made her want to ask Faith a million questions.

Mercy's phone buzzed and she sighed, looking at the screen. "Caleb," she explained. Rianne rearranged the stuff on her dresser. The red lacquered jewelry box, which contained her first learner's permit and her passport plus all sorts of other stray bits she had collected over the years, stayed in the center. Beside it was a little silver dish full of ponytail elastics and a pleated fan with a painting of Mount Fuji her dad had got her back in junior high. A little set of tiny ceramic kangaroos her aunt Emma had sent her from Australia formed a protective row in front of all of this.

Finally, Mercy sighed, and put her phone in her hoodie pocket.

"I gotta go," she said. "Thanks for letting me eat and bitch."

Rianne followed Mercy out. Her dad was no longer in the living room; her mom was in the kitchen. Mercy stopped and said good-bye to her; Lucy Hettrick smiled kindly while she wiped down the grease from the sausage pasta on the stove top. Her mother was always so fake-polite to her friends, which annoyed the shit out of Rianne.

And she was angry at Mercy for planting herself here for Caleb. Rianne couldn't ever get pissed off out loud. Though Gabby always did. But Rianne did the exact opposite: gave her friend a plate of food and listened to her talk. Pretended she wasn't disappointed. Pretended everything was fine. She'd toss all the apartment listings and do another search for something cheaper. Could you rent just a room, not a whole apartment? And maybe she could take the bus instead of buying a car?

The second the door closed, before she could sprint back upstairs to her room and start up a new Google search, her mother said, "Rianne? Can you come here?"

The living room was just off the kitchen. It had been a deck at first, but her mother had it remodeled into a dayroom and this had become her main space. There was a sofa full of pillows but Lucy Hettrick sat in a chaise lounge where she read and watched television and drank wine in the evenings after grading her students' papers. Since junior high, Renata's piano had taken over the downstairs TV room; she'd often sleep on the sofa down there to be closer to her "studio space." Her preppy clothes and school papers and tennis racket string kits clearly marked the territory as Renata's.

The studio space, this dayroom? Neither was for Rianne. The dayroom was only the setting for getting bitched at.

Lucy Hettrick wouldn't have used those terms. Though her mother wasn't shy about swear words, she usually didn't use them. She didn't need swear words to underscore her point. She knew her way was the right way, the sane way.

RATIONAL: *nail, rat, ton, trial . . .*

Rianne sat on the couch, happy her dad had moved the pointless throw pillows to one side. She lay back, as if she was relaxed about this. She could have been; she'd been through this a million times before.

These talks started up after ninth grade, when she got caught drinking at Cattail Park, with a hickey on her neck from Devin Trauger. After that first "talk" came all sorts of annoying, stupid solutions: the weekly check-ins with the school guidance counselor and the family therapist and the "girls-only" camping trip where Rianne was bored out of her mind from listening to her mother's friends gasp about nature's beauty all week. From these talks came the birth control pills that Lucy Hettrick insisted upon after finding condoms in Rianne's backpack in tenth grade. And the joint membership to the YMCA that Rianne never used because she didn't want to run in place on a treadmill or take fitness classes with a bunch of old women. It seemed to Rianne that her mother went through life reading a handbook on raising a daughter she didn't like. Which was maybe why it seemed as if Lucy Hettrick was half assing all these stupid ideas herself. Sabotaging them, even. Renata hadn't needed all this effort; Rianne could tell her mother found the whole thing tiring and pointless.

Her mother started talking about her dad. He was here for a while, they should all try to be welcoming, it's important to make time for family.

Rianne said nothing.

"Regarding where your friend Kaj said to find you."

"Gullwing Lake."

"Yes. The Pinskys own that cabin there?"

Rianne shrugged.

"It was on the mailbox, Rianne," she said. "Don't act like I'm stupid."

"I'm not acting like anything!"

"Regardless." Her mother cut her off. "Never mind that I'm embarrassed as hell to have Mai Vang know how you've lied to me. And her, too."

Rianne regretted involving Kaj. Again. Not just because Kaj's parents thought she was a good person. Obedient. Honorable. Smart. But also, her mother had met Kaj's mom at a business conference where Mrs. Vang was doing something for her smoothie shop and Lucy Hettrick was running a booth for Wereford Community College's communications program, where she was a faculty member. Their mothers weren't exactly friends but they saw each other around, sat by each other at volleyball games. Gabby's mom was always chasing her little boys; the Kovashes worked night shifts and often weren't able to get to the games at all.

"We're not doing this again. I'm done." Lucy Hettrick sighed and leaned back. Her glass of wine on the side table was empty and her library book closed beside it.

Rianne stared at her mother. She wore black yoga pants and striped hiking socks and a super thick cardigan that looked like it was knit from raw sheep wool. Her mother's style was the crunchiest, boring-est style ever.

"Okay," Rianne said finally. "Great. Good enough." She started to get up.

"Sit down," her mother said. Voice like stone. Rianne froze and sat back. This time she didn't pretend to be relaxed.

"There won't be punishment from me. If your father has ideas, he can share them. But, all this?" Lucy Hettrick waved her hand around, as if Rianne's sins were floating in the air. "I'm just too worn out. You'll be eighteen soon. You've got friends. You're on the pill. I just don't know what else I can say or do to get you to make rational choices. To think for just one goddamn minute about what you do. Or don't do."

That last was about school. School was all about what Rianne didn't do.

"So. You don't want college?" her mother asked. "You and Mercy are doing Saint Paul in the Fall?"

"No," Rianne said, feeling gloomy. "Mercy's staying here."

"Staying here. Hmm. Okay. Fine. But there will be no car for you."

"You got Renata a car."

"Renata had the grades. She earned it."

"Of course. Renata's basically perfect. What else is new."

Her mother blinked but didn't stop. Her volume increased. "What's new is *me*. How *I* plan to act. There will be no wondering where you are. You do your thing, you finish school, you do your sports, your job. Whatever. But you figure out how you get to all those places. You arrange it, you pay for it."

"Fine."

"And while you're doing that, you'll need to get ready to move out. To leave. Doing all the estate stuff for your grandmother, I've decided that I'm going to get things in order for myself. I'm going to sell this house too."

"What?"

"I'm downsizing," she said. "I don't need all this space."

Rianne pulled back like she'd been slapped. Her mother continued.

"Because it's come to this, Rianne: graduation and then you're out. June first is your date. You need to find somewhere else to live after that. Which means you've got to figure out something solid. I've done way too much for you, that's the problem. For once in your life, you need to think ahead."

This made her want to kill her mother. Kill her with her bare hands. Her mother had no idea about how long she'd been thinking about Saint Paul in the Fall. She'd been doing all of it. Now that plan was garbage. Not that she'd ever say so. Telling her ideas to Lucy Hettrick never went well. Her mom questioned, debated, argued. Pointed out all the flaws of any of your possible decisions until the only thing you could actually decide was to never tell her anything again.

"Where are you gonna live then? In Wereford?"

"Yes, probably. There are some developments in Dalby I'm considering too."

"And I can't live with you."

"There won't be room for either you or your sister, no. Renata doesn't need a place to live, though. She's figured that out for herself, you see."

"Then, what? I'm just supposed to go live under a bridge or something?"

"I don't know, Rianne. It's not up to me. It's up to you. It's always been up to you."

"But can't you just . . ."

"No," her mother said. "I can't 'just' do anything further. You'll need to figure this out."

"Oh, that's it? That's all?"

"It's very simple. It's also very hard. That's the trick of growing up. Letting go." Her mother laughed but it sounded completely unhappy.

Rianne didn't say anything. *Growing up, letting go?* It made no sense. But there was no give-a-shit left in this Lucy Hettrick and it felt dangerous, like walking over a cliff. She had ruined it,

Rianne had, by being who she was, doing what she did. She heard her mouth say, "Well, okay," and then her mother left the room, her library book under her arm, the empty wineglass dangling between her fingers.

FOUR

BACK IN SCHOOL, Kaj was so apologetic Rianne felt like a total asshole. Though Kaj hadn't gotten caught doing anything, her parents had taken her car away for two weeks. All Rianne's fault, which Gabby couldn't stop pointing out.

"So, Kip's going to have to take his mom to work if he wants to drive her minivan?" Gabby asked Kaj.

Kaj shrugged.

"And you'll have to walk to work," Gabby continued.

"It's not that far," Kaj said, glancing up at Rianne from her turkey wrap. "I'm cool with the exercise." They both worked at Planet Tan, which was close to school. But the forecast was below zero for the coming week. Rianne gave a halfhearted smile to her friend.

"Some people don't give a shit about who *drives*," Gabby said, stabbing her caf fries into a puddle of ranch. "They just bum rides like it's nothing."

Since this was the first time since Christmas break that Gabby had hung out with them, no one said anything.

Then when Luke stopped to say hi, Gabby rolled her eyes and left the table. Luke watched her go—Gabby made sure to be dramatic and noisy about slamming her tray around—and though he looked like he wanted to say something else, he just shook his head and went to sit with his friends.

"God, he just said *hello*," Mercy said. "Why is she being such a baby?"

"She keeps saying she didn't even like him," Kaj added. "Are you guys going out now officially or something?"

Rianne shrugged. "Not that I know," she said. "But maybe Gabby knows."

"She does seem to know everything today," Mercy said. The three of them laughed but inside Rianne felt gross. Going back to school after Christmas break was hard enough; now it was like Gabby had overturned the table and stomped all over their lunches too.

The next day they had their intramural community college league. Things started off decent: Gabby picked Rianne for a partner during practice and they did some basic passing. With friendly, basic chatting. But then Gabby started smashing down spikes at her during two-pair. It wasn't like it was wrong to challenge your partner in a warm-up but the other players were looking over at them as Rianne went after everything she could—digging and sprinting across the floor.

As punishment for this, during the actual game Kaj quit

kicking sets to Gabby. Which only made Gabby sulk more. They lost the match after a series of stupid block errors. Rianne felt embarrassed about it because it was their first loss. Some of these players were adults that Coach Paula knew too. Gabby acting all pouty was so babyish, though not really that out of the ordinary. Coach Paula had lectured Gabby for not being a team player before.

But intramural league wasn't the same as the school team. There was no locker room hangout, no JV squad, no post-match coach lecture. When it was over, a churchy group of singles had the court and they all had to clear off to the sidelines to grab their stuff. Gabby put on her warm-ups and coat and went straight to the reception desk to talk to Claire Andale's older brother, who worked there whenever he was home from Iowa State on school breaks.

"God, what is her problem?" Kaj said, after they passed Gabby giggling with Claire Andale's brother, who had a stupid goatee you could tell he was proud of. "It's like, if you don't even care, get over it."

"She's a hypocrite," Mercy said. "And she doesn't give a shit if how she acts hurts other people's feelings."

Because people didn't call Gabby names like they did Rianne. Even if Gabby didn't have a boyfriend long-term, she always seemed to have guys who couldn't get enough of her. Getting them to start shit, to pay attention to her, was a matter of Gabby Vaccaro hollering something snarky down senior hallway. Gabby was the reason people started calling Rianne "Hat Trick Girl" in tenth grade—she'd been the one to tell everyone how Rianne was with three different guys in one night at a party at Cuddy's. Even if she just kissed one of them (Cuddy's roommate, Pete Novotny) on a dare and another (Pete Novotny's cousin) because he said something funny.

The third guy was the only one that Rianne regretted. That was Aidan Golden. And then Gabby told everyone Rianne gave Aidan Golden a hand job in the basement, behind the orange-striped sheet that Cuddy hung up to keep people out of his laundry. Which wasn't untrue, but Gabby didn't bother to mention how it happened after Rianne and Aidan had done a bunch of Jägermeister shots. Instead, Gabby made it seem like Rianne had done some threesome orgy. Of course, Aidan Golden laughed about it; he had nothing to be embarrassed about, being a guy. Rianne worked hard to avoid him ever since. She even asked Guidance to switch her schedule last year so she didn't have Studio Arts with him.

The next day, Gabby stopped talking to Rianne in any of their classes. Instead, Gabby talked to everyone but her. Devin Trauger in psychology, Aidan Golden in the hallway, Claire Andale in Global Studies. Claire Andale! The prissy Homecoming Queen girl who did a speech about living with the disability of scoliosis for one year in sixth grade and how hard it was. Fucking Claire Andale, with her glossy dark hair and little ruffly dresses that barely covered her bony non-ass and her perfect grade point average. Claire Andale, who everyone was nice to but who no one could actually stand. Claire Andale played tennis and sang solos in choir and at her and Gabby's church. All their lives, all four of them had thought Claire Andale was the most boring girl in Wereford and possibly the entire world.

But now Gabby talked to Claire like she was hilarious and exciting. Gabby wore a flippy scarf just like Claire's, only hers was black and Claire's was gray. The whole time, Gabby made no eye contact with Rianne. Rianne had become invisible.

This wasn't exactly a new feeling. When it came to actual classes, Rianne had a special talent for becoming invisible. She listened to the lecture, kept her book open to the correct page, sorted herself into group work activities, didn't have a habit of being late or absent. Her talent, despite appearing attentive and involved, was that she was somehow able to think about everything beyond the topic at hand, all without participating or getting called out.

Take World History. The topic might be types of classical architecture—Corinthian columns, something Rianne found beautiful and worth more thought. So, when the class lurched ahead, Rianne would just stay back in the pages of ancient architecture, imagining building something from dust and stone, while the rest of the class marched ahead to the Punic Wars. In Spanish, she could only mimic, not spell anything, so she got points in verbal tasks at least. In photography this fall, she ended up reading the appendix in a Robert Mapplethorpe biography instead of roaming the school grounds doing the various assignments like everyone else was, taking pictures of their feet, or close-ups of dew on leaves, the slanted light layers under the bleachers. And of course, in English, she'd take vocabulary words and wring them out into little lists of other words.

PORTENTOUS: *tent, poor, store, tore, sore, spent, out, port . . .*

DISCORDANT: *card, and, rant, trod, act, oar, soar . . .*

ESOTERIC: *ice, site, sire, tire, ire, rose, erst, rest . . .*

This wasn't great for her grade point average. But it made going to classes tolerable. At times even sort of interesting.

At the end of the day, Gabby brushed past them all, talking on her phone and ignoring them as they stood by Mercy's and Rianne's lockers. Ignoring the day's-end ritual of talking on their way out of school.

"She didn't say hi this morning, either," Kaj said. Being alphabetical, Vang and Vaccaro were next to each other.

"She's acting like she's in a fucking movie or something," Rianne said.

"She'll get over it," Mercy said.

Kaj shook her head while putting on fresh lip balm. "Whatever. Fuck her."

Mercy finished loading up her backpack while Rianne zipped up her coat. Through the window by the Art Showcase, she could see that outside it was snowing like hell. Down the hall, Gabby was looking at something on Aidan Golden's phone and clutching his arm in a way that was obviously on purpose. They both looked up at Rianne at the same time and started laughing.

Rianne looked down, felt her eyes water. Felt Mercy and Kaj looking at her.

"Fucking bitch," Mercy muttered.

"I wonder if she'll say anything to me during the meeting today," Kaj said. "I hope she does." Kaj shoved her lip balm into her handbag all crabby. Gabby and Kaj, always good students, had National Honor Society after school twice a month.

"It's like she's trying to make a point about something," Mercy said.

"About what, though?" Rianne asked, still looking down at her feet, willing her eyes to dry.

"Don't even look at her," Kaj said. "She gets off on being wondered about."

Then Luke came over.

"Hey," he said, his back to Aidan and Gabby, clueless about what was going on. "What's happening?"

"I'll be at your game tomorrow," Kaj said, not missing one beat. "But I can't drive Kip. He said you'd give him a ride. Is that true?"

"Sure," Luke said. Oblivious to the way Kaj had to manage Kip's life, Luke nudged Rianne. "You coming too?"

"I don't know," she said, glancing up at him, then looking over his shoulder at the fire extinguisher case on the wall. "What time is it?"

"Same time it always is, silly girl. Same place too."

"Rianne doesn't do hockey," Kaj said. "Aidan Golden's not exactly her favorite dude in the world. Remember?"

He didn't acknowledge the Aidan Golden comment. "You want a ride home?" he asked Rianne.

"Mercy was taking me."

"I can take you too," he said.

Rianne felt everyone looking at them for a minute and wanted to die.

"She's had a shit day," Mercy said. "Be nice to her, Pinsky."

Luke never took his eyes off Rianne. "I'm always nice," he said. "I'm the nicest goddamn guy in this whole school."

He opened the truck door for her, and once he got in, she started to cry. It came out of her so quickly that she couldn't believe it was happening. Luke looked shocked but he couldn't have been more than she was. One minute, she was willing her tears to disappear, the next they were gushing.

"Oh man," he said. "Mercy wasn't lying. What the hell happened?"

Rianne shook her head, swiped tears out of her lashes, wiping her hands on her jeans.

"Can we just drive?" she asked, looking down at her nails, which were unpolished and jagged.

"Yes. Yes, I can," he said, pulling the old gearshift into reverse and hauling ass out of the lot.

"My house?" he asked. She nodded, still struggling to control her stupid tears. She looked out the window at the gray sky over the snowy fields. Luke lived out in the country with his mom and grandparents. When it snowed too much, kids out there didn't make it into school; the buses couldn't get out that far. She hadn't thought about it much, how she lived so near "town" and he was so "rural." Rustic. Country boy.

They pulled up to a little white house with red shutters and blue trim and a big gravel drive. A big truck and a little Jeep were parked in front.

PASTORAL. *Think of pasture, not religion*, she'd told Mercy when the word came up in English.

"Is your mom around?" She ran her fingers through her ponytail, hoping to unsnarl the ends a bit.

"No one's here. My grandma works at the animal clinic in Dalby on Wednesdays. And my mom and grandpa are still at the office."

"Hey, speaking of your grandma—is your dog okay? Sorry I didn't ask before."

He didn't answer right away.

"Ruby was fifteen years old," he said, his voice sounding sandy. "And it was . . . my grandma didn't think surgery would help any of it. Her lungs were totally giving out."

"Oh, shit. I'm sorry. I'm so, so sorry, Luke," she said. "God. Why the fuck am *I* crying here?"

They both laughed it off, but she could see he was trying to act cool about it. "She listened to Lance more than me, anyway," he said. "And at least we got to say good-bye to her before . . . you know."

"Yeah. That's good."

Rianne had never had a pet. So she didn't really know what he meant, but she'd watched enough TV to know it sucked when they died. She couldn't imagine putting down your grandson's dog, however. It made her itch to ask if his grandma had done that part or if Ruby had died naturally. But she didn't think they needed any more crying at this point.

Once inside, she could tell it was a dog house. There was hair all over the hallway rug and a faint doggy odor. There was also an undernote of the citrus spray she used to wipe down all the various surfaces at Planet Tan. In the front hall, there was a wooden mirror with little stenciled ducks on it and piles of boots and skates were heaped on a rag rug.

Luke took off his shoes and she did the same, then followed him to the kitchen, where he began to rummage through the refrigerator.

"Coke, Diet Coke, Dr Pepper, or orange juice?" he asked. "We're out of Mountain Dew." The bottom of the fridge was loaded with pop, which was totally bizarre to Rianne. Lucy Hettrick never bought pop. Too much sugar, too much caffeine. Only when they went out for dinner could they have it and only stuff with no caffeine. She shook her head and asked for orange juice, and he poured two large glasses of it that they drank while standing in front of the sink. The phone rang and Luke answered it, a big black cordless thing whose ring shook the walls. He was talking to his grandpa or maybe his brother. Rianne half listened while she took in the Pinskys' house.

There was a placemat near the back door that had a big red bone on it, but no dog dish. A suncatcher of a sparkly frog in the window above the sink. The yard behind the house had a big blue shed with a giant woodpile stacked beside it. Beyond the chain-link fence was a plowed-over soybean field. The house wasn't grandmotherly, like Grandma Hettrick's had been. But it was girly in some ways. A blueberry-muffin-scented candle sat on the counter. A china cabinet with flowery plates, angel magnets on the refrigerator. Framed pictures of Luke and Lance everywhere: in their church clothes, in their school pictures, in their hockey gear.

Around Wereford, Luke and Lance's story was well-known. Their mother, Lorraine Pinsky, got pregnant at sixteen. She had stayed in high school, lived with her parents, and raised Lance, and then, two years later, Luke, in their house. Who the fathers of Luke and Lance were was still a mystery, though some people had floated theories: it was the same guy; it was a dozen other guys. Lorraine Pinsky had been kind of wild.

When Luke hung up the phone, he dug around in a cupboard and came out with a box of Swiss Cake Rolls.

"Nice," he said, tucking the box under his elbow.

"Do you always eat that much after school?" she asked.

"Sometimes I eat more," he said. "We got late practice, gotta keep the metabolism going, you know?" He smiled at her through his shaggy bangs and then led her down some stairs.

It was a typical basement. Laundry, a canopy of women's bras hanging from a rack above the dryer, a workbench with a broken chair on it, hampers full of dirty clothes, three old olive-green suitcases stacked on top of one another and covered in dust. He opened a door and she went into a dark room with just casement windows for light. He didn't bother to turn on the lamp, just tossed the Swiss Cake Rolls on his desk and sat down on his giant unmade bed.

He took off his hoodie and patted the bed for her to sit. None of Luke's room looked particularly nice, but the bed was soft. He put his arm around her and she leaned into him. She didn't feel like having sex with him, but she knew she would, anyway. This is what made her a slut, in her heart, really. That she would be fine with it, either way. The whole thought depressed her even more.

"What's up?" he said softly, his hand curling around her waist, slipping under her sweater. She twitched; she didn't need him getting acquainted with her love handles right now. She wasn't sure where to start. Tried to gulp back the crying feeling.

"I mean, I'm not the only one with a dead dog story, am I?"

"Oh . . . ," she started. "No. No. I'm sorry. I mean, I don't know. Today just sucked. A lot of things suck."

"Okay. Like what?"

"Do you . . . I mean, I could make a list, Luke," she said, trying to joke.

"Go ahead," he said.

"Well. First. My mom's kicking me out when I graduate. And she's selling the house."

"So?"

"Well, Mercy and I were going to get a place together, up in Saint Paul this fall. But she's probably moving in with her sister. And so now I've got to figure something out for the summer. Money. And a plan."

"All right," he said. "What else?"

She looked at him in the gloom of the room. Unsure he was really up for this. Active, supportive listening was pretty out of character for Luke Pinsky, the party guy of Wereford.

"Well, for some reason, my dad is back living with us now."

"Your dad living with you—is that something bad? Are you okay?" He said it like he was asking if Dean Wynne beat them or something.

"No, he's fine," she said. "He's in the army, so he's never really lived with us, anyway. They've been divorced since I was five."

"Okay. What else?"

"And Gabby's acting like a giant bitch."

"Ha! Gabby *is* a giant bitch. No acting required." He got up and grabbed a package of Swiss Cake Rolls from the box and unwrapped it for her.

She laughed, not expecting that. She hadn't really wanted to bring up Gabby, get into why she might be jealous of Rianne. But he'd asked for the list. And Rianne didn't know what she had with Luke. Even with him handing her the chocolate cake, even with his hand stroking the skin above her hip. She had never had a thing with a guy where she cried and told a list of things that upset her. Though she knew that was how it worked, from watching dumb shows on television. And from Caleb and Mercy and Kaj and Kip.

She sighed a little. Leaned into him. Bit into the Swiss Cake Roll. It was nice to sit on his soft bed and eat junk food and unload her life on someone. He smelled like the kind of cheap shampoo her dad kept in his Dopp kit when he traveled. The kind that made her hair dry as fuck.

"Don't let Gabby get to you," he said, his voice soft, his arm squeezing her to him.

"I can't help it," Rianne said. "She can be such an asshole. And only to me."

"She's just jealous of you," he said. He flopped back on his bed and watched her pluck apart the chocolate from the frosting innards of the Swiss Cake Roll. She fed him a thin strip of cake striped with the white icing, which he accepted easily.

"She's not *always* a bitch."

"Right. What about the Hat Trick thing? Her starting that with Aidan?" he said. "I remember that." Little peels of glossy chocolate had landed on his T-shirt. She brushed them away, though he didn't appear to care.

She wiped chocolate crumbles off her mouth. Felt like a pig for eating so messy. For being so messy and bad. For being Hat Trick Girl. All of it.

Her hair was falling out of its ponytail, and he ran his fingers through it.

"Girls are such bitches to each other," he said. "My mom says that all the time."

Rianne couldn't argue. "Well, yeah. But who else can they be bitches to? Not guys. Not you."

He shrugged, pulled her down to him. Licked the bit of chocolate off her upper lip.

"So, here's a story. Okay, so, you know, the first time I had sex, I was thirteen?"

"What? Does everyone know this?"

"No, just you. And the girl too, I guess. She was thirteen too, just so you know. But, anyway, immediately after we're done, I've barely pulled up my shorts, I can't believe it's happened, I'm super geeked out about it, you know. And like, the next thing I know, her friends are telling her she's a whore."

"Who was this?"

"This chick at hockey camp. You don't know her."

"Oh."

"Anyway, I haven't even said one thing about it to anyone before I've got all her friends giving me shit looks. But, at the same time, they won't even eat with her in the dining hall anymore or pass her any pucks and it's all stupid."

"Jesus."

"And the kicker? Then they're all lining up to get with me themselves! What the hell is that?"

She laughed. Lay beside him, her head in the nook of his arm. She had no answer for him about why girls were the way they were. Not one she could explain very easily, at least. Gabby had hooked up with Luke, so had Rianne done it later, just like the hockey camp girls? There was no way to explain girls to him, she realized. It was easier to talk first times.

"The first time I did it wasn't at camp," she admitted. "But with a guy I met there. He was a lot older than me, though. He was like nineteen? Maybe twenty."

"Jesus," Luke said. "What a sleaze."

"He was okay," Rianne said. "He did an okay job coaching. I mean, he was all-conference in basketball, I guess."

"He was a *coach*? That's even worse! What kind of shitty camp was that?"

Confessing this to Luke was making her feel so gross. She could never tell him it had all happened on Gullwing Lake, just across the water from his own cabin. He sounded so outraged and his whole body was rigid, like he might ask her to leave. Or get up and go kill Eli himself. Was Eli still in Colorado, where he said he was going to school so he could snowboard between classes? He'd surely graduated by now.

"We weren't at camp, at the time. It happened later. Sophomore year. I was super wasted when it happened, actually," she said.

"Jesus, Rianne," he said. "Was *he* wasted?"

"We smoked out together, so yeah, I guess."

"Rape-y fucker."

"Luke, come on."

Luke started ticking shit off on his fingers. "Okay, one, he's older than you. Two, a coach. Three, you're fucked-up when it happens? He's lucky you didn't call the cops."

Luke lecturing her about this was pretty insane. Especially when he was usually fucked-up when he got with girls. The Pinsky cabin was known for that shit.

But she didn't want to argue. She wanted him to let it go, just like she had. So she rolled over him and then, a few minutes later, they'd moved the relevant clothes out of the way, and he got a condom in his nightstand, and she had sex with him. Him on top the whole way, because though it wasn't bright in the room, it wasn't dark, either. Her being on top felt like everything would show.

When they were done, Luke took off the condom, tied it into a knot and spun it in a little white globe above their heads, and then chucked it toward the wastebasket by the television.

"Two points," he said softly, and laughed. He pulled her back under his arm and covered them with blankets. The bed smelled like Luke, and a little rank too, like he never changed the sheets. She felt as gloomy as his room. Usually, she liked the fun of sex. It was exciting and interesting, seeing what someone might do. Guys did lots of things, when they wanted sex. They trembled. They said your name so soft and kind. They shut their eyes and squeezed you like they didn't ever want to let go and in that moment you were important. Valuable. Everything they wanted or needed.

But sometimes she felt crappy afterward. It became too clear how short the glory would be. How basic and boring everything actually was. How it had been just something to do when you didn't have anything else going on. Because no guy had ever made her come the way she could make herself come when she was alone in her bed or the bath. That was the shameful part, in her mind. That she did these things, and they were fine, and fun, but unlike the guys, who always got off, she never did.

She closed her eyes. The room was darker now. She wondered how long they could be down there before his family came home. She wondered how many girls he'd brought back to this bed. How many condoms were stuck to the side of his wastebasket. It was kind of hypocritical to wonder. She was a girl just like him, in that exact way, her coral orange packets of pills that her mom brought home to her and insisted on her taking were in the bathroom drawer. Even if Rianne suspected they made her gain weight.

A knock on the door. "Luke? You in there?" His mom.

"Yeah, me and Rianne are here," he said. His voice was as lazy as Rianne's body was tense. She tried to sit up but Luke pulled her back down.

"It's okay," he said into her ear.

"I've got dinner from the chicken place, so come on up," his mother continued. "Your grandpa's setting the table."

"Okay. Be there in a minute."

After the footsteps went back up the stairs, Rianne sat up. "Luke! I'm so embarrassed!"

He shook his head. "It's fine," he said. "I told them you'd be coming over."

"Today?"

"In general." He grabbed a T-shirt from his dresser and put it on. She saw the strip of his stomach above his boxers and thought how cute he was sometimes. Like a little boy, cut into a man.

She shook out her hair, rigged up her bra beneath the sweater, dumped her boobs into the cups, untangled the straps with a snap. Put on her jeans and socks. Rubbed on some coconut moisturizer from her purse, wiped on a stripe of lip gloss, flicked on a bit of mascara. Ate a piece of gum.

"God! I look obvious, don't I?"

"You look perfect," he said.

"Shit."

"It's fine," he said. And then he took her hand and they went upstairs where he said, "Mom, Grandpa? This is my girlfriend. This is Rianne."

FIVE

"YOUR MOTHER'S STUBBORN," Dean Wynne said, after he picked Rianne up from the YMCA after yet another lost intramural league match. Gabby hadn't even bothered to show up to this one. "But I'm working on her. Don't worry about it."

"Yeah," Rianne said. Her dad acted like he hadn't been divorced by this woman. That he somehow had any pull with her at this point, that her mother was one who didn't think long and hard before saying something. Rianne had heard her mother say it for years: Lucy Hettrick hadn't wanted a life of travel and moving. She wanted stability and routine, a small-town life that simplified raising a family.

Simplified was right. Rianne's dad had been simplified out of the whole situation. But obviously he still didn't realize it.

"I think it's just talk, though," he said. "There's gotta be a work-around, I'm sure of it."

He was, in a word, OBTUSE. A good, fancy word for him.

Because, how long had he been gone? Did he not understand how stubborn her mother was? She was as stuck to her ideas as her father was loose. Dean Wynne had cliff dived and rock climbed and sailboated and zip-lined all over the world, with his kids, and without them too. Was he really that dumb to not see his ex-wife for what she was? A grouchy, bitter woman, forever dug in about being right. She made decisions that she liked to be final.

"It doesn't matter, Dad," she said. "I'm fine with it." The last part was a lie; she wasn't fine with it, she was a panicked mess, searching all of study hall today on the library computers for apartments in Wereford, apartments in Saint Paul and Minneapolis. She had called about a caretaker position in an apartment building in Dalby that had a low rent in exchange for basic duties around the place. But the dude answering the phone hadn't even let her finish her question:

"How old are you, sweetheart?" he said in a growly, mean voice, and she'd hung up.

"It *does* matter," he said. "I can tell it matters to you. How are you going to handle being on your own?"

MAELSTROM.

"I'll figure it out."

"How? With no one around to help?"

A situation or state of confused movement or violent turmoil.

"Mom doesn't think I need help. Mom thinks it's got to be all my decision."

"Well, technically. But there's no reason you have to be on your own. We're your parents. We can help you. We can . . ." She stared at his mirrored Oakleys, the light bouncing from the sun, from the rearview mirror.

. . . storm, seam, roast, rots, least, stem, most, male . . .

"Dad? Can we not talk about this right now?"

"Honey, come on," he said. "I'm just trying to help you think about it. Be a resource."

Rianne hated the word *resource*—it was a dumb school word teachers liked to say. A word that didn't want to be clear about what it was. *Resource* could be a fucking book in the library or it could be a stupid "Do You Have Attention Deficit Disorder" quiz hanging on the wall of the guidance office at school. It could be a seam of coal or a telephone book in the recycling bin or a magazine article on police dogs. It could be anything, really.

Anything besides her dad driving them in his Kansas-plates truck, wearing his awful rainbow-lens Oakleys. Her dad, with tattoos on his bicep of an eagle clutching little ballistic missiles in its talons and the flag on his heart. The worst. Better to have no tattoos than ones like that.

He turned to the strip mall for Planet Tan; he was going to buy beer while she turned in her schedule request for work.

"Meet you back in five?"

She jumped out of his truck and went inside. Gwen, the owner of Planet Tan, was making appointments. She held up a long, French-tipped nail when she saw Rianne, smiling her wide white veneers. Gwen was a redhead with orange skin and blue eye shadow and her clothing style was what Kaj liked to abbreviate as STC: short, tight, cheap.

Rianne was tired, she was annoyed, she had to do a presentation in Global Studies the next morning on desertification in Africa. Every extra dumb word Gwen said to the invisible person on the phone was making her want to scream. All she wanted to do was take a shower and go to bed.

Gwen hung up the phone. "What's up, doll?" Gwen called everyone stuff like that. *Doll. Honey. Baby. Sweetie.*

"I brought in my hours for the schedule."

"Perfect," she said. "I was waiting on you; I'll have February's schedule posted tomorrow. I've done some new things with the formatting and the shifts."

But before Rianne could hand it over, the desk phone rang again and Gwen was back on it.

"Planet Tan, this is Gwen, how can I help you . . . ? Thursday . . . ? At one . . . ?" With one hand she hiked up her top, adjusting her boobs, while the other started flipping through the paper calendar on the desk. Gwen was saving up for fake boobs; her last boyfriend had promised to finance them, but he'd dumped her and moved to Seattle. Not that Gwen let this stop her. Like Dean Wynne, she was always talking about the importance of goals. How Kaj and Rianne needed to believe in themselves, find their happy place, follow their dreams.

Then the little ding that signaled a new customer entering the place went off and Gwen looked past Rianne entirely. Another customer, a guy in a puffy coat and sweatpants.

"Can you hold, please, my computer's being slow," Gwen said to the next invisible person on the phone.

"Hang on, baby girl," Gwen said to Rianne as she stood to set up the guy in his booth. Her tall bony body rippled; she straightened the wide black patent leather belt that bisected her red top and short skirt.

Rianne sighed. She looked out the window. Snow piled up on her father's truck and the other cars in the strip mall lot. Two boys came out of GameStop with their parents, pushing and shoving. A woman lit a cigarette the second she stepped out the door of Tobacco World and then stood looking at her phone.

And then the big black Buick of the Russians drove up in front of the smoking woman. Rianne watched to see if the woman got in the car, but instead, Sergei and one of the other Russian guys got out of the car. Rianne's skin went shivery seeing him: Sergei so tall, the car so low he almost had to unfold his body to stand. The black car rumbled toward the Liquor Barrel, the other Russian went into Tobacco World, but Sergei stayed beside the smoking woman. Snow piling up on his head. He was wearing a black peacoat and, from the looks of it, his same Levi's, same shiny black shoes. She would have bet he was wearing his pressed white shirt too, though from a distance all she saw was a flash of red scarf.

The woman was talking to Sergei now; her face smiled into life as she did, full of laughter and attention. She slipped her phone into her purse and crossed her arms and tapped her cigarette ash with a casual, cool flick.

Sergei turned so his back was to Rianne. All she could see of the woman past the black back of his coat was her bright lipstick mouth blooming smoke out the side, like she didn't want to contaminate him.

A minute later, the woman tossed her cigarette on the ground and stamped on it with her black boot. *Bitch*, Rianne thought. *Way to pollute the earth.* Rianne hated smoking cigarettes. They didn't even get you fucked-up and they cost a ridiculous amount. The woman offered him a cigarette from her pack, but Sergei didn't take it, which made Rianne secretly happy.

At that moment, her father came out of Liquor Barrel holding a big sack in one arm and a case of beer in the other. She watched him scan the parking lot for her, looking toward Sergei and the girl. Dismissing them. Instantly, she felt sad. A deep-down depression. She couldn't forget the hangover remedy on her skin, the experience of waking up feeling so good. She wanted to ask Sergei more about it because it was impossible to Google it. How could you Google something that you didn't know the name of?

She looked again at Sergei and the woman. Her father was now brushing snow off his car with his big yellow suede glove. Sergei was someone who didn't exist. Just background. Just an extra in a movie, filling the space, making no difference.

That night, after she had raided the internet for articles on deserts in Africa, clipped pictures from *National Geographic* and glued them to a tagboard poster, she got in bed and thought again about Sergei.

Had Sergei ridden a train in Europe? He must have. She thought of how he looked, black coat, black shoes, bright shining blond hair, red scarf. That tucked-in fancy look was weird here, but probably normal where he lived. She wondered how he'd look in all those places she had never been. In the waiting area of Planet Tan, and on the walls of the individual booths, there were framed posters of tropical locations: Costa Rica, Monaco, Greece, Tahiti. Places you'd go with your fake-tanned skin and your bikini body. Fake and stupid and expensive, like the tanning itself. Thinking of Sergei in Russia, somewhere dark and cold, a place where an old woman made magic medicine in a silver tin, where he would stand and wait, exhaling cold breaths on a train station platform, where shadows stacked up around him like mountains and the disastrous economy of Russia they read about in Global Studies, everything all grimy and dark and desperate. That setting made more sense for him.

She ran her hand down her neck. Despite Gwen's urging, she never paid to use the beds at Planet Tan. It was ridiculously expensive, even with her discount, when you compared it to the summer sun that was always free. She tanned easily, playing on the sand court near Cattail Park, running laps out on the track in the off-season with Mercy. Swimming on Gullwing Lake, near the camp where she had first met Eli.

Her palm went over her left boob, and down her stomach. There were silvery stretch marks on the sides of her boobs, down the sides of her hips, and on the top of her thighs. You couldn't cover those with tanning bed light; you could only ignore them and hope no one saw. In the summer, they still winked under her browned skin. They had been there forever and there was no getting rid of them, though it was better now than when they first appeared at the start of sixth grade, the year she got her period and a growth spurt that sent her shooting up taller than Renata and her mother both. Her father didn't see her until later that summer. Dean Wynne had been shocked to see his youngest girl look less like a middle school girl and more like a teenaged one.

Her father had been at tonight's game at the YMCA, and so had Luke. Both of them had whistled and yelled from the sidelines, though there really wasn't any place for spectators. Luke had met her father, briefly, afterward. He said, "It's good to meet you, sir. Your daughter's amazing," and her dad's eyebrows went up to his shaved hairline, but he shook Luke's hand all the same.

This is my girlfriend, Luke had said to his family. Then they all sat down to roasted chicken and Styrofoam cups of mashed potatoes and biscuits with honey butter and his mother, who she didn't know what to call—Lorraine? Mrs. Pinsky? Ms. Pinsky? Miss?—asked her questions that only felt curious, not mean: where she lived, what sports she played, did she like hockey. Luke's mom had hair that was pretty terrible. Silvery blond with a sprayed puff of bangs that looked like a deep-fried dandelion wishflower, and a ponytail braided high on the back of her head, like she was going to be a genie for Halloween. But still, at least Luke's mom was sort of interesting. Lucy Hettrick would probably let you kill her dead before she'd have a hairstyle that required more than just running her hand through it.

At Luke's they had talked about her job at Planet Tan—his mother knew Gwen, somehow—and his grandpa talked about their family's business, the snow removal season in full swing. Then it had been all of them making references to things she didn't know about, but she sensed it was a way of them showing off.

Now, from downstairs, she heard her father laugh. Why was he here with them? She had remembered the years before they divorced in a haze. She'd been a kindergartner, new in the school in Wereford. Though she had bragged about it when she was younger, how she wasn't born here, the truth was that she didn't remember Germany that much. Just odd little bits. Taking the train, walking in winter-cold squares with statues in the center of them, strange modern art, shopping, playing in parks, the blue of her bedroom on the walls, and the diamond pattern on the carpet. The little machine on the corner that sold cigarettes like some kind of strange robot.

Fingertips under the elastic of her undies, Rianne listened to the sounds of a house with two parents. Her father's pushy laugh. Her mother's answering murmur. The dishwasher door banging down, the crisp snap of a beer opening, her mother's slippers smacking the wood floors. Sounds that were familiar, sounds that weren't. Sounds she wouldn't hear after graduation.

She thought of how Luke felt inside her. How it always felt, someone inside her. It felt good, important. But it didn't do what she could do with her own hand and fingers, her thighs squeezed

98

tight. The old word Mercy had taught them back during that first year of camp at Gullwing Lake in seventh grade. Cha: the silly-nothing word, now used constantly and without care by all four of them.

Do you shave your cha yet? Or just your legs? Mercy had said it like a dare.

Mercy, god, what are you even talking about? Gabby, always annoyed, even then.

Chaw? Kaj always wanted to get things right.

No, chaaaaaahh, idiot. That's what my grammy always called it. Mercy spelled it out on the floor with lipstick and Rianne laughed and wiped it away with a towel wet from swimming.

Getting herself off took her no longer than a minute. Her fingers were quick, specialized. The only sign of anything happening was her thighs clenching repetitively under the thick heap of her comforter.

Always for a while afterward, she felt complete. Strong. Tight as a wire. Everything that upset and confused her dissolved from her body, evaporated out of her skin, through the smooth chutes of her pointing feet and curling toes.

But then came the small lump of guilt over this particular habit. Of how she needed it to fall asleep every night. It made her gross, she was sure; it made her a freak apart from tidy girls like Claire Andale. Even girls like Mercy and Kaj, who had steady boyfriends.

Her hand curled on the sheet, smearing wetness off her fingers, and she tipped into a perfect sleep. The kind where sad stories leaked into dreams and made you cry all night long, leaving you to wake up the next morning feeling lonely and not knowing quite why.

SIX

IN PHYS ED, they were playing water polo. In the middle of January. Because everyone needed to know how to play water polo for a life skill, Kaj joked.

"I think Gabby's blocked me on her phone," Rianne said after class in the locker room. "I text her and hear nothing back. But she'll talk to you and Mercy?"

Kaj twisted her hair into a topknot. "She talks to me, yeah. But she's totally got a pitchfork up her butt still. I don't think this is just about Luke, Ri. I think you're going to have to just ignore her."

They were hollering, because their lockers were by the wall of screaming hair dryers, with one blaring over a girl named Ariana Richter, who seemed hell-bent on getting her hair back into the perfect blowout it had been before.

Idiot, Rianne thought, looking at her. Ariana had an older brother, Gabe, who graduated the year before from Wereford.

Rianne had had sex with Gabe at a party at his house. Ariana was gone, visiting some college in North Dakota she was overeager to attend. She had never spoken to Gabe again, even though he said hello to her, because the whole time they'd been doing it, she hadn't been able to get over this big collage of his sports pictures over his bed, a metallic strip with little magnets of all the athletic versions of Gabe. Little Gabes in baseball uniforms and basketball jerseys and soccer shorts. Above that, a little shelf with all his basketball trophies that trembled as they fucked. It wasn't like having sex with him had hurt or anything. But something about the whole thing made her so sad. Killed the buzz that had made her flirt with him to start with.

Rianne turned away from Ariana. Ariana had the same dark hair as her brother and she was brushing it out carefully. METICULOUSLY. Rianne only had one more class after phys ed—stupid Spanish III. There was no reason to look fancy anymore.

"How the hell am I supposed to ignore her?" Rianne asked. "She's in two of my classes. Plus intramural league."

"She's quitting intramural," Kaj said.

"Great," Rianne said. "How nice of her to tell everyone. Or just you."

"I can't help it if she talks to me, Ri! It's not like I think she's being nice or anything! She's acting like a total brat. And about Luke Pinsky, for fuck's sake." She said his name like it was something equally babyish, like "a Barbie doll" or "Pokémon cards." Then she said, "Sorry. No offense. But you know what I mean."

Rianne divided her hair into two loose braids. Always, with her friends, she imagined the shit they said about her privately in little secret snotty duos: Kaj and Gabby, Gabby and Mercy, Mercy and Kaj. Things might be different, now that Gabby was out of the normal loop, but generally, she could easily guess the shit all three of them said to each other. The angle always changed depending on who you were talking to: with Mercy it would be how spoiled Gabby was by her parents and their money; with Kaj it would be how bitchy Gabby would act in front of guys; with Gabby it would be how Kaj was married to Kip, how that was so boring and predictable. She assumed they all had their way of talking about her too: how she acted at parties, how she was slutty and stupid when she was wasted.

"It doesn't help to have Luke hanging around you at lunch," Kaj said.

"It's not like I invite him!"

"You should tell him not to."

"This is so middle school, Kaj!"

Kaj sighed. "I know. Believe me."

As they headed to class, Kaj said, "Gabby told me Caleb was acting all creepy in the library the other day. Like, he wouldn't stop staring at her chest."

Rianne rolled her eyes.

"Gabby is so conceited," Rianne said. "She can't stop bragging about how gorgeous she is."

That was another thing about Gabby: she was a bragger. Especially about her family—her father was a doctor and her mother stayed home with her little brothers—Gabby was always discussing everything great about them: their vacations to Italy and Mexico to visit family, their new flat-screen, Dr. Vaccaro's new boat, her older cousin who went to college at UCLA. Rianne knew that this bugged Kaj too, because her dad was also a doctor, but he was a dentist, not an MD, which Gabby liked to point out. Kaj wasn't one to brag about anything, especially her family.

There had always been distinctions about their families. You went to Kaj's to eat good food, because Mrs. Vang always had good fruit and stuff around from her smoothie shop. You went to the Kovashes' to be girly and veg out in their deluxe rec room entertainment center they'd built in the basement. You went to Rianne's if you wanted to hide in her room and be invisible, because Lucy Hettrick didn't do more than say hello and goodbye to any of her friends.

But every single time you went to the Vaccaros', you'd just feel shitty about everything you didn't have while also wanting to smack Gabby's little bratty brothers.

At the end of the day, Rianne's hair was still half-damp. It was sleeting out and everyone was freaking about the slippery stairs to the parking lot because some ninth grader had wiped out and had to go to the ER to get stitches.

"Hey, girly," Luke said, coming up to her as she dumped her stuff into her backpack. He called her that now, because he said that his grandpa called her that "nice little girly" since they'd eaten dinner together that one night. It was a kind of inside joke, at least for Luke. She didn't like to think of Luke as a grandpa.

"Hey."

Luke was standing too close for just normally talking. She was still as he kissed her, first along her cheek, near her hairline, then on her mouth.

"What are you doing this weekend?" he asked.

"I don't know."

"Let's do something."

"At the cabin?"

"No, Lance and Tana are painting. They're moving in next month."

"So that's the end of the Party House, huh?"

"Yeah," he said. But he grinned. "It had to happen eventually."

"We could go to Cuddy's on Saturday," she said. "There's always something going on over there."

Luke made a face. "Cuddy's is fucking nasty on Saturdays, with the ladies' night thing. Nasty girls, nasty beer. Just . . . whatever, I'm not up for it. Let's go do something cool. Just me and you. Alone."

"Okay," she said. She felt like he was asking her something big. Like for them to do something grown-up and fancy, like Kip and Kaj did. Go out for dinner at Outback Steakhouse. Buy each other special gifts: Kaj got the corny jewelry, Kip got this watch that supposedly you could dive underwater with and figure out your directions if you got lost in the wilderness. Kip even bought Kaj Victoria's Secret underwear, which Kaj hated and only wore so he wouldn't feel bad. Would Luke do stuff like that too? She didn't know if she should feel happy, that she was in this club now—The Girlfriend Club. She wondered if Luke understood how far away from being here she had been her whole life.

At dinner the night she and Luke were going to hang out "alone," her mother asked about her friends' plans after graduation. Which was bullshit, because Lucy Hettrick didn't give one shit about any of her friends. She was nice to them only when they showed up. They could have been dead otherwise.

Still, while Rianne dipped bread into her soup, she told her parents vaguely about her friends and their plans.

"St. Thomas is a good school," her mother said brightly, wiping her mouth with a napkin.

"Yeah," Rianne said.

"Which one of them is the amazing athlete?" her dad asked. "The one with the killer arm?"

"All of my friends are amazing athletes, Dad," Rianne said. "But Mercy's got the wicked arm."

"She's not going to St. Thomas?"

"No. Kaj and Gabby."

"Is Kaj that little Asian gal?"

"Dad. 'That little Asian gal'? Really? Who says 'Asian' about someone? She's Hmong."

"Okay," he said. "That's nice."

"Nice? Someone's nationality is nice?"

Her dad glanced at her. "Hmong were based in Laos. Not a

106

nationality. A people. They were in China, before. You think I'm some kind of dunce. The Hmong have quite a history for being warriors. Worked for the CIA in the 1970s during Vietnam. Though we totally fucked them over on that enterprise. And they've got a very complex, very old religion with ghosts and spirits and whatnot."

"Kaj doesn't believe in ghosts. Her family goes to the Presbyterian church over by the hospital."

"Quit biting my ankle, girl. Don't act like it's impossible that I might just know more about this than you."

"They're basically American, Dad," she said.

"That's easy for you to say," he said.

"Except, I guess, for food," she admitted.

Rianne started describing how she went to a cookout with Kaj's entire family two summers ago. Kaj had worried that none of them would want to eat the food and had even bugged her mom to pick up a pizza. Rianne refused the pizza and instead ate everything else, even the green papaya salad that nearly burned her mouth off. But she was the only one of her friends to finish her bowl of it. Gabby had gagged. Mercy had turned bright red and had politely swallowed her bite but didn't take another.

"Papayas are green?" her mother asked. "I thought they were orange."

She shrugged. "Look it up if you don't believe me."

"Where's Mercy going to school?" her dad asked.

"I don't know," Rianne said. "I think she'll probably just move in with her sister."

"Faith goes to Wereford Community," her mother noted. "Maybe she will too?"

"Maybe," Rianne said. She put down her spoon.

"What about that Luke kid," her dad said. "What's the deal with him?"

"He's going to work with his grandfather's business," Rianne said.

Her dad wiped his mouth, swigged his beer. "No, I meant, what's the deal with you and him?" He pointed to her with his spoon and winked like it was some funny joke.

"He's my . . . we're, like, you know."

"No, I don't know. Enlighten me."

"Dad! God. I mean . . . I guess, we go out."

"Dean, stop," her mom said, bringing her bowl to the sink. "At least you've met him. Am I ever going to meet this boy?"

"What do you care?" Rianne said.

"Rianne." Her dad's face was angry.

"Sorry," she said.

Her mother dropped the subject, though, and started loading the dishwasher. Rianne and her father resumed eating their soup. Her father kept looking at her as he ate, making her worry that he was going to scold her for real.

"Dean, you want another beer?" Her mother, at the counter, was pouring a glass of wine. Soon it would be book and chaise lounge time. Soon this soup-slurping dinner would be over and

Rianne could escape from trying to be good for both her parents.

"Sure," he said to his ex-wife. "Okay, so this Luke. He play any sports?"

"Hockey."

"Oh. Sure. Of course."

"He's very good at it."

"I'm sure he is."

IRATE: *ire, rate, rat, tear*

"We're going ice-skating tonight."

"That makes sense. He'll want to strut his stuff for you, I'm sure."

Rianne wanted to punch him. Not to hurt him. To wake him up about how he was being an idiot. And also for how he had become this weird thing, this strange guest walking around shirtless in her mother's house, making them blueberry pancakes and filling the bottom of the fridge with beer. None of what he was doing made sense. She had sat through his silence about his work and his long raving descriptions about places he'd been living. The beauty of this or that culture, the strangeness of the geography, the price of milk or walnuts or meat. The way everything smelled and felt.

She had bugged him as a little girl to tell what he did: "Do you kill people, Daddy? Do you shoot them? Or just blow them up?" And while he'd never gotten mad at how shitty those questions were, how any of them could have been true and she was this little snotty girl, asking them in her singsong baby voice, he'd never told her, either.

Luke coming to get her turned out like something you'd see on a TV show. Rianne had tried to answer the door and just run out, but Luke came inside and then her dad showed up and Luke took off his snow-covered Sorels on the rug. Her father and Luke small talked until her mother called, "Stop cramming yourselves in the doorway and come inside like civilized people!"

Rianne, who had been stuffing her feet into her boots, hung back as Luke walked deeper into the house. Dean Wynne ushered him into the living room where he introduced him to her mother. For all her interest in meeting Luke, her mom didn't bother to get up from her lounger in the living room. It wasn't even seven o'clock and Lucy Hettrick was in her yoga pants and slippers and hoodie.

Luke sat on the couch in his bright white socks on the wheat-colored carpet, his big hands on his knees, smiling and talking and acting like this wasn't some shitty job interview but something he'd been waiting for his whole life. Her dad sat next to him and Rianne stood in the archway, her skates over her shoulder, folding her arms and finding it impossible to know what to say.

Which didn't matter. Luke was talking hockey and the nursing home that Grandma Hettrick was in—his aunt worked there—and how great Rianne was at volleyball and yes, he was going to take her skating.

"Rianne hasn't been skating since grade school," her mom said. "Unless you took her skating, Dean?"

"Nope," her dad said. "We tended toward the warmer weather vacations." To Luke he said, "Rianne's mom and I are divorced."

"Oh, right," Luke said, his eyes wide, his blue hockey cap bunched in his hands.

"Dad. God. Luke, come on," Rianne said. She grabbed Luke's hand and pulled him off the couch. Lucy Hettrick rolled her eyes and murmured that Rianne was always in a big hurry to leave all the time.

"Have fun, you guys," her dad called.

Luke kept talking and she pulled him back to the door ("nice to meet you!") as she grabbed her mittens and hat. Everything Luke said—it all came out so easy for him. She hadn't behaved as confidently when she had met his family. Even the fact that they were going skating! As if that were normal, standard behavior for them! When really, what she and Luke did, what they *were*, was something completely different. He had fucked her in his cabin while people got wasted in the next room; she had sucked him off at a party in the bathroom. They had sex in the truck parked right now in her driveway. Why did he get to be so calm and easy in this world when she could not?

But of course, he wasn't in the same stressed-out rush. Of course, he stopped to open the passenger door for her, as if he knew her father was watching from the kitchen. Which he was.

Luke gave her the keys and told her to turn on the heat so she wouldn't get cold and then she sat in the cab with the headlights aimed at the garage door while Luke carefully brushed the snow piled on the windshield. The radio was on the sports-talk station, which she hated, but she just turned down the volume. She wanted to be as good and polite as he was being.

"You're all stressed about your parents," he said when he got in the truck. "I don't mind parents."

She nodded. He turned off the radio.

"Put your seat belt on, girly," he said, putting on his own. "Besides, I don't even know who Lance and me's dad is," Luke added. "I mean, think about it. It's not a big deal, your parents being divorced." He checked his mirror and then pulled out of the driveway. Finally.

"Your mom never told you who he is?" she asked, once they were clear of her street. "You never asked?"

"We've seen our birth certificates," he said. "They're both just with her name on them."

"But you've never just asked her?"

"No," he said. "It's kind of a touchy thing, with my mom."

She felt like a dick for being so nosy. She wondered how he could be so unconcerned about who his dad was. Wasn't that a thing all boys cared about? Instead he seemed unbothered.

BLASÉ. NONCHALANT. LAISSEZ-FAIRE.

As he drove toward the rink across from the high school, they talked about other stuff. Kip's latest with his mom's minivan, which involved him taking a corner too fast and knocking the spare tire off the bottom of it. And then not telling her until she got a flat the other day. Kip had panicked and called Luke to come help her.

"The spare tire's on the bottom in a minivan?"

112

"Well, on Kip's mom's minivan it is. That fucker is *old*."

Rianne thought about how dorky Kip was. Compared to Luke, at least, who knew about things like flat tires. She was surprised Kip hadn't called Kaj. Kaj drove a little Honda that she kept in perfect shape. Her dad had made her change a tire in their driveway the day they drove it home from the car lot.

"I don't even know if I can skate anymore. I'm probably going to fall on my ass a lot," she said as Luke parked on the hill overlooking the rink.

"You'll be fine," he said, his hand on her knee. He said it with so much certainty. Like they'd been together for years.

Below them, little kids skated under the blaring light from the warming house.

"Little rink rats," Luke said. "That one is Kip's little brother. Little baby Jelinek. I think his name's Kyle."

"Does Kip only hang out with people with names that start with *K*?" Rianne asked. "Kyle, Kaj . . ." Luke laughed.

"He's got a little sister too. Her name's Kayla."

"Shut up!"

"Not even kidding. You ready?" he asked.

She grabbed his hand. "Not yet. Come here."

"Come where, Hat Trick Girl?" He had this little sneaky smile and his hat was nearly falling off his head, his hair bushing out at the sides in big golden blobs.

"Don't call me that," she said. But she was already scooting closer to him and then they were kissing.

That things happened so quickly with Luke turned her on like

113

crazy. There was no waiting around, no wondering.

She pushed his hair behind his ears and his hat fell off just at that second. His hair was very soft. Golden as beer in the warming house light. The kids' skates scraped and clunked in the distance. She could feel the truck cooling off without the heater blasting but she didn't care.

"You smell good," he said, rubbing his face against her ear, her neck.

"Thanks." She thought he smelled good too, but didn't say so. Did you tell a guy that? Even if he was now, supposedly, her boyfriend? Probably not. Though he only probably smelled good by accident. It wasn't like guys set out to smell good. Mainly, he smelled like he'd taken a shower and put on deodorant. Sort of the bare minimum, really. How strange that you didn't ask much of a guy, that he look a certain way, that he smell not like flowers but like leather or musk. Whatever "musk" was.

The herbal scent of Sergei's hangover remedy came back to her. Sergei brushing menthol and mint around her hairline, beneath her eyes. Why she thought of him now was startling. His polished black dress shoes. The foreign, beautiful scent of the hangover remedy. Her strange brain suddenly popped with the thought: *I want to smell every guy for the rest of my life. Store up the memory files like perfumes.*

Luke's perfume: deodorant and cheap drugstore hair gel, with hints of the grime and gasoline from his Carhartt coat, notes of toothpaste on his tongue. It made her imagine him in his bathroom before he came over, a mouthful of toothpaste suds,

114

checking himself out in the mirror. A laugh bubbled in her. A wish to sit on his sink counter to watch him floss and shave and comb the gel through his hair. Seeing how he went about making himself ready to be seen.

Thinking this made her feel extra guilty that she had never told him about Sergei and the hangover remedy. She had kept that secret like a sin. She resolved, not for the first time, to be better. To be the girl her mother wanted. To be a girlfriend who was good.

But not right now. Later. Much later. After graduation.

She shrugged off her coat and unzipped his. If the little kids on the rink looked up, they could see them all over each other in his truck. But who really cared, anyway? They were dumb little kids, smacking and shouting at each other. She put her hand on Luke's crotch.

"Fuck," he said, looking down at her hand. "I swear, I meant to take you skating."

"We can go skating in a minute."

His hands went under her shirt. She sucked in her stomach, hoping to flatten it. Wanting him to feel ribs, not flab. Between kisses, he said, "You just make me so crazy. Hat Trick Girl."

"That's never going to be my nickname."

"Watch. I give everyone nicknames." He sucked on her neck like he was going to give her a hickey. She hoped he wouldn't. Mercy thought it was trashy. Devin Trauger had given Rianne the only hickey of her life. And it hadn't gone away for a long time. It had still been there, on the edge of her collarbone, when she and Renata were at a water park with her dad in Wisconsin. Rianne had lied that she'd been hit with a basketball.

"What's *your* nickname, then?"

"Everyone gets one but me," he said. He pushed his hands under her bra and squeezed her boobs. She didn't like how he scrunched her bra up over her collarbone but it was kind of cute how desperate he was acting.

She started unbuttoning his jeans and he shifted so she could do it, his hands caught in the net of her bra. She lifted his thermal up, running her hands on the little scrim of hair around his belly button, then under his boxers.

"This is the worst place to get easy, I swear."

"I think we can handle it."

His hands slid down. Fingers slipping under the waist of her jeans. He looked straight at her, his eyes dark and steady, then glanced down at the kids.

"Okay. But, just, don't lean back. The horn's kinda touchy."

She laughed. They kissed more. She was wondering how to take off her jeans in a way that wouldn't look stupid when they heard a little girl's scream. The kind that sounded like a horror movie. Luke wiped a hand across the fogged-over windshield. One of the rink rats had wiped out on the ice and now was struggling to get up.

"Oh man. That can't be good."

"What are you doing? Luke?"

"Little girls' crying kills me," Luke said, doing up his buttons and putting on his hat, reaching in the back for their skates.

"That's not blood. Is it?" There was something dark spreading across the ice.

"We better go see."

He hustled down to the rink, hollering to one of the little boys, who was standing with his arms crossed over his chest in front of the screaming girl. Luke walked on the ice like it wasn't slippery, but when Rianne stepped on it she almost fell on her ass. Watching him so confident had made her believe it was not a big thing.

"Explain what happened to your sister, then," Luke was saying to the boy, as if he was a dad in charge of this skating rink and had every right to know. The boy, who must have been Kip's little brother, Kyle, started flipping out excuses but the girl—Kayla—wasn't having it. She screamed, "No, you didn't!" a whole bunch and Rianne just wanted some parents to show up and deal with this already. It reminded her of herself too much. Having tantrums that her mother stood calmly in front of, pressing her lips together in silence. Renata made fun of Rianne's tantrums, told her she was mental, defective, psycho. She never had tantrums in front of her father.

Luke knelt down in front of Kayla and looked at her knee. The little girl was wearing a skating costume with thermal tights that were smudged a little, but there was no blood. The blob on the ice was a juice pouch that had been slashed open with a skate. The air smelled like fruit punch.

"Give me your phone," Luke said, interrupting Kyle, who was hollering something at the girl. At least his sister wasn't screaming anymore.

"Why?"

"I'm calling your brother, that's why."

Kyle skated over and handed Luke his phone. She couldn't believe how easily he gave it up. Kyle wore black hockey skates, smaller versions of the ones Luke had hanging over his shoulder, and he repeatedly poked the tip of the blade into the ice, making divots. Sulking and shrinking, all grouchy misery. She had forgotten how much older high school kids seemed to her at that age. In addition to throwing tantrums, she had always been the kid other people bossed around. The baby. If Renata told her to do something, she would of course do it. Usually it was something Renata would never do, some dumb thing that she wanted her little sister to try. It didn't hurt when Rianne got in trouble for it, either.

Done crying, Kayla started twirling around the rink while Luke talked on the phone. About ten minutes later, Kip Jelinek and Aidan Golden showed up.

"Oh, hey, Rianne," Kip said, and went straight to yelling at his little brother, while Kayla hid behind him. Luke stood at his side, his arms crossed over his chest. They were like two dads ganging up on the little kid, who looked humiliated and pissed, though he was still sassing back excuses. Aidan Golden didn't say hello, just stared at her, spitting dip into a can of Red Bull.

Soon enough, the kids started rampaging toward the opposite embankment, where some other kids were sledding. Kip watched to make sure they linked up with the sledding kids and then all four of them went into the warming house. Rianne first, then

Kip and Aidan, then Luke. The guys put on the same skates as Luke and Kip's little brother, black Bauers. They all sat on the long bench to lace up.

"Where's Kaj tonight?" Rianne asked Kip.

"At her cousins'," Kip said.

"She gonna scrimmage with us now?" Aidan Golden said. He grinned at Rianne and Luke. Like he was going to say something about them being together.

No one said anything. Rianne quietly laced her skates.

"Good old Hat Trick," Aidan continued. "Good luck for everyone."

Luke looked up at Kip first. Then Aidan. The whole warming house was quiet except for the clanking fireplace heater. Aidan's skates were already on and he pulled out his chew tin to pinch a fresh dip.

"Shut the fuck up before I kick your ass," Luke said. His voice was completely calm, not even a little bit of anger in it. He could have said, "Pass the salt" or "What time is it?" in the same exact voice.

Kip turned away. Aidan Golden grinned again, like the asshole he'd always been. It made her sick to remember liking him back in tenth grade.

Luke grabbed the big blue shovel leaning against the wall and banged out of the warming house. Aidan glanced back at her, and then followed Luke out. Then Kip.

She kept sitting there, remembering Aidan's dick in her hand in Cuddy's basement, remembering how there was puke on her

119

jeans from Pete Novotny's cousin, remembering how Gabby had told everyone in first-hour algebra to call her Hat Trick Girl, and Aidan laughed about it all day long. She wanted to set the whole warming house on fire.

Instead, she teetered around the warming house with her blade guards still on, breathing the hot stale air until she felt less murderous. Part of her imagined Luke punching Aidan out. Real blood on the ice. That was crazy and stupid. Life was not a goddamn movie. Life was not dramatic and all about her. She knew that, but it took a while to calm herself down before she went outside.

There was no fight. Just three guys on the ice. Luke was shoveling back the little scruff of ice along the edges of the rink. Picking up the juice pouch and tossing it into the trash barrel. He skated like he walked, fully at ease. She couldn't imagine how he played hockey and skated. How did you manage other people crashing into you while keeping up with a little slippery puck? She took off her blade guards and took a tentative step onto the ice and felt like she was in a cartoon, her arms flapping in panic.

But Luke was there, steadying her with his hand at her back.

"You okay, Rianne?" Kip called. Aidan Golden was on the other side of the rink, dribbling a puck.

"I'm okay," she said.

"Takes a minute to get used to skates," Luke said, and then he pushed her slightly forward, his arm around her hip, his mouth at her ear. He told her to think of her skates as making wide slashes on the ice, to think of them as skis, to think of it as widening her influence so that her center of gravity was settling deep in her stomach. All sorts of shit that sounded like yoga, not hockey. Kip and Aidan were trading shots back and forth, while she and Luke slowly circled the long oblong shape of the rink.

It was snowing again. A couple other guys showed up and a game started getting organized. But Luke shook his head when they asked him to join in; he kept his big hand curled around Rianne's back as if it wasn't even an option. Every time they circled around, she felt stronger and surer.

"You can play, if you want," she said. "I'm good."

"I'm good too," he said. "I don't need to scrimmage."

"There's a scrimmage tonight?"

"Nothing official. And I don't give a shit," he said.

She thought, INTERMITTENT. How he could be one way, then another. But always Luke. In himself, fully.

term, time, enter, net . . .

His hand gripped her hip. Steady. Solid.

Rianne had a brain that cycled in and out. Her outside might look strong, but inside her skull were waves, sloshing and crashing. Lists and ideas. Snowflakes circling, snowflakes in straight lines. But Luke was like ice. Even when he changed his mind, or his mood turned one way or the other, he was still the same, essential stuff.

What any of that meant, she didn't know. Was she in love with him? Was that how it started? She had no idea. The night was really beautiful, though. Beautiful in a way that she'd remember years later. Stars in the deep black, a bit of moon.

LUMINOUS: *to glow from within a deepness, a darkness.*

She liked how this felt with Luke. She could see herself, being this. With him.

She liked how their breaths frosted out together. How blue his eyes were. How fast they skated, the snowflakes clotting in her hair, the quick scrape of sharp metal on heavy ice. How he bent and kissed her, so fast and precise, right on the lips. Like he could do anything, be anything, on skates, going this speed. His mouth was warm and his nose was cold and they circled, her eyes on her feet because she couldn't look at him direct for too long.

LUMINOUS: *light as it is perceived by the eye, versus its actual energy.*

Could she have met Luke in the returns line at Walmart? Could they live here in Wereford like Mr. and Mrs. Kovash and be happy? Luke mowing lawns and shoveling driveways and landscaping the medians around strip malls and gas stations. What would she do? She couldn't be a teacher like her mom; school was not her thing. She couldn't be a nurse like Mrs. Kovash—blood disgusted her—and she hated customer service enough to know running a smoothie shop like Mrs. Vang was out of the question. So what would she do? Run after their kids like Mrs. Vaccaro did all day?

slim, sum, us, no . . .

Always, the words skittering around in her mind. LUMINOSITY was in Science 9, and you used it differently than LUMINOUS in English 10. The same basic thing, in different shapes.

Her mother had been born in Wereford. Her grandmother too. If Lucy Hettrick hadn't joined the army and met Dean Wynne from Tampa, Florida, Rianne would not be here. *You couldn't just park it in one place*, she thought as they whirled around the rink in circles. She could feel herself getting stronger, more confident in her skating. It was all coming back to her now and the dark helped, knowing she wasn't completely on display, knowing the stars and moon above were fixed and glowing.

Why do people fear the dark but want to see in it too? That's the point of luminosity. What makes something luminous, what makes it glow, is the surrounding dark. That is why seeing in the dark is such an important adaptation for animals. Why humans never lose that fear; they're in danger, but they know something's out there. And they want to know what it is, and why it's there.

Kind of a no-shit realization. But even after Mr. Hanson, her Science 9 teacher who said this, left to go teach in Thailand, the words rocked through her for days. *That is why we need the dark. That is why the light matters. That is why.*

SEVEN

STILL, EVEN AFTER the skating night, she didn't call Luke her boyfriend. Even if that was what he was. Even if that was her now: his girlfriend. His girlfriend in the hallway between classes. His girlfriend at his hockey games. His girlfriend at his house, in the living room where they'd watch movies after eating with his mom and grandparents, and later, in his basement bedroom, where he convinced her it was fine for them to have sex, even with his mom watching TV upstairs eating popcorn and drinking beer, his grandfather's heavy boots clomping in and out, getting wood for the fireplace, his grandmother banging open cupboards while she put away clean dishes.

When Lance and Tana moved into the cabin on Gullwing Lake, she was his girlfriend too, sitting beside him at the table while Tana served up slices of the cake Luke's grandma had made for their "housewarming." She bought Tana some baby clothes from Target; she and Luke helped Tana paint the nursery bright yellow with little orange sun stencils.

When Tana left the room, Luke nudged her about what they'd done in this same room on New Year's Eve.

"What happened to the beer bottles and sleds?"

Luke shrugged. "Tana probably pitched them. She's not having any of Lance's packrat bullshit."

There was something about being with Luke's family that made her feel good, but also bad. AMBIVALENCE was what streaked across her brain when she thought about it at night in bed, her hands feeling along her belly and boobs, feeling parts of her that Luke felt. Reminding herself that he liked those parts. Liked *her*. That it wasn't fake. That he invited her, all of her, into his truck, into his house, into his bed. That he wasn't seeing anyone else but her. It felt good to think of this. But also a little scary. It meant she had to be better than she was. As good as he thought her to be.

The week after the nursery painting, Rianne walked in on her dad hugging her mom. His hands around her waist, cinched where her yoga pants met her hoodie. Her mom's palms on her dad's bare chest, her right hand covering the flag tattoo over his heart. They were standing in the middle of the living room.

Rianne said hi. Her parents moved apart. Her dad rubbed his eyes with the back of his hand but he was smiling. Her mother said hello and went into the kitchen.

"Hey, honey," her dad said. "How was school?"

"Fine," she said, turning up the stairs as fast as she could.

She stood in her bedroom for a long while, holding her

backpack, wondering what to do. Did she have to do anything? Was anything wrong? Kaj had given her a ride home in her mom's Prius, which was quieter than Kaj's car, so they hadn't noticed her coming in, probably. But still. It was the creepiest thing. She had no memory of her parents as a couple. It had always been them as separate beings. Her dad swooping in for vacations, or picking her and Renata up at airports as they traveled as unaccompanied minors to meet him for summer visits. Her mother always in Wereford, living out her days as a college professor, a rotation of library books and wineglasses and crises with their grandmother. They were never in the same zip code, the same house. Never mind the same square footage, their arms around the other.

The next Friday after school, she and Kaj went to pick up their checks from Planet Tan, and then headed to Mercy's house to hang out, and for Mrs. Kovash to measure Kaj for her prom dress. Mrs. Kovash's family used to own a tailor shop and she had made dresses for girls in the past, though never her own daughter. All four of them had always been very anti-prom. Prom was for girls like Claire Andale who gave a shit about things like renting a limo and going out somewhere fancy for dinner. But now Kip was insisting that he and Kaj go, because it was their senior year. Kaj, as usual, was putting up with it.

On the way, Rianne told Kaj about her parents' weirdness. Kaj didn't think there was anything that alarming about it.

"I had an aunt who divorced her husband twice. But it was all super strange, because he'd already been divorced once and they were raising his kids and the kids were assholes to her."

"Why did she marry him again?"

"I can't remember. The older kid went to college somewhere else and then they fell back in love or whatever. But that aunt's a freak. She's one of those extreme-coupon people, for one thing."

Rianne laughed. Kaj had a thing about coupons; they made her crazy. She especially had no patience with the people who came into Planet Tan with the coupons from the back of the receipts at the grocery store, which were a pain in the ass to calculate.

When they got to Mercy's, Mrs. Kovash answered the door, but she was on the phone and held a finger to her lips in a *shhh* gesture. Rianne and Mercy went in, taking their shoes off. The Kovash house was pretty tidy. It always smelled like bleach and flowers to Rianne. Which was also what Mercy always smelled like. Her sister Faith's apartment smelled the same way, which made Rianne wonder if there was something genetic about it. Like it wasn't just a matter of what cleaning sprays people used. Faith's roommate, Allie, had recently gotten a cat; she wondered if the apartment would smell less like bleach-flowers and more like cat funk, like Gabby's house smelled. Gabby's mom had three cats that no one ever saw, but the front entryway always knocked Rianne out with how gross it smelled. Especially when you considered how much money the Vaccaros had, how big and rich their house was. The smell wasn't necessarily like cat piss or shit, though there was that note. More like a cat's sweaty armpit. If cats' armpits were like human armpits.

"You're such a space case, Ri," Kaj said, plopping down on the Kovashes' sofa while Mrs. Kovash ducked into the kitchen on her phone call. "You just zone out and stare like that. Like you're super wasted."

Rianne shrugged. Her friends always said that, but she couldn't help it. Why were people expecting her to pay attention to what they thought was worth attention? It was stupid. Everyone was different.

"Is Kip's tie gonna match your dress?" Rianne asked as Kaj pulled out the magazines she had marked up to show Mrs. Kovash for the prom dress.

"No," Kaj said. "Nobody does that dorky shit anymore. Plus I want the dress to be black and white, anyway. With just a little bit of red."

"What are you guys doing after prom?"

"I don't know," she said. "He says we should just go to his house. My parents aren't going for that since the New Year's thing. Why does he want to do this? I mean, it's nice and everything but . . ."

Rianne felt guilty. Like it was her fault Kaj had to go to the dumbass Wereford prom, in the shitty VFW hall. Last year on prom night, she and Mercy had watched a show on serial killers on Netflix. Gabby had picked them up later after she'd finished working at Caribou and they'd all walked down to Cattail Park, where Kaj met them with two bottles of wine she'd stolen from a party her parents had the week earlier. They drank them behind the changing rooms by the pond.

"Fuck prom!" Gabby had made them holler, more than once. Then they told gross sex rumors about people they knew. Channa and Ana and Devin Trauger (which was verified). Ariana Richter and Claire Andale (which was not). Then Gabby started complaining about Dylan Garcia, who was a year old than her. They weren't going out, but Gabby liked him. The thing was that Dylan was sort of religious and wouldn't have sex with her. Other stuff, but not sex. He'd asked her to prom, though, and Gabby refused. Then he quit talking to her completely and when he graduated that June, he joined the marines.

Dylan Garcia was kind of lucky, in a way. It seemed like Gabby had shut him down. But he'd really been the one to have the last word.

Finally, Mrs. Kovash came back from her phone call.

"Hey, girls," she said, sitting down and sighing in a way that was very unlike Mercy's mom. Her mom was always offering snacks and generally seeming upbeat. This time she just set her phone gently on the coffee table.

"Where's Mercy at?" Kaj asked.

"On her way to the hospital."

"What?"

"It's not her! She's okay. But Grayson picked up Caleb this afternoon, downtown." Grayson was Mr. Kovash. Mrs. Kovash's name was Nicola. They had weird names, the whole Kovash family.

"What happened?"

"He got into a fight with someone in the Pumphouse?"

"What?" Rianne thought of Sergei immediately.

"But how did they let him in?" Kaj asked.

"Well, that was part of the trouble. I guess he went in to pick up some food, and when they didn't have his order, he went into the bar. They don't really keep it that separated during the day? He started playing pool and that's when they asked for his ID. He got belligerent and the manager called the police."

"Was Faith there?"

"Yes. She was the one they asked to come talk him out of causing a scene. But he was acting like he didn't know her. Anyway, he wouldn't let go of his pool stick and then the bouncer came and so did Mercy's dad and . . . well."

"What happened next?"

"I'm not sure," Mrs. Kovash said. "Faith said it looked like Caleb was trying to break the pool stick over his own knee? The bouncer tried to take it from him. And then the bouncer got hit in the face with the stick."

"What was the bouncer doing there in the day?" Rianne interrupted. "Don't they only need a bouncer at night?"

"Good question," Mrs. Kovash said. "I don't know. But, anyway, then Grayson and his partner had to restrain him. He wouldn't stop screaming the entire time. It sounded like praying. Lots of asking for Jesus to help him."

"Wow," Kaj said. Rianne saw her fingers twitch toward her phone on the coffee table. Thankfully, so did Mrs. Kovash, who finally started turning back into herself and asking them not to say anything until she got the full report from her husband. There was a ding from the microwave in the kitchen.

"I'm making hot tea for myself. You want any?"

They shook their heads; Mrs. Kovash went to the kitchen.

Kaj reached for her phone the second Mrs. Kovash left.

"Don't," Rianne said. "You can't say anything."

"Just to Kip, though."

"No," Rianne repeated. "You have to talk to Mercy first."

Kaj sighed, like she thought Rianne was being overly sensitive. But she put her phone down.

"Is Mercy driving herself, Mrs. Kovash?" Rianne called into the kitchen.

"Faith's driving her," Mrs. Kovash said, coming back with a mug of herbal tea that smelled faintly like soap.

"Is she okay?"

"Well, yes and no," Mrs. Kovash said. "But it's Caleb she's worried about. He apparently hurt himself in the back of the police car. So he's being admitted to the psych ward first."

"Will they let her see him?"

"There's no way," Mrs. Kovash said. "I don't work on that floor anymore but I used to, and there's a pretty strict procedure. He'll have security and a police escort with him while they treat him. Then, when they stabilize him, he'll be taken to jail."

"What?" Rianne was stunned.

"Oh my god," Kaj said. "Mercy must be freaking out. Is she completely freaking out?"

Mrs. Kovash nodded, and tears started dripping and Rianne could see how she'd been holding it all in so well. Telling the details had kept her calm. But now Rianne could see how she knew her daughter was going to be disappointed. And how she was letting it happen. Letting Mercy see exactly what she had seen on the psych ward floor.

"What's Caleb's problem?" Rianne asked. "Do you know?"

Mrs. Kovash wiped her eyes, grabbed her mug of soapy tea.

"I do," she said. "Some of it, I know. But I can't say."

"Oh," Kaj said, sitting up straighter.

For a few minutes it was just the quiet except for the tick of the clock above the bookshelf. Finally, Mrs. Kovash asked Kaj to show her what she was interested in for the dress and there was no more discussion of Mercy or Caleb, though Mrs. Kovash kept glancing at her phone as she looked through the magazines and then went for her iPad to check on some pattern ideas.

Rianne sat like a lump on the sofa while they talked about dresses. Caleb was crazy. Caleb was on drugs. Maybe both? She wondered if Sergei was in the hospital too. If he had ended up hurting Caleb. How did that feel, to be expected to hit people for a job? She supposed her father would know, and so would Officer Kovash. She wondered if Sergei liked it. She had always assumed her father did but knew he'd never admit that. Officer Kovash she doubted enjoyed it. He wasn't one of those dickhead cops like the one that hung out at the school for the purposes of overhearing who was doing what fucked-up criminal shit.

She had no idea how Kaj could sit there and go over ruffles and skirt slits right now. Something horrible had happened to Caleb, and to Mercy. Something none of them could fix. Maybe it was just like Mrs. Kovash telling the story. Rianne remembered the night she met Sergei and how careful she had tried to be with words. What if something horrible happened and you were somewhere where they didn't speak your language? Was that why some people were so stressed out when they traveled? Because they didn't have the exact right words? Maybe the hard part happened when you ran out of actual words. Anything that was too distressing or too magnificent to express actually had its own word: INEFFABLE. Her English teacher last year liked to use that word when someone said something extra disturbing or gross. Once he'd written it in the margin of Rianne's paper on *The Tempest*, when Rianne said that Ariel being granted freedom was like a teenager getting to leave home after so many years of servitude.

INEFFABLE. Even when you were at a loss for words, you didn't have to be, turns out. But maybe, when there weren't any other words to say, then you were like Caleb. Banging your head inside a cop car. Bleeding. Praying. Screaming.

That night, after the hockey game, Kaj drove Rianne to Faith's apartment. Mercy was staying there overnight, because she was pissed at her dad. Accusing him of hurting Caleb. The Kovashes allowed it, because they knew she needed someone to blame, and the word on Caleb was that he'd gone "psychotic." This was from Mr. Coyle, who was the only one who would talk to Mercy at the hospital. Mrs. Coyle said Mercy needed to stay away from her son, that it was all a private matter.

"Are you sure you want to go in there?" Kaj asked. She had talked to Mercy, who had basically just sobbed on the phone.

"I want to at least try to be nice."

"Do you want me to hang around?" Kaj asked. "I can wait." But she was already scrolling through messages on her phone and Rianne knew it was easier to tell her to go hang out with Kip. Luke was kind of salty that she wasn't going to meet up with him after his game. They'd gotten into a pattern of where she'd come over after a game, talk with his mom and grandparents while he showered, and then lie around on the couch with him, watching TV and eating snacks.

"No, I can call my dad, it's fine."

She didn't know if it was fine. Nothing like this had happened before to any of her friends. She wasn't going to sit in Luke's living room eating chips and flipping through the channels. Rianne had never thought of herself primarily as a "good friend" but she knew it was shitty not to check in with your friend the night her father arrested her boyfriend.

When she pressed the button for Faith's apartment, no one came. She called Mercy's phone but no one answered. She was about to turn back and see if Kaj was still in the parking lot when Faith barreled through the door, holding her purse and keys. She was still wearing her denim shirt from the Pumphouse.

"Oh, thank god," Faith said. "I don't want to leave her alone! I have to get fucking tampons. Mercy just got her period and we're totally out. Can you hang out with her? She's going to take a shower. Her jeans got totally slammed. This day has been unfucking real."

Rianne said okay. She wanted to ask a million questions, but Faith was already jogging down the sidewalk to her car.

Faith's apartment building wasn't old, really, but it was far from modern design. The hallways had a sad green striped carpet and everything kind of smelled crappy. Like burnt popcorn and beer cans sitting too long in the recycling. Faith had lived here for about two years now, with flaky roommates always rotating in and out. While it wasn't the greatest, it made sense that Mercy would want to escape here from her parents and move in, too. Mercy loved this place mainly because of its proximity to Taco John's, which was one hop past the building's Dumpsters in the back parking lot.

On the sofa was an orange cat, whipping its tail and staring at Rianne, while the TV blared one of those shows where grown women bitched at each other and drank giant glasses of wine. The coffee table was covered in magazines and dirty dishes; the place had the familiar cat-butt smell that seemed to thicken as she stood there. Finally the cat shot off the couch down the hallway and Rianne hung up her coat on the rack of hooks by the door. She walked through the kitchen, which was strangely clean, and headed toward the bathroom. She could hear the shower running and thought about barging in, just to say she was there. But she felt shy about it, in a way that was odd. How many millions of times had she seen Mercy naked? Dressed next to Mercy? Gotten caught without tampons and had to hit up Mercy for some herself?

She rushed back into the kitchen. And Sergei was there, wavering drunk.

"Jesus fucking Christ! What are you doing here?"

135

"I live in building. On the top floor. I work with Faith, yes?"

"Oh. Yes. Right," she said.

His left eye was swollen and red, a bruise darkening beneath it. Two butterfly bandages, one on his cheekbone, one by his eyebrow. Caleb had got him good with the pool stick. While she stared, Sergei gripped the back of the kitchen chair. Tried to keep his body steady.

GOBSMACKED. Not an official vocabulary word, but in a list of Briticisms she'd seen online. According to Google, *gob* was British slang for "mouth."

"I am sorry. I am very drunk now. Rianne. I must make some food. Rink has eaten it all. I see Faith just now; Faith says this is fine; Allie is not here now. May I do this?"

"Sure," she said. It wasn't her apartment, after all.

"I am sorry," he repeated. He took off his coat and hung it on the hook beside hers. His eyes were half-open and there was a large wet stain on his pressed shirt, not white this time but a pale blue button-down. Through the stain, she could see the outline of his nipple. Part of her wanted to laugh. His eyes ran all over her, down to her feet and then back up again. Slow. She tensed, feeling self-conscious and embarrassed. And a little bit scared. When you were sober and other people were drunk, it was so obvious how out of control they were. Something she didn't notice when she was wasted herself.

"Faith's sister is here," she said. "She's in the shower."

He didn't seem to care. "I need coffee, some bread. I may do this?"

Rianne nodded.

"I am quiet," Sergei continued. He pressed his palm against the wall, his pale forearm covered in blond hair. His silver watch shined.

Slowly, purposefully, he began frying eggs in butter, dropping bread in the toaster. To help him, she scooped a pile of mail and magazines to the side of the table to clear a space. In response, he set two plates on the table.

"Oh, no, thank you. I'm not hungry," she said.

"You will sit with me? I will make coffee." She watched him pour water and measure out the grounds. The coffee gurgled while he finished frying the eggs and buttering the toast.

He slid everything onto his plate, and again offered some to her as she sat across from him. She shook her head and he insisted on her having coffee. She didn't like coffee, but accepted it. She wondered how he knew where everything was? Had he made breakfast like this before? Back when he was fucking Faith's roommate, Allie?

He heavily salted and peppered the eggs, then pushed them around with the buttered toast. She wondered if this was a Russian custom, which made her want to ask him about the hangover remedy, but he didn't speak, just ate seriously and slowly, like someone preparing for a test. After he finished eating, he drank his coffee, draining it quickly.

She asked him if he wanted more coffee and he said yes. She refilled the cup, happy to have a job. He drained the refill and then wiped his sweaty forehead. He stared at her so intensely that the hair on the back of her neck sprang up, and she looked down at her bare plate.

"Thank you," he said, exhaling. His breath was greasy, boozy.

"You're welcome."

He cleared the dirty dishes noisily into the sink and went to the door. Steadying himself against it, he closed his eyes for a moment. She wondered if his eye hurt. Maybe that's why he'd gotten so drunk? The shower was still going in the background. Was Mercy ever going to get out of there?

"I go now," he said. "I am sorry." He put his coat on.

"Why are you sorry?"

"This . . . I am disgrace. Not good. Drinking like a . . ." He said some words in Russian, spit them out like each syllable disgusted him.

"I heard about the kid at the Pumphouse," she said. "I know him. I'm sorry. It's terrible."

He turned toward her. Slow. He breathed in slow too. Like it was all very difficult, the turning, the remaining standing, the looking at her. Waiting for whatever she was going to do next.

She pointed to his shirt, where the wet spot was.

"What happened here?" she asked.

He leaned closer and kissed one cheek, then the other. The way people in Europe greeted people. She remembered that bit from living in Germany, one of the few things. Her mother lifting her face to greet Renata's piano teacher in the same fancy way.

But after he kissed her cheeks, he kissed her mouth. Lips closed first. He leaned away again. They looked at each other. She could see the little scar on his temple. Then she kissed him again, her tongue in his mouth. He tasted like she expected. Greasy breakfast and booze.

Again, they stopped.

Then, he smiled. There was a space between his front teeth that was exotic to her. Perfect straight teeth but for that space. Was he born that way? Maybe Russians didn't fix teeth like Americans.

He kissed her again. Pulled her near. Her fist went against the wet spot on his shirt. His hands gripped over her boobs: squeezing, pressing, reaching under her sweater. Touching her like he had the right to. Like he knew she wouldn't object. She could feel him smiling while they kissed.

She let him move his hands down. Straight for the button of her jeans, the zipper. They were low-rise, so it didn't take long and then his hand was beneath her undies, palming her cha. Petting it, almost? Like he was trying to be gentle, nonthreatening.

She hung on to his shoulders. He pushed her jeans down her hips. They weren't kissing anymore; now he worked his fingers up inside her. His booze breath spread over her cheek. She kept her eyes closed while he worked his hand in her. Somehow, his height, the position of them standing made it so she could feel everything ten times more intensely, his fingers making the same tension she gave herself in her own bed.

How strange that it could be here now as well, in front of the door at Faith's apartment. But not with someone who called her his girlfriend. Somehow Sergei was getting her there. Her thighs tensed, her back straight. She could hear how wet she was on his fingers. She thought of Mercy in the shower. They had to stop. But he was touching her in exactly the way she liked. She tried to be quiet. Failed.

He pressed harder, like he didn't want to fail either. Drunk as he'd been when she first saw him, he wasn't stumbling any longer. He rubbed with one hand, the other steadied at the small of her back. Her calves tensed, and she knew it was going to happen. Going to, going to, going to . . .

Happening.

She heard her own toes crack. Or maybe it was her ribs? The vertebrae in her neck? An entirely perfect, embarrassing moment.

As the feeling fizzled out of her skin, she opened her eyes, staring at the pale blue of his shirt, the wet spot fading away. She was afraid to look at him. She could hear him breathing, feel the hotness of it on her neck. Slowly his hand came out of her, leaving her undies in a twist, her jeans at mid-thigh. She felt dizzy. This was so dangerous. The shower wasn't running any longer.

He pressed his mouth on her neck. Kissed it, once, twice, three times. She made another sound she tried to hide, a kind of sigh. Then she looked up at him. His eyes reminded her of the ice at the park, frozen gray-blue. She couldn't stand it, how good she felt right this second. He didn't smile, but there was a little twitch from the side of his mouth.

Then there were sounds in the hallway, and he stepped back from her. Stood up tall, to his full height, until she was looking at the buttons of his shirt, the open lapels of his coat. He wiped his hand on his shirt, coughed into his fist, and stepped back from the door. She turned to zip and button her jeans. They were silent as they listened to the noise move down the hall to another apartment. Keys jingling, laughter. A girl's voice saying, "Hey! You're the dumbass who wanted to go there!"

He was about to say something, but then her phone, still in her coat on the hook, started jangling. Luke's ring. She pounced on it, looked at the picture of him on the screen that she'd tied to his number, and though she had yet to see Mercy, to tell her anything, to be a good friend in any way that mattered, she hit the mute button, grabbed her coat, and rushed out the door.

EIGHT

LUKE GOT A new puppy and named her Sally. She was a Lab mixed with German shorthaired pointer, which meant she basically wanted to run every minute she was awake. This high energy also meant she would fall asleep instantly in a totally batshit unpredictable way, like right on top of your foot under the dinner table. She was a beautiful chocolate color, with spritzes of white like foam on top of hot cocoa and the cutest, sweetest face. Luke's grandma explained that the reason people love puppies and dogs so much was a phenomenon called *neoteny*. Which basically meant humans bred dogs for juvenile or babyish characteristics and features. All dogs were kind of perpetual Peter Pans.

"We don't want them to grow up," Luke's grandma said, watching Sally tumble over Luke's boots to gnaw on the laces. "Stop that," she said, lifting the puppy up and setting her on the sofa. She petted the puppy with her wrinkly hand and Sally fell asleep a minute later, her little pink tongue sticking out like a stick of red cinnamon chewing gum. Basically, Luke had a new baby before his brother. A furry baby that was still learning not to crap on the carpet.

On Valentine's Day, Rianne went over to his house to eat spaghetti he had cooked for her, because it was her birthday. Luke's mother was out of town for work and his grandparents had gone to San Diego for their winter vacation. Alone in the house, they had sex, ate dinner, and had sex again. After that they were out of ideas. Rianne suggested walking Sally. So they took her out on a long walk down the country road, until Sally tired out and Luke picked her up and stuffed her inside the front of his coat.

Sally sleeping beneath his coat, Luke took Rianne's hand and they walked along in the quiet as the empty fields covered in snow darkened under the crescent moon.

"I love this," Luke said. Sally made a snoring sound, scrunching her nose.

"Who doesn't love a puppy?"

"Not gonna argue there," he said. "Am I, Sally?" he added to the snoring puppy. "No, I'm not.

"But I meant, here," he said. "I love where my grandparents live. It's fucking perfect. So many stars. Totally quiet. I'm going to train Sally to hunt."

"I'm sure Sally'll love it too."

"Yeah," he said. She was scared he'd say something big. Something important. It was her birthday and he seemed close to making a gesture. Because it *was* beautiful out here. She loved the wide, dark sky over the fields covered in snow. She loved the quiet, though it wasn't quite quiet. She could hear the rumble of trucks in the distance near the soybean plant. Every so often, one would come down the road, its headlights blinding them while Sally slept oblivious inside Luke's coat.

But he didn't say anything. Just kept holding her hand as the white streams of their breath crossed in front of them. Just kept walking, looping around to the side road bisecting the field behind his house. No traffic, less noise. Snow sparkling everywhere.

It was only after they'd gotten back inside and she suggested watching a documentary she'd seen about coral reefs a few weeks ago, that he did the big gesture. Sally wiggling under one arm, he gave her the ring.

It wasn't *that* kind of ring. He said that up front. But it was a nice one. Silver. With a little purple stone.

Amazingly, the ring fit. And she liked silver. But she didn't really wear rings. Or purple. But here it was, looking intimidating in its little velvet pouch from J.A. Hankens, the jewelry shop over by the courthouse. Where people went to buy engagement rings and wedding bands. The diamond earrings her mom still wore had been bought there, on a visit home to Grandma Hettrick's one Christmas, before Rianne was even born.

"Like it?" Luke asked, wrapping himself around her so her hand was stuck between their chests while she fiddled with it so the purple stone faced front. Sally stomped around on the floor by the sofa, fiddling the peanut butter out of her rubber toy.

"Yeah," she said. "It's really pretty."

"I want you to have it, not because it's your birthday," he said. "Or Valentine's Day."

"Okay."

"Though, you know. Obviously, those days count too."

She nodded, not sure where he was going.

"But you're like, you know. The most awesome girl I've ever been with. And I want you to know that. I didn't really know how to say it. Because, you know. You might think about all the shit your friends say about me and whatever."

"My friends?"

He shrugged and then Sally whined at their feet. He sat down on the sofa and pulled the dog up with him.

"I just really like you," he said.

"I like you too," she said. And they didn't watch the show on coral reefs, but went downstairs to his bed, trailed by Sally and her slimy dog toy, which made everything smell like a peanut butter sandwich. Sally's fangs scraped on the rubber toy in a way that made Rianne's hair stand on end. Luke kept pulling her clothes off, slowly, like it was a ritual, and he kissed her everywhere: mouth, arm, shoulder, belly button, knee, and all she could think was that nothing real had been in her brain for weeks, not ideas about where she could live, not for-sale ads for cars tacked up in the grocery store bulletin board, not Mercy fighting with Caleb's parents, while Caleb was being sedated into a walking coma in the psych ward. Not Luke's puppy or Tana's baby that kept hauling in the cute outfits and big boxes of baby equipment. Not her mom and dad laughing quietly down in the living room after she went to bed.

All she could think about was Sergei and what he'd done to her the night he was so drunk. All she could think about was how much she wanted to see him again. And ask him, with words or not, everything he knew about the entire world.

By the end of February, the drama of Caleb had settled down, and he was being homeschooled and attending therapy constantly. It was easy to see that Mercy was depressed. She had given up on intramural volleyball; she was barely attending classes. She slept on the sofa in her basement entertainment room and watched hours and hours of television, glued to her phone for any news of Caleb. Caleb didn't have a cell phone; his internet access was totally cut off. Mercy didn't know if this was for religious or mental health reasons.

Because Gabby had decided to spend every extra second of her life with Claire Andale and Aidan Golden, it was basically Rianne working to cheer her up constantly, watching endless television with her, trying to get her to do homework, make cupcakes. Do anything at all. Kaj helped out here and there, but she was less close with Mercy. And people being sad and depressed and silent was something Kaj didn't get.

But then on the way to the last hockey game of the season, Kaj got all emotional herself.

"Rianne, you can't tell anyone I told you this. Promise? No one! You can't say anything."

"What is it?"

"Promise first!"

"Okay, I promise," Rianne said. Thinking that it would be completely bonkers if Kaj had been a cheater with some other guy, just like she had. Hoping it, almost. Because she was dying to tell someone about Sergei. Dying to even just say his name. But there was no way to bring it up that she could think of.

"I don't want to stay with Kip when I go to school this fall," Kaj said.

This was so not news. Of course she wouldn't. She'd be at college! In a new place.

"Well, no kidding, Kaj."

"Can you tell? Does it seem like that from how I act?"

"No, but . . ."

"I mean, not that I don't love him or anything," she said. "Just that, I don't think it makes sense for us to be officially together when he's going to North Dakota and I'll be in Saint Paul."

"Well, yeah."

"Yeah, what? 'Yeah, that makes sense'? Or 'yeah, it doesn't'?" Kaj was unusually cranky right now. Clearly stressed.

"Yeah, it makes sense. It'll be hard for you guys, being in different places. Doing different things."

"That's just it. I think doing different things is the part that'll kill it more than different places. He doesn't get that."

"Can't you just tell him? Talk to him?"

"I've tried," Kaj said, her mouth turning down again like she might cry. "But he got so upset that he . . . he just freaks out. He starts *crying.*" At this point, Kaj started crying herself. "He won't let go. He acts like . . . like he can't stand the fact that we're going to be adults now. And it's time to do adult things."

"Does he not want to go to North Dakota or something?"

"He says he does. He says he wants to do construction. But I think it's all for the wrong reasons. He wants to save up money so we can get a place of our own."

"What about you being in the dorms and stuff? You'll have volleyball. And your classes. Doesn't he get what college is about?"

"It's like he thinks college will be this quick little blip and be over soon," Kaj said. "Then we'll move in together and get married."

"Seriously?" Rianne felt the ring Luke had given her under her mitten. She hadn't shown it to anyone but Kaj, who knew about it from Kip, anyway. Kaj said it was pretty, but also gave Rianne a weird look. Like she wanted to say something but then held back. Mercy didn't even notice it on Rianne's finger. And Gabby was basically not their friend anymore.

"He figures he'll drive down every weekend to see me. That's like a twelve-hour drive. I don't think he's thinking it through."

"He's probably only thinking about you having your own place and not having to worry about parents," Rianne said.

Kaj laughed, and wiped her tears on the collar of her jacket. She turned down the street where the ice arena was and took the Kleenex Rianne dug out of the center console. Rianne was glad it was the last game of the season. They'd gone to so many of these games together lately and she liked hockey fine, but it was always a long night. A long experience where she was expected to cheer and smile. Which made her think having kids in sports must be such a giant drag. All the paying attention, all the sitting on cold hard bleachers, eating oversalted popcorn, burning your tongue on cocoa in Styrofoam. Just to see basically the same thing, over and over?

And there wasn't much chance of seeing Sergei at a high school hockey game, either.

She wished she knew what Sergei did for fun, besides study grain agriculture and work at a bar and make his own vodka. There were no more parties at the Pinsky cabin, no reason to go to Faith's apartment, either. She'd been researching making alcohol earlier today when she was supposed to be doing the assignment in Dishonorable Math, clicking through her school laptop not on the Trigonometry for Idiots exercises, but the distillation process. How did he do that while living in an apartment? You couldn't keep a still inside; the hazard for fire was so great. Did he not care if he accidentally burned the whole building down? Was that something she should tell Faith about? But then, would Faith have to tell her dad? According to the internet making alcohol was illegal. You could brew beer and bottle wine for your own use, as long as you didn't sell it. But making moonshine was totally fucking against the law, no matter if you only drank it yourself or didn't sell it. There was no way making vodka could be part of his college studies. Was there? She loved these questions. She hated how they gnawed at her.

They got to the bleachers right as the national anthem started. Kaj put her hand over her heart like most people, but Rianne always felt like that was corny. Even if her dad officially fought for the United States. She'd been born in Germany, on an army base, and she was an American citizen. But there was something arbitrary about being devoted to your flag. When just one step off the base would mean, what? That she was German? It wasn't that she couldn't remember the capitals and countries of the world. It's just that she'd seen how they changed; her non-AP, Just-Regular-Dumb-People social studies class had a series of globes on the back shelf, which showed Africa changing lines all across the continent. Germany held apart, then glued together. Names in parentheses Myanmar (Burma) like the globe-makers were trying to knock that into their heads, *it's Myanmar now, even though we don't like the military taking it over, even though we still think of it Burma, privately.*

GEOPOLITICAL. That was what those globes showed. Political lines. Not the lines of sand flowing over a desert, not the rivers or lakes that didn't give a shit what person decided who was where.

Next year at this time, Kaj would be in Saint Paul, in a school founded by Catholics, in a town on a river where Minnesota had been born. Kip would be in North Dakota, building apartments with his cousins, and Luke would be in Wereford, training Sally to hunt and shoveling snow for a living. Or mowing, depending on whether spring came early due to climate change. Luke believed in climate change, at least. His family's business had proof from years of mowing lawns and scraping snow off parking lots that the seasonal patterns were changing. He didn't need to see pictures of skinny polar bears to know it.

Had Sergei ever seen a polar bear? Were there polar bears in Russia?

Stupid questions. Constant questions.

She watched Luke take his place in the face-off, his blond hair flipping out of his helmet. Her dad had told her that hockey players used to not wear helmets. She couldn't imagine. Just hearing the bodies slam against the boards made her startle. Ache for the bruises sure to come. When she told Luke that, he laughed. "I wear a lot of padding, don't worry, girly."

The players scraped and slid and sped across the ice. The crowd was loud, the announcer was annoying. She looked around and saw Gabby sitting with Claire Andale, and the whole Homecoming, Honors English, AP Calculus crowd. Gabby was here for Aidan Golden. Rianne had heard that Gabby had finally formally accepted Saint Thomas's offer and would be going there in the fall, same as Kaj. That she and Aidan Golden were going to prom. That would be hilarious. Ms. Fuck Prom going with Mr. Fuck Face.

Next year, Gabby would be at St. Thomas. Would she and Kaj talk? Eat lunch together? Study the same stuff? Where was Aidan Golden going? Anywhere? Nowhere? Did it matter?

Next year. Who knew about the rest of them. Caleb's parents planned to send him to relatives in Stillwater who ran a religious carpentry business; the trucks all had giant crosses painted on the sides. This was how he was supposed to "screw his head back on straight" and get right with the Lord, with Mercy hours away and unable to corrupt him.

Mercy would live with Faith. Mercy, who would get to see Sergei in the same building. Sergei, who would be her neighbor. Maybe not for long. He could finish his studies here and move any time. Back to Minneapolis. Back to Russia. Even so, she had looked at rents for Faith's building and there wasn't anything available. But she was jealous of Mercy living in Wereford with Faith, probably destined for Wereford Community College.

How stupid she was. She had Luke's ring under her mitten; she had Luke as her boyfriend. Luke was nice and sweet and cute. Luke, who had a job, a plan, goals and dreams for After Graduation. Would he care if she worked at Planet Tan, still? And would he expect to live in her place, if she managed to get one on her own?

She had looked at classified ads in the back of the PennySavers that sat in stacks by the front door of Planet Tan. Even the lowest rents, even if she didn't eat or have phone or cable or anything, were beyond her. Renata lived very cheaply in New York, herself. But she had two roommates and they didn't live in the city. And her mother helped her with bills, because Renata was such a perfect student. Such a rational, high-performing, academically inclined daughter.

Kip scored a goal and the crowd jumped up to scream, Rianne and Kaj along with them. Sports did that to you; you couldn't not feel it. Even Kaj was still excited, even if she wanted to be done with him in the fall. Not in a mean way, probably. Just . . . wishing the whole situation didn't involve feelings. A boy crying. Rianne couldn't imagine Luke crying.

Before the first period ended, Rianne got up to beat the concessions rush for some hot cocoa. And of course, there in her tidy toggle coat was Gabby, standing next to Devin Trauger and some of Claire Andale's stupid friends.

"Hey, Rianne," Gabby said. She flipped her hair, which was unbelievable to Rianne. A hair-flip? *Really, Gabby?*

But she just ignored her and bought two cocoas.

As Rianne was grabbing napkins, Gabby walked over. Her eyes were super red and Rianne instantly knew she'd been smoking weed. Wow. Talk about corruption. Claire Andale's big cause was Students Against Destructive Decisions. Maybe once you put crap like that on your college applications, you didn't have to practice what you preached.

"What's this shit about Caleb going nuts?" Gabby asked. Flipping her hair again. Rianne could see why now; it was caught in the collar of her dumb coat.

"I've only heard what everyone else's heard," Rianne said.

"But, he's like, what? Schizophrenic? Or bipolar?"

Rianne didn't know. Mercy was constantly coming up with a new diagnosis from psychology websites she obsessively studied. Every day, there was a new thing: "pot-induced psychosis" or "schizoaffective disorder" or even Caleb being on the autism spectrum. The main thing was that he wasn't in school, Mercy wasn't allowed near him, and his parents had cut off all his communication to the world. He was like a prisoner. Mercy was out of her mind herself, not knowing. Not being able to talk to him.

"Why do you fucking care, even?" Rianne said. It felt great to finally be angry for once. She imagined tossing the hot cocoa right in Gabby's face. All over her dumb toggle coat. But she'd just paid eight bucks for this cocoa. And she wasn't a goddamn episode of *The Bachelorette*.

Gabby looked sick. Shocked. She glanced around, twitching, to see if anyone was watching them.

"Are you paranoid as fuck right now?" Rianne asked, grinning, sipping the foam off one of the cocoas. "I hope you are. You should be. I can tell looking at you from a mile away that you've been smoking. Everyone can tell."

"Rianne . . . ," Gabby started. And then she put her hands into her coat pockets and looked smaller. Hunched. Rianne grinned bigger. She knew exactly how Gabby felt right now—horrible, freaked out—and it was delicious. She took another sip of cocoa. Licked her upper lip.

Suddenly the crowd inside the rink went "Ooooooh!" The announcer stopped talking. Then started up again: "Looks like a bad collision. Players from both sides down."

Rianne and Gabby both rushed to the rink, Gabby holding open the door so Rianne could get through with her hands full. She couldn't see who was down, because the referees, coaches, and medical trainer, a woman from Gabby's dad's clinic, were bent over one of them.

She wanted to believe it was just the red lines on the rink.

But it was dark. And in spatters, not straight lines. Blood. The word surfed all over the people in the stands, people were pointing, covering little kids' eyes. One of the referees skated out of the way and Rianne could see who it was. Luke. Luke's face beneath his helmet. His mouth was open and Rianne knew he had to be screaming.

CONTORTION. WRITHE.

The crowd was on its feet; the players were on their knees, lined up beside one another, watching silently on the ice as was their habit when someone got hurt.

Gabby exhaled. "Oh god, Rianne. Rianne. Oh god. I am so sorry. Please. I am. Really. Oh god." Her words were short and whispered. She repeated them, as if she was worried they wouldn't take effect. Rianne couldn't respond. Through the Plexiglas boards she thought she could hear Luke crying. Wailing. Moaning. Was it him? Or someone else?

The player from the other team slowly stood up, giant from his padding, and skated with his arms around two of the coaches in their street shoes and clothes. The crowd clapped weakly as he left the ice.

But Luke remained down. The creeping of the blood was stopped somehow, covered, but Rianne couldn't unsee it. The Wereford coach and lots of other people came and went. The announcer mentioned, grave and serious, that it looked like the Faribault player was okay. But he said nothing about Luke. A minute later, EMTs came on the ice with a stretcher board.

Rianne watched it all as if she were the one who'd smoked the weed, not Gabby. Luke seemed to be resisting at first, his head out of the helmet, rolling back and forth. Like he was objecting to something. More people surrounded him now, like it was embarrassing to see a person broken this way. As if it were a surprise that a sport so fast and so rough would do that to you. Hockey made volleyball seem silly. A rope-skipping routine or a square dance, in comparison.

Someone in the crowd around him shifted again, and she could see him on the stretcher. He looked unconscious. She wondered if they'd given him something. She felt like she might throw up. And then the stretcher was surrounded, was pushed through the Zamboni gate, and the other players got back on their skates. But the crowd didn't clap.

"Jesus," Gabby said as they watched the referees swirl between the teams on the bench. "Are they really gonna just keep playing? They are, aren't they? Oh my god, Rianne. Oh my fucking god. Can you believe this is happening? Why is this fucking happening?"

She was sitting in the hospital waiting room with Lorraine Pinsky when her father walked through the automatic doors.

"Honey?" Dean Wynne asked. "What happened?"

Lorraine looked up from her phone for the first time in a while. Rianne introduced her father to Lorraine and let her tell the whole story, even though Lorraine had been stuck at work and hadn't been to the game for the actual event.

Luke was being prepped for surgery. He'd suffered an open fracture of his tibia, which accounted for the blood on the ice, and also shattered some ankle bones that they would have to pin back together with screws.

"I'm so sorry," her father said. "Jesus."

"At least it's the end of the season," Lorraine said. Like *she* was the one who should be comforting Dean Wynne.

"Well, I tell you—we just like Luke so much," Dean said. "He's a great kid. I know he'll mend quick. He's a strong guy."

"Thank you," said Lorraine, as if she was responsible for her son's strength and greatness. Rianne turned as her father patted Lorraine on the back; his mother had started crying again.

"Let us know if there's anything we can do," her father told Lorraine. Then Luke's grandparents came through the automatic doors and Lorraine rushed to them and they hugged and the whole story was repeated, Dean Wynne was introduced, polite hellos made to Rianne. Luke's grandpa said she was "a sweetheart" to be here with the family at such a time. His grandma said, "Yes, honey, it's so good of you!"

"We would have come sooner but Sally got loose," Luke's grandma said.

"Oh, for Pete's sake," Lorraine said.

"I told your mother it was because that damn dog wanted to come with and see her boy in the hospital!" You could tell that Luke's grandpa really thought that was amusing. They all gave him throwaway laughs.

A very tired-looking nurse came and told them they were

moving Luke to surgery and invited them to wait on a different floor if they liked. Dean Wynne looked at his watch and said he'd take Rianne home.

But she said she'd wait until Luke was out of surgery. Again, the Pinskys smiled at her like she was angelic. Grandma Pinsky even patted her arm and repeated, "So good of you, dear." Rianne shrugged, asked if anyone wanted anything from the cafeteria, a move that Luke's grandparents and mother thought sweet—of course—but they all said no, they were fine.

Dean Wynne scratched his neck while the Pinskys headed over to the elevators with the nurse.

"It might get late, Rianne," he said. "I mean, that sounds like a pretty bad break. He's in tough shape."

"Like how you sugarcoated it to his mom, though."

"Aw, come on," he said. "That's what you do at a time like this. Now, seriously. What's your plan?"

"I don't know. What's yours?"

"I'm heading out. I think you should come with."

"I can get a ride back with the Pinskys."

"Honey, they live clear out on the other side of town. You really want them to have to cart you to our house and then drive home?"

"Dad," she said. "It's what you do at a time like this."

He pinched her cheek, pissy and gruff.

"Fine," he said. "But call me. I'd rather you wake me up than put out those poor folks. Okay?"

She said okay and he put on his knit cap, turned to leave. She thought of how she yelled at Gabby earlier. How good it felt to just *say things*.

"Dad? What's going on with you and Mom?"

For a second he didn't move. She thought he'd get mad, start shouting. Or insist she come with him so they could talk. Maybe he'd even make her mom talk too.

But then he winked and pulled down his cap over his ears, fished the keys out of his pocket and jingled them all sassy.

"Wouldn't you like to know."

NINE

MAYBE MOST PEOPLE aren't good, Rianne thought as she ate Reese's Pieces from the vending machine and wandered the hospital. She wasn't sure what floor the Pinskys were on, but since Lorraine had her number and could text her, she was in no hurry to find them. Her mission at this point was to walk away from the pukey cafeteria smell, which reminded her of her grandma Hettrick's nursing home.

Maybe most people just do the things that look *good, because they don't want anyone to bother them.*

Rianne hanging around the hospital had nothing to do with Luke. Or his family. But just how she wanted people to see her. See her as The Girlfriend Who Was Nice. A real sweetheart.

She went out a door that wasn't the one she came in and found herself in an empty parking lot. It was cold but the air was fresher than inside the hospital. She walked along, watching for ice patches. She was wearing her winter coat but unzipped it now. The hospital had been so hot. As if the air itself was feverish and infected.

The hospital in Wereford was surrounded by houses that did not look good. It was the kind of neighborhood where people had four cars in their driveway, with two of them looking like they hadn't run in a long time. Christmas lights still sagging under the roofline. Yards full of kids' toys and bikes and bags of recycling. A trampoline under wet snow.

It wasn't that she didn't want to be good. Who didn't want to be good? But she tended to put it off for later. Now that she was alone and thinking about it, she decided that it wasn't that she was bad. She just didn't always want to do what was asked of her. She was lazy, maybe. Or easily bored. Or sick of listening to lectures.

Or maybe that wasn't it at all. Maybe she just wanted to *feel* good. Not *be* it.

Turning around the corner of the building, she saw a Dumpster and some recycling bins and a snowblower thing, the kind the Pinsky brothers used to clear big parking lots for schools and office buildings in Wereford. Then a loading dock, with a giant garage door, except way bigger. A glint of platinum hair. The shine of dark shoes. A man sitting there. Sergei.

Before she could react, he looked straight at her. Called her name. Waved, like he wasn't sure she recognized him. He wore the same peacoat, same shiny black shoes, same jeans.

Probably I am bad, she thought as she walked toward him. *I am bad, but that's who I am and it's easier to just be who I am than pretend.*

"Hello," he said. "I am happy to see you."

"What are you doing here?"

While helping her to sit beside him on the loading dock, he explained that Rink had a thing for one of the nurses, so they'd come together to get her to check Sergei's bandages.

"I wait now," he said. "Rink eats with her in the cafeteria on her break."

"Why wait out here? Why not inside?"

"I do not like hospitals," he said.

She accepted that; she couldn't imagine having a date in the horrible-smelling cafeteria. She couldn't smell the wintry mint medicine scent of him here, but she didn't care. She worked hard to hide how excited she was to see him. To be invited to sit by him.

She asked him one question that had always bugged her: *Why didn't he drive? Why did he have to wait for Rink all the time?*

"Rink's car does not please me," he said. "It is not because I cannot drive. I drive at home. Everywhere. Here, I do not." He shrugged.

"I can't wait to get my own car," she said.

"This is not a big place. You can walk this city and see everything very fast."

"There's not much to see."

"It is small city. Why I picked to study. Better than Chicago.

162

Too much things to do. No, wait. That is incorrect. Not 'much,' right?"

"I think you mean 'many' instead."

"Yes, thank you. Too many things to do. Things I should not do. I am better to be studying."

"Not making vodka?"

He smiled. Slow. The last time he'd smiled at her, he'd been drunk, with his hand inside her. The fact that now it was her, her words that made him do it, gave her a surge of power. Happiness. Delight. She made fists of her hands inside her coat pockets so hard that the knuckle on her index finger that she always jammed in volleyball cracked painfully.

"Vodka is my study. It is also my disgrace. You remember, yes?" They looked at each other direct now; the curve of his white-blond hair up close looked like a kind of flossy decoration you'd put on a Christmas tree. How could he be so good-looking? Though that wasn't the word. He wasn't handsome. Not like Luke was. There was something uncomfortable about how he looked.

"It's not a disgrace," she said, not blinking away from him.

He looked at her mouth, at her eyes. "You are right. It is not. And I am not *alkogolik* like my brother. My vodka is very good. But now, you say it, Rianne. It is your time to say it."

"Say what?"

"Such a *pochemuchka*," he said. Laughed.

"What does that mean?"

He ignored the question. "Now you say why you are here. Now

I am asking you the question: Why is Rianne here, at the back of a hospital? Late at night?"

She hesitated.

"A friend of mine got hurt," she said. "He's in surgery. Luke."

He nodded. "You hurt him?"

"No!"

"I joke."

"Oh. Ha. No, he was playing hockey. His leg is broken very badly."

"Hockey is not an easy sport."

"Did you play?"

"Only when I was very young," he said. "Not with a serious way. I am bad with goals."

She asked if that meant goals in the scoring sense? Or the other way? She liked that about talking to him. That everything could mean so many different things.

"Ah, yes. I see. Both, I think. Both kinds of goals. My oldest brother—Dima is the athlete. He is concerned with his fitness."

"Are you?"

"No," he said. "I am not careful enough to plan my days like Dima. Dima has a patience."

"Is Dima the alcoholic?"

"No. That is Aleksander. Alek is the happy brother. But like me, Alek has not patience. We have not the brain for patience. No, that is wrong. The mind." He said this last word like he was correcting some long note-taking court reporter in his head.

FORTITUDE: *a kind of willful patience.* She liked how he

couldn't see it in himself. How he didn't see himself the way she saw him. How he underestimated himself.

"You must be patient to make vodka, though."

He shrugged. "Why are you asking me about driving? Do you want to go someplace?"

"Always," she said.

"Where would you go?"

"Anywhere but here. But Wereford."

He looked around. The loading dock was littered with trash.

"It is a small place," he said. "But it is not bad place."

"I hate it here," she said. "I don't want to stay here my whole life. I don't want . . ."

She ran out of energy to explain it. She yawned.

"What don't you want, Rianne?" he asked.

"I don't know," she said. "I am always wanting something, I guess."

"I know this," he said. "I have the same wanting. Also anger that is always there. Always fighting, me. Disgrace. More of that."

She thought of Mercy, who worked her pissed-off feelings out by smashing the holy hell out of the ball on the court. Gabby, who just sprayed it all over other people. Kaj, who seemed too above it all to ever get mad. It made her wonder where her and Kaj's anger was. Maybe Kaj didn't have that much. But thinking about how great it was to let it out on Gabby earlier, Rianne knew she had lots of anger inside her. She always had. She was the sister who tantrummed while Renata stood calmly, rolled her eyes, and called out in a tired voice, "Mother?" Rianne was the one known for throwing food from her high chair and screaming until she fell asleep facedown on the floor of her nursery room after jumping out of her crib. These were the stories told about her, by her aunt Emma and Renata and her mother. As if she were the same girl now. As if Renata had never even been an actual baby, but just slid out of their mother perfectly formed, wearing a white tennis skirt and holding her violin, ready for the Suzuki method she learned from the German woman who lived in the house next door, the one who kissed both cheeks. The woman who was always praised for her power and strictness, her excellent teaching of Renata. Her mother called the German woman "unflappable."

"Do you like fighting?"

He paused. "How do you mean this?"

"The Pumphouse. Hitting people?"

He sighed. "Yes, I like. I like this very much. Yes, you should move yourself far from me, now. Caution." He leaned the other way, as if she should be repelled.

"No, come on!" she said. She reached toward his leg and then settled her hand on her own thigh. "I'm not afraid of you. I'm only asking a question."

Now he went quiet. Moved his mouth a little like he was testing out which words to use.

"It is not good work. But I am liking this work. It is not good to like it. Me, I have a trouble with boredom. You understand?"

"Yes," she said. "That is why I hate Wereford."

"You are not seeing what this place is," he said. "You are not giving it fairness. You only see the small part."

166

"Maybe," she said. "But I've lived here longer than you."

"This is correct," he said.

"And why have such a big world if you cannot see it all?"

"Also correct," he said. "But traveling costs."

"That's why I have a job," she said. "Why you have a job too."

"I choose this work for what it is. Not any other. I do not need to make money," he said. "I am disgrace, also, in this."

"A good one, though," she said. "A good disgrace, maybe?"

"This," he said. He stopped, said a word in Russian. "I cannot explain. There is a saying: *Net khuda bez dobra*. I cannot explain."

"Spell it," she said. "I can look it up on my phone."

From his pocket, he pulled out a pen and then reached for his wallet in the back pocket of his jeans. He found a receipt and flipped it over on his thigh, wrote the words in a slanty script.

"You can find online," he said. "The proverbs are difficult for translation."

"I like things that are difficult," she said. "Words, especially."

He looked at her mouth, handed her the receipt. Now he might easily kiss her. They were close enough. But she decided she would not kiss him. Not because Luke was a few floors up, getting screws pinned into his bones. But because she wanted to be picked, by Sergei, again. Just like the time in Faith's apartment. Except he'd be sober, not drunk like that time.

"Seriy!"

Rink, standing and waving. Sergei's head snapped up and he jumped down from the loading dock. Held out his hands to help Rianne down.

"He calls you 'Siri'?" Rianne asked. "Like the lady on the iPhone?"

Sergei looked pissy for a minute. "Is nickname." He replied to Rink in Russian and they exchanged words, much more quickly than he spoke with her. She thought of how slow she spoke in Spanish class, how quickly the people in the audio lessons spoke. How long it took to accumulate a language, to soak everything up, only to spit it out like gunfire. How much people would never know about others, the whole world, because of this. How could she explain, for example, how Gabby was being a bitch? You'd have to explain why calling a girl a "bitch" was so mean, where it came from, that it wasn't that she was a dog, because dogs were cute.

And never mind about words like *cha*. Even if he had touched hers.

Again, he reached to touch her shoulder. Lightly. The watch under the cuff of his coat winked.

"Rink asks can he drive you to your home?"

"Oh," she said. His hand was still on her shoulder. "No, I am okay here. I will stay."

"Another proverb. This I do not write," he said. Then spoke some Russian. Rink, in the background, laughed quietly.

"What did you say?" she asked.

He shook his head.

"Luke," he said. "You are his girl." He nodded, as if it were a fact. Not one that made him happy. But not one that appeared to disturb him. It flooded her with shame, though, when he tapped her chin with his finger and said "Good night, Rianne," and walked toward Rink into the dark of the parking lot.

It was a week before Luke could even take a shower. Another week before he didn't need constant pain pills. Almost the end of March before he started coming to school half days. His mother and grandparents all took turns driving him to doctor appointments, physical therapy, tutoring sessions. Buying him protein powder shakes to help his bones heal faster. Even if that was bullshit, according to Mrs. Kovash. He would be lucky if he could walk normally by graduation.

In the middle of all this, something good had happened. Her father had to fly back to Virginia for something and in the meantime, he had given her his truck. He put her on his insurance, which he said wasn't that expensive.

"Even with my bad grades? Mom says it's expensive with my grades."

"I've got better insurance, it's fine."

Rianne was completely nuts with happiness. She drove everywhere she could. Picked up Luke's homework assignments. Drove Kaj instead of bumming rides from her. Squashed both Kovash sisters onto the bench seat the night when the Dairy Queen opened for a little cheer-up session for Mercy.

She drove everywhere around Wereford in his huge red truck. Gwen paid her to drop off flyers for tanning all around town and she zipped in and out of stores, leaving them in the windows of Laundromats and coffee shops. She stopped by the donut shop and got a dozen of them for Luke and his family on Saturday mornings. The weather was warming up and things were wonderful. Every day, she could go somewhere in Wereford and not have to wait for anyone or anything. Which was just what Sergei was maybe trying to tell her. Wereford was small, but she hadn't been seeing it. Not all the way. Not everything had to be beautiful to be good.

The only one who didn't care about this was Luke. Mainly because he was so absorbed in getting better, walking on his own, that he couldn't think about anything else. He was positive to a degree that was ridiculous. Or maybe admirable. Rianne couldn't tell. He didn't get mad when people would point out the extent of the injury, tell him to be patient. He would just blink at them like they'd said something in another language.

Underneath the positivity, though, he was getting impatient with Rianne. She wasn't sure if it was part of his own annoyance with his limitations or just the fact that they hadn't been together all that long yet. Or the ring that she kept forgetting to wear. Maybe it would've come out anyhow. But he was always a little irritated with her. Basically, because they hadn't had sex since the accident.

One night she'd gone out to his house to pick him up. Earlier on the phone, Luke had said he might even be up to going out somewhere.

But when she got there, nobody answered the door. She went in and saw half a pizza in a splayed-out box from Pizza Palace on the counter. Immediately, she felt gaggy.

"Luke?" She went downstairs and saw the light was on in his bedroom.

"Are you in there?" she called, knocking on the door.

"Come in, girly," he said.

"What's going on . . ."

"Quick," he said, shutting his laptop and setting it on the floor. He stood, only in boxers and a T-shirt. He hopped on one foot, not bothering with his crutches. He grabbed her arm and tugged her backward toward the bed. "My mom had to go out to Dalby with my grandpa and my grandma's at bowling. Get over here."

"What?"

"You know *what*, girly," he said. She stood in front of his half-made bed and he started rubbing up behind her.

"Luke, are you sure that it won't hurt you . . . ?"

"I didn't break my dick, Jesus!" he said. "Come on."

He took off her sweater, then the dress she wore under it. Her boots were up on the front hall rug. She had worn something cute in the hopes they'd go out.

When she turned around, he was taking off his T-shirt. She could already see his boner in his boxers. He took those off too and sat on the bed, his back to the headboard.

"Just get on top."

"Can't I just . . . maybe I can just give you . . ."

"No," he said. He was past the pity blow jobs she'd given him. "I want the whole deal."

This was the last thing she felt like doing. Mainly because she didn't want to undo all the work she'd done to feel cute. After weeks of just sitting around, tonight she'd made an effort. Her hair was nice, she'd spent time on her makeup. In addition to all that, she'd done Pilates with Mercy earlier that day, in an effort to cheer her up about Caleb. Mercy was a disaster. Caleb was now staying with some relatives but Mercy wasn't able to find out where. Mrs. Kovash was regularly asking Kaj and Rianne to come over for dinner, to hang out, just to get Mercy off the couch. They'd done the workout all the way, no excuses, and though she'd felt jealous of how easy it was for Mercy in some parts, now she felt tight and fit. Energized. Her muscles punished and sore in the way that made her feel good about herself. She wanted Luke to admire her, see and say that she looked pretty, not just get her naked in two seconds. She reached over and turned off the nightstand light.

"Come on," he said, watching her settle herself over him.

Her thighs burned as she got in place, her whole body tense to make sure she didn't hurt his leg. But they'd barely started kissing when he told her to get a condom. And when she moved to get off him, he made a sound like she'd hurt him.

"Shit! Luke, are you all right?"

"Yes! I'm fine! Hurry up!"

She opened the condom still standing up. Above them, they could hear Sally's babyish barking, her little puppy claws clicking on the floor.

"Should Sally be loose like that?" she asked. "What if she gets into something?"

He snatched the condom out of her hand. "She's fine."

Only after he was inside her did his crabbiness cease. Then he was sweet again. Gentle. Whispering into her ear how good she felt, and how pretty she was, and how much he missed her, and needed her, and *goddamn, Rianne, do you even know?*

And yes, she did know. She totally knew. He was so handsome, Luke was. And nice. And sweet to his family and his puppy and to her, mostly. Except lately, maybe.

She wondered if they'd actually go out. She was feeling so uncomfortable and bored lately. Even having this sex was boring. Uninteresting. She tried to make good sounds so he wouldn't notice. She knew how lucky she was. How sad Mercy was to be without Caleb. How tense Kaj was feeling about knowing she wanted to break up with Kip.

But Luke? Here he was loving her and wanting her to be with him. Desperate for sex with her. But she knew that his wanting extended past that.

"Goddammit. God. Thank you, baby," he said, pushing her against him harder. Like he was driving something. A car, a truck. Not a person. She pressed her hands against the headboard so it wouldn't knock as loud against the wall. He took this movement as a sign for him to kiss her boobs, rub his face between them, and she wanted to laugh out loud at how fucking crazy life was. His leg in its cast was a heavy weight behind her on the bed, like one of those balls prisoners wore on their ankles in cartoons. A jailball, she had called it until Renata had teased her and told their mom that Rianne didn't know what a ball and chain was, how stupid. Like this was some big proof of how much of a dummy Rianne was.

Was Renata a virgin still? After all these years? There'd been no boyfriends for Renata through high school. And no one asked or cared if she had one now. Renata could be gay for all they knew.

It had never occurred to her, Renata having any kind of sex life. Any relationships, really, beyond family and her music. It would kind of explain a lot, though, if Renata was gay. How controlled she was about everything. How careful. Maybe everyone else *did* see it, except Rianne? She would have to ask her father, probably. He would talk about that kind of thing. Her mother, just like Renata, would dismiss it with an eye roll.

But how cool would that be, to see Renata surprise them all! Renata being an actual human being, with human behaviors for once. It made her almost . . . interesting. More than the high-achieving, rule-following, scolding older-sister grouch that she always had been.

Why hadn't he come yet? She shut her eyes and pressed down harder. He said, "Yeah, baby." She opened her eyes and he was staring at her. Looking up at her. His blue eyes so wide in the semidark. His hands reaching past her boobs and up around her shoulders, holding her face. Rubbing his thumb over her mouth. "Fuck," he said. "You feel so good."

She felt so guilty. It wasn't a good sign to be riding your boyfriend's dick while wondering if your older sister who you couldn't really stand might be a lesbian. But there was only so much pretending she could do while sober. She hoped he wasn't thinking that he was making her come. Because she couldn't pretend that anymore. They were so far, far away from that.

DISSEMBLE: *seem, bleed, side, meld, miss, less . . .*

He said her name. She said his. He said, *I love this, I love you,* and when he shut his eyes while he came, she could hear Sally barking and scratching above them. The only blue eyes she wanted to see were not Luke's, but off somewhere she didn't know about. Some other place than this basement bedroom entirely.

TEN

ON GOOD FRIDAY in April, she didn't have school. But instead of sleeping in, she was mopping and sweeping her grandmother's house. Her father had flown back for the weekend and he was loading boxes and furniture and plastic Rubbermaid tubs into a storage pod. This was her trying to work off his goodwill about him giving her the truck. The day was sunny and chilly and beautiful. Her father had stripped down to a T-shirt, sweating while he carried load after load out of the house.

She squeezed out mop water with her hands. The night before she'd gone out to eat with Luke and Kaj and Kip to Brewery Grill, but the place was packed with a groom's dinner. So they'd ended up at Pizza Palace, where she drank Diet Coke and tried not be a buzzkill.

"Who doesn't love pizza?" Luke asked her, the millionth person in the world who had asked her this. "Who orders the turkey sandwich at a pizza place?"

Some things took too long to explain. Some things were not worth explaining. Some people just asked questions when they didn't want an answer.

When everything had started with Luke felt like decades ago. She was just a party girl then. This totally up for whatever chick. Now the whole world had tilted like a bucket spilling out into a drain and nothing felt the same. She was as energetic as the mop water too. Pretending she was in love with him—he said it all the time now and she would just kiss him back as an answer—pretending she wanted to have sex, pretending she was happy for his every bit of progress (physical therapy goals achieved, stitches taken out, no more painkillers) wore her out.

All she could think of was Sergei and the for-sale sign in the front of her house. The boxes from the liquor store that her mother was piling up in the living room.

"Start sorting through your things," her mother reminded Rianne every time she came in the front door. "Anything you want to get rid of, let me know and I'll donate it to the Goodwill. Just leave it by the back door and I'll take it on my way to work!"

Her mother was so cheerful lately. Even boxing up Renata's old stuff made her happy and full of energy in a way that seemed strange to Rianne. Lucy Hettrick had her phone stuck to her ear every second, talking to Renata, going over what things could be tossed, what needed to be stored. The leftover clothes could be donated, the sheet music needed to be stored so she could go through it later, the piano was going to be donated to Renata's piano teacher who lived in Dalby.

It hadn't been so simple for Rianne. Digging through just her own closet meant several depressive evenings reviewing ugly clothes from middle school, volleyball team photos she'd never taken out of the plastic order sleeve, her old retainer in its watermelon-colored case, the busted-out pill packs from her first few months of birth control. Gabby had wanted to make a sculpture with them a long time ago, as a joke. Seeing the soft plastic wheels in a shoe box made her wonder if Gabby even remembered the whole stupid idea. Then there were the YMCA camp photos. Eli, standing behind her. His ears stuck out in the worst way.

"Looks good, honey," her father said, passing through the kitchen with another box marked "RIANNE" that he set on the counter. He swiped his forehead with a dish towel that had a faded goose wearing a sun hat on it.

"What's that?" she asked.

"Just setting aside some of your grandmother's stuff for you," he said. "You know. Dishes and cups and stuff. Basics."

"Did Mom tell you to do that?"

"No, but I doubt she'd mind. Your grandmother has two whole pallets of toilet paper in that bathroom."

"You should give them to Mom, then."

"Your mother can afford her own toilet paper, honey."

Rianne shrugged. "You could buy this house, maybe?"

He looked at her like she was crazy and rummaged in the fridge for a can of mineral water. When he wasn't drinking beer, he was drinking that fizzy tasteless shit. "Hell no. I hate this house."

"So you're moving in with Mom?"

He paused with his nasty drink. It was "blackberry-flavored" sparkling water. To her, it had more in common with what was in her mop bucket than an actual blackberry.

"Did she tell you that?"

"No."

He put down the can on the counter, which she had just wiped clean.

"Would you be upset if I did?"

"Oh god, Dad!" she said, dropping the mop into the dirty water. "Really? You're really back with her? I'm not just seeing things?"

"What did you see?"

"Would you stop asking *me* the questions for a second? I mean, grow up, please! I'm not an idiot. I have eyes. You're both totally ridiculous if you think I can't tell what's going on."

Her father sighed. Looked up at the ceiling. Rubbed his jaw. Nodded. Made every gesture that suggested he would say something. Tell her the truth. Own up to the fact that he was here, back with her mother. Rianne knew she was supposed to want the fairy-tale reunion. That they would love each other and make a whole family again, not Hettricks or Wynnes, but Hettrick-Wynnes, all of them.

But she didn't want that. She didn't see how her mother deserved her dad and she didn't care if Lucy Hettrick got her way. Lucy Hettrick always got her way.

As for her dad, well. Moving in with his ex was pathetic. Nothing but a comedown for Dean Wynne. He was way more interesting than his ex-wife. He was way more interesting than living in some apartment in Wereford, or Dalby. More interesting than someone like her mother.

She tugged the mop out of the water and pressed the squeeze lever until it stopped dripping. She would sit here forever, she decided, until he said something. No dropping it this time.

"The truth is, honey, that I don't know. I'm not sure whether to retire or what. I'm waiting."

"What in the hell? You've been here months!"

"I have a lot of leave saved up. I barely use it, you know. I work my ass off, honey."

She nodded. She knew. He was always saying that. "I work hard, I play hard," was his thing. Such a cliché. You could have that for your life, though, if you didn't have a house or a family. If you had a flag tattoo on your chest and an eagle holding missiles on your arm.

"You're still not telling me anything I'm asking, Dad."

"My next billet's probably in Colorado Springs. It's not the one I hoped for, but it's the last one before I retire. I'm just waiting for confirmation. You can keep the truck, anyway, if that's what you're asking."

"No, I'm asking what's going on with you and Mom."

"Things are up in the air. I know that's not a good answer."

"Does Mom think it's a good answer?"

"Your mother is much more independent than you give her credit for."

What the fuck, she thought. In psychology, they'd read a thing about how babies don't know they're separate from their mothers. Rianne couldn't imagine feeling that way with her mother. Lucy Hettrick had always been a person apart from Rianne. Always independent of everyone. Less like a mom, more like some British nanny who insisted on using napkins and pinched you for being noisy and carried an umbrella.

Dean Wynne had taught her the army way, which was that umbrellas were for pussies: *it's just goddamn water*, he always said. And now he was acting like Rianne saw her mother as some kind of precious girl who loved him in some sob story, desperate way. Like Rianne might be, if she weren't his daughter. He was like the old shitty computer of Grandma Hettrick's, the one they couldn't even turn on because the software wouldn't run on the operating system anymore. Dean Wynne had been gone so long "gathering intelligence" that he didn't even know what updates had already happened in the middle of the night.

"Okay, so you admit that you're back together at least?"

"We'll always be together, honey," he said. "Renata and you; you keep us together."

She laughed. "Oh. Right. Yeah. That makes me feel so special."

"It should. It's true."

"Dad, don't you find it a little ironic that you've got a built-in place to stay, no matter what you decide, and I've got to go live under a bridge once Mom sells the house?"

"Your mother is being hotheaded about that, I told you. The stuff with your grandma really made her want to go the other extreme. Downsize, get rid of all her stuff. She's just getting an apartment, not joining a convent. And apartments can have more than one bedroom, you know. I think just talking to her once in a while will soften her."

"I don't want to talk to her! And I think the feeling's mutual!"

"Honey, come on."

"She doesn't talk to me, because she really doesn't want to know. It's a fact."

"Rianne, sweetheart, that is simply not true. I'm telling you. You just need to reach out."

Rianne slammed the mop down on the floor, skimmed it along the baseboards to loosen the dirt in the woodwork.

"And if you're worried the house will sell right away, well, don't," he continued. "The market here isn't that strong. And she should really drop the price if she's that aggressive about . . ."

"There were two showings last week!" Rianne yelled. She'd had to clean her room within an inch of its life. Take down all her pictures off the corkboard so that it looked generic. Like a room anyone could move into and make their own. Stuff all the crap back into her closet and try to pretend her life was tidy for strangers.

"Rianne, you're being impossible. You're not listening."

She finished the next baseboard corner, and the next, then slipped the mop back into the bucket. Rinsed her hands in the sink. Looked out at the storage pod blocking her view of the street. And then, wearing only her hoodie, she walked out. No good-bye. Not even a slam of the door.

But she couldn't drive off. Her dad had driven them and the

flatbed was loaded with junk headed to Goodwill. Only a few weeks of having her own transportation and she had no idea how she'd ever lived without it.

First she walked. Then she ran. She felt her phone buzz in her pocket. She didn't answer. Instead she called Mercy.

"I'll come get you."

"No, I'll be there in another ten minutes."

The Kovashes had lived near Grandma Hettrick. Mercy had come over and played at Grandma Hettrick's since elementary school. Was that where they became friends? Or was it school? It was a blur to Rianne. She started running, passing the familiar boarded-up gas station on Leroux, then the block past the sad park where no one ever went for a picnic, then down Holly Lane, Mercy's street. Officer Kovash's squad car was in the driveway, Mrs. Kovash's minivan was not. Rianne let herself in, taking off her sneakers, being quiet and calm, despite her heart beating fast and wild. Officer Kovash had to be sleeping ahead of the night shift.

Mercy was in the downstairs rec room entertainment space, under a giant quilt on the couch. Only her head and hands, phone between them, peeped out. The television was on but muted. One of those cooking shows where they ate nasty diner food all over America.

"Who're you texting?"

"Caleb's little sister."

"She has a cell phone?"

"I guess," Mercy said. Rianne sat down on the end of the sofa, pulled up the quilt over her legs.

"What does she text you?"

"Stuff. She misses Caleb. She says he talks funny now. She says he cut his hair really weird."

"What does that mean?"

"I have no idea. She's eight years old. She can barely spell."

"Want to do Pilates?"

"Now?" Mercy asked.

"Yes."

Mercy sighed. Chucked her phone on the carpet. Then sat up and pulled the quilt around her, around Rianne. They watched a man with a very sweaty face eat something that looked like gravy diarrhea poured over a waffle. Mercy leaned her head on Rianne's shoulder. They both sighed.

When the show went to a commercial, Mercy got up, pulled the quilt off Rianne, folded it into a neat square.

"You queue up the DVD," she said, her voice heavy but determined. "Let me put on a sports bra."

The first weekend in May, Rianne decided they would all go to Cuddy's. Kaj, Kip, even Mercy promised to come. Most importantly, Luke said yes. Finally, something interesting besides going out to eat or sitting at his house.

Though they showed up early, around six p.m., Cuddy's was already loud and full of freshmen who stood in little clutches holding their beer cups and looking afraid to make any sudden moves. Kaj rolled her eyes and Kip made fun of them, going up to the girls with braces and too much makeup, who leaned away from him nervously, and asking them how the beer tasted.

"Is it good? Or do you prefer something more hoppy?"

"What . . . ?" one of the girls asked, glancing at her friends, who laughed nervously. Kip didn't even wait for the answer, just walked along, smiling to himself. Kaj punched his arm. Luke wasn't paying attention. He was still talking to Cuddy, who was working the door with his sleeve of cups and wad of dirty ones, a big lump of dip making his mouth hump up like it had a tumor. Luke had crutches tonight but he kept them tucked in his fist, as if he were just holding them for someone else.

"Quit being a jerk," Kaj said to Kip as they moved through the crowd. "They're just little kids."

Rianne remembered being that age, remembered standing around waiting for the buzz to kick in, for the fun to begin. She felt sorry for these "little kids" who she would never bother to get to know, and who would replace her and her friends at Cuddy's in the next years to come. The thought made Wereford seem so big and yet so tiny at the same time.

Sitting on Cuddy's kitchen table were Gabby and Aidan Golden, both wearing giant green leprechaun hats, even though Saint Paddy's Day had been weeks ago. Rianne tried to think of what she'd been doing on Saint Paddy's Day and couldn't remember. But Gabby looked pretty, even so. She wore a very tight blue dress and big rubber rain boots. Aidan looked totally fucking wasted. And sweaty. He stared at Rianne's chest in an obvious, gross way. Rianne felt disgusted at ever liking him. Even if she'd only been a sophomore at the time.

"Mercy's here," Gabby said to Rianne. She jumped off the table and it wobbled under Aidan, who swore.

"Already?"

Gabby slung her arm around Rianne's neck. "I called her. We drove together."

Rianne couldn't believe Gabby was touching her. Talking to her. Acting like they were friends. *Gabby had called Mercy, Gabby drove with Mercy.* Rianne glanced toward Kaj who was also taking this information in.

"What's with the hats?" Kaj asked. "You and Aidan gonna get married or something?"

"They're for good luck," Gabby said. "Rianne, come on. Where's your cup?"

"Luke has it."

"That's a cute shirt," Gabby said. She held back a burp. "Sorry."

Rianne said thank you. Gwen had given the shirt to her, from a pile of clothing she was getting rid of. It was a little tight and had a weird asymmetrical tie that Gwen had to show her how to do up the right way, but it was cute. This was the first party Luke had wanted to go to since his accident and again she felt the desire to be pretty beside him. For him. Even if it was just a show. If she was going to be in Wereford, she might as well be out in it. Seeing it. Not in anyone's basement, watching television.

A tiny part of her also hoped to see Sergei. Other than hanging out with Faith or sitting in the parking lot around Planet Tan, waiting for Rink's car to stop by Tobacco World, a party

186

like Cuddy's was the best chance she had of seeing him. Not a big chance, but better than anything else. Tonight she had shaved her legs and cha, put on makeup, blown out her hair, took her time on picking out clothes. She was trying, really, to be good.

Gabby tugged her through the crowd again, toward the basement where they kept the kegs. They passed Luke, who was still talking to Cuddy by the door, and who knocked up an eyebrow when Gabby snatched Rianne's empty cup from him. Rianne sailed along, waving at Luke and at Cuddy. How old was Cuddy, even? How fucking long had he been having these shitty parties, anyway? Didn't anyone wonder why he was doing it? And why was Luke looking at her like he was worried? He looked ready to follow them down the stairs. As if she and Gabby were freshman girls and didn't know what they were doing.

Cuddy's basement always smelled like rusty water, moldy socks, and beer. Always beer. The orange striped sheet still hung between the keg area and a rumbling washing machine. Only people who were tight with Cuddy could get away with sneaking off behind it, otherwise he got pissed about it. Obviously Aidan Golden had been cool with Cuddy even back in tenth grade.

Mercy was sitting at the keg with a bunch of Cuddy lifers, older fat guys who wore the same Wereford hockey hoodie for their whole lives. Not Pete Novotny, because he'd moved up to Ely to ice fish and hunt. But the same *kind* of guy as Pete Novotny. Big, gross, badly dressed, dumb. The complete opposite of Caleb. Now Mercy was talking to them and laughing at their jokes as if they were fascinating, beautiful human beings, not sweaty losers whose best years of their lives were in high school.

"Hey, guys!" Mercy yelled to Rianne and Gabby, and then ran to hug them. Bouncing the whole way. Rianne noticed how Cuddy's gross friends watched Mercy's ass, the back of her shirt riding up as she swung her arms around her and Gabby's necks.

"Ladies," said the one with the goatee. "Can I fill your cups?" Goatee Guy proceeded to fill all three of them at one go, his big ham-colored fingers stabbed into each cup, the tap tubing running from his fist like some kind of futuristic pissing accessory.

"I love your shirt, Ri," Mercy yelled. "We're just killing it with the Pilates, aren't we?" She winked and Rianne felt stupid and watched by the guys at the keg. As they waited for their beers Mercy kept talking about how great it was to see them and how cute Rianne looked and how pretty Gabby's dress was until Rianne took the cups back before they were all the way full; things were stressing her out down here. Plus Luke was slowly making his way down the steps, doing some strange hop-with-crutches move, his eyes scanning for her the whole time. She smiled at him, trying not to make him feel self-conscious. She was hoping he wasn't hurting, at least.

"Where's your cup?" she asked, when he made it through the crowd.

"I'm not drinking tonight," he said. He looked toward the guys by the keg and nodded at them. Then he scanned toward where Mercy and Gabby were talking to some other girls and said in a low voice, "You guys should come upstairs. Seriously."

He glanced back toward the keg again. "You shouldn't be down here."

"But how were we supposed to get our beer?"

"I'll get it for you," Luke said. "Just, come on."

But Mercy didn't want to go and Gabby was talking to Claire Andale's little sister, giving her a sort of older sister advice act about being at this party and *what would Claire say if she saw you here.* Luke just stood there, holding his crutches like they didn't belong to him, waiting for Rianne to herd everyone upstairs again. He was the last up, going slow up the steps that were slippery with beer.

After that, though, things got kind of fun. The beer warmed quickly in her cup, which was gross, and the house was steaming hot, since Cuddy could never open the windows or neighbors would complain or call the cops. And she was sweating and not drinking that fast, either, because she didn't want to make Luke get refills.

But they were laughing and being idiots, which was the main point of a party, for Rianne. And Mercy was happy, at least. Mercy was sitting on the dirty floor chatting with Channa and Ana, while Erica and Anika played beer pong next to them. Rianne didn't know how they all could sit on the floor and not think about all the crud and puke that had accumulated there. Channa and Ana were drunk too, and Anika kept tipping over into Erica's lap in a dramatic way that made everyone laugh every time.

Rianne would have sat with them, but she was wearing a little skirt, which would have meant her bare legs would touch the nasty floor. Plus Luke was beside her every second, hopping, holding his crutches, asking her if she was having a good time.

Finally, she broke away from him to stand in the bathroom line. Two sophomore girls were in front of her, whispering in each other's ears. They both had their hair in matching braids and wore jeans and T-shirts that said "OVER IT" right across their boobs. The matching made them confident and ballsy, which made Rianne feel old and nostalgic. Like she was looking at her own self.

Once in the bathroom, she squat-hovered to pee over the nasty toilet—people said you could get herpes from sitting on the seat at Cuddy's—and then she stood looking at herself in the mirror. She did look cute. And the top was weird and a little tight, but she liked it. Liked how just tugging the one tie would make it fall off. Her cheeks were bright from drinking and the heat and she thought that it might be easy for other people to be jealous of her. Luke's girlfriend. Cute outfit. Nice hair. Her friends all together.

Are you having a good time, Luke kept saying. *Still having a good time?*

When she came out of the bathroom, the good time was over. Gabby was yelling at Luke. People were quiet and staring at them. Gabby was sticking her hand in Luke's face, telling him he was a dickhead, an entitled loser. A hopeless townie. That he might as well move in with Cuddy.

"Born to live and die here!" she yelled. "And guess what's hilarious? You'll never see why that's sad."

"No, *you're* hilarious, Gabby," Luke said, not even riled. He smiled at her. "How you think anyone gives a shit about your opinions. That's what's funny about you."

Rianne was frozen. Frozen listening to Gabby shout while Luke grinned and yelled back.

Frozen until Claire Andale's little sister tugged at her sleeve and said, "I think your friend might need you? She's in the basement . . . ?"

Rianne walked past Gabby and Luke, who barely noticed her in their shouting. As she headed downstairs, she saw Aidan Golden approaching the whole argument, like some sweaty, drunk peacemaker.

Fuck.

In the basement, the keg was unmanned. The whole place was quiet and still, except for the music. And then she realized Mercy was behind the orange striped sheet. Not alone.

She didn't notice which of the Cuddy lifers it was. It wasn't Goatee Guy but what did it matter. The Cuddy lifer looked totally idiotic with Mercy's hand in the fly of his jeans. He receded away from the dryer where Mercy sat, her shirt off, her bra dangling open.

"Mercy, come on," Rianne said.

Mercy put her arms over her boobs. Shut her eyes. There was shouting and screaming from upstairs. Thumping on the floor.

Fuck fuck *fuck.*

"Mercy. Jesus."

She took her hand and Mercy did up her bra and shirt. Then she started crying.

From the dark, back toward the water heater, the Cuddy lifer said, "Jesus Christ."

"Yeah, fuck off, asshole," Rianne said, her anger pushing out, pulling Mercy toward her. Her need to spit fire at the whole world dragged them out from behind the orange striped sheet, up the sloppy stairs. Mercy was still crying.

In the middle of the room, Aidan Golden stood by Gabby, his mouth bloody.

"Where's Luke?" Rianne asked, holding Mercy against her.

"Fucking dick," Aidan said.

"What did you do?" Rianne yelled at Gabby.

"I didn't do anything," Gabby shouted back. "Cuddy kicked his ass out."

"Where's Kaj and Kip?"

"They went to McDonald's like an hour ago. What the fuck is her problem?" Gabby said, motioning to Mercy.

The room started to hum again with private conversations. Which were probably about whatever caused Aidan's bloody mouth. Aidan was now spitting into his cup, his mouth dripping strings of blood and slobber. And he was smiling, talking to the sophomore girls wearing the "OVER IT" T-shirts.

Rianne felt murderous. She shuttled Mercy against her and went to look out the little window by the door where Cuddy usually stood guard.

She saw blinking lights, red and blue. Cops. And Luke's truck pulled over up the street.

"We're leaving, Mercy," she said. Realizing she'd left her coat in Luke's truck. "Where's your coat?"

"In Gabby's car. She's parked out there."

"We're going without it," she said. "The cops are here. Come on."

They went out the back door of the kitchen, which was blocked up by the overflowing recycling bin. While Mercy stood passively, Rianne pushed aside the bin, causing a tinkle of cans to lurch on the floor while she undid the locks. The back step was slippery from the afternoon rain shower. Rianne told Mercy to be careful.

They walked silent but quick through a series of backyards, past woodpiles and charcoal Weber grills and tossed-aside sandbox toys and plastic sleds. The ground was soft and squishy and Rianne was happy she'd worn boots and not flip-flops like Mercy. The whole time, cop sirens whined and blue and red lights flashed through the driveways of the houses. Mercy kept stopping to look into the windows of the houses they passed and Rianne kept pulling her by her shirt's sleeve and saying come on until the lights and sirens faded and they were out of Cuddy's neighborhood.

"Where are we even going?" Mercy asked, panting.

"To your sister's," she said. "Faith will figure something out."

"All the way to the hill? She's not even home! She's working tonight!"

"I know," Rianne said. "But she'll figure it out. Your dad could be there right now, for all we know."

"Do you think he's busting Luke?"

"Luke didn't drink tonight."

"Please don't tell anyone about that guy and me, Rianne."

Rianne stopped. She took Mercy's hand.

"Are you kidding? I would never."

Mercy started crying. "God. What if Caleb knew . . . ?"

Rianne hugged her friend. Pulled her tight again, hoping if she held her strong enough, if she calmed her down, Mercy would stop being sad. Stop loving Caleb in a way that made her do dumb things. Not make good life plans. Get too drunk. Hook up with old gross guys. Guys who should be the ones getting busted, not Luke. And not for underage consumption, but worse.

"I totally kissed that guy. Me. I did it first. He wasn't even expecting it!"

"It doesn't matter."

"I don't even think he's cute! I barely liked him! He's like twenty-six years old!"

"It's okay."

"He even had a condom in his shirt pocket, Ri. Seriously. He said so."

"Shhh," Rianne said. "We've got to go."

"I'm freezing to death," Mercy said, her mouth hot on Rianne's shoulder. "How are you so warm?"

"We're almost there. Come on. Another block and we'll be fine."

ELEVEN

WHEN THEY GOT to the Pumphouse, there was no one working the door, just an empty stool. Rianne pulled Mercy inside. The place smelled exactly like Cuddy's house. The same blast of old beer.

They couldn't see if Faith was at the bar, but the manager dude in a denim shirt with the Pumphouse logo stopped them at the hostess podium.

"Uh, girls. We're gonna need to see ID. Otherwise, you need to leave. State law."

"We need to talk to Faith, that's all," Rianne said. "Can you tell her that her sister's here?"

She expected the dude to argue—he had that prickish, snappy restaurant manager look, where he lived to remind people of rules. But the look on Mercy's face convinced him and in a minute he came back with Faith. The three of them huddled off into a storage area in back and Mercy told the bare bones of the story.

Leaving out the Cuddy lifer guy, mainly.

Faith handed Mercy a cocktail napkin from her short black apron. "Go to the bathroom over there," she told Mercy.

"Hey, thanks for bringing her," she said to Rianne. "Good thinking. Because Dad finding her this way? God. But my manager's a dick and you'll have to find a ride home. I mean, I can talk him into letting Mercy stay until I can figure something out. But both of you?" Her voice lowered. "And you've been drinking? We could seriously lose our liquor license."

"It's fine," Rianne said, taking her phone out. "I get it. I'm fine. I'll just . . . I'll figure it out. Just take care of our girl, okay?"

"Of course," Faith said.

When Mercy returned from the bathroom, Rianne kissed her cheeks, one, then the other, as if she were foreign. Mercy leaned back and blinked.

"Call me tomorrow," Rianne said. "We'll go have tacos or something. Okay?"

Mercy curled up on the floor by a stack of empty kegs and nodded.

Rianne walked through the Pumphouse, her head down, moving quickly so that Faith's prick manager wouldn't see her. She had no idea what she was doing. Where she was going. But she pushed open the double doors, anyway.

And there was Sergei. Sitting on the bouncer stool, holding a flashlight in one hand and a magazine in the other. Pressed button-down shirt, a dark navy this time, but the same Levi's, the same black shoes. Same strange Russian as ever.

"Hello," he said.

"Hi."

"What are you doing?"

"Walking home," she said.

He stood, set down his flashlight and magazine on the stool. "May you wait? One minute? I will return. Yes?"

She nodded. Smiled. Couldn't help it. The beer, fleeing the party, panic about cops, and the nerves and sadness for Mercy made it so she couldn't hide anything anymore.

He went inside the bar. A minute later he returned with a big bearded guy in a leather vest and thermal shirt who took position on the stool, spinning the flashlight's little strap around his finger.

"Now we go," Sergei said, nodding to the guy, who was already clicking on his flashlight as people approached the entrance, IDs in hands.

"Where?"

"Somewhere. Here? There? I walk with you." He took her elbow for a minute to steer her away from a big crack in the sidewalk that was filled with mucky rainwater.

"Thanks," she said.

For a while, they walked in silence. Away from the main street. Past the library and the Holiday Inn. Past the Gas & Grub and the high school. The sun was almost completely down and the streetlights were taking its place. The sounds of squealing tires and slamming screen doors drifted around them, along with the scent of backyard grilling and soft-serve ice cream. Summer was coming. He seemed to know the way she was going, as he over-ruled one of her turns.

"That guy—he'll work the door for you?" she asked.

"He thinks I am gone ten minutes," he said.

She was surprised at first. Then laughed. He laughed after a second too.

"I do not care," he said. "I leave soon."

"When school ends?"

"In a few weeks."

"Will you go back to Russia?"

"First Chicago," he said, sighing. "My father does not want me yet."

"Why not?"

"Because he marries a new woman, yes? I tell you this. And she is younger than me. She has twenty-two years?"

"How old are you?"

"I have twenty-five."

She nodded. Slipped her handbag across her body so it would stop sliding down her shoulder.

"My father has two ex-wives," Sergei continued. "He thinks I make problems."

"Do you?"

"No," he said. "I do not care about this wife. She is idiot. Her family owns a factory my father buys. But he is old, bald. And I am young. He thinks I am . . ." He stopped to recall the word.

"Competition?" Rianne suggested. He nodded.

"What kind of father thinks his son will fuck his wife?"

"This is why I like you," he said. "Because you have so many . . ." He said a word in Russian. "I do not know English. But this is your nature." He pronounced the last word *natchure*.

They came to the bridge crossing the river. She realized he was slowing down to match her pace and she tried to quicken but he noticed right away.

"Is okay, Rianne," he said, putting a hand lightly on her arm. "You go how you are."

The cars that raced past made it too loud to talk. The unknown Russian word pulsed in her brain. Him saying "This is why I like you." All of it repeating at the same steady rate as their footsteps.

Her thighs brushed against each other, her purse bounced against her hip. And her cha itched now too, like the stubble was already growing back in, which made her feel urgent. Like she should slow down or go faster. Something.

The wind from the passing cars whipped her hair across her face. At the end of the bridge, they crossed through a neighborhood of little houses full of random lights and barking dogs. And now the hill, all the way up toward her house, they started up the long curve labeled Belle Crest Way. It was fringed with trees and rock and green things pushing up through thick mud. They followed a cracked curl of sidewalk. He rolled up his sleeve and looked at his watch.

"What time is it?"

He held out his wrist. Two minutes past nine.

"This looks like village near my dacha," Sergei said.

"Dat-*cha*?"

"Sorry. Dacha: this is a traditional home. Not where you always live, but in the country. For simple life. Like the house on the lake where I first see you. Smaller house, though. No running water. For relaxing. My favorite place to go."

"Do you miss that home?"

He shrugged. "Years ago, trees have no fruit," he said. "The pollution from factories of Communists. Nothing grows. And now, fruit everywhere, flowers, women make sweets. My father starts a brandy company, so much fruit. It is a beautiful brandy. Best I have tasted."

"Will you help him?"

Sergei shrugged. "My father is . . . always his own plan."

"What about your mother?"

"She has died," he said. "She has a cancer."

"I'm sorry," she said.

"I do not remember her so much. I am the youngest," he said. "My brothers remember."

Rianne had walked this hill so many times. Up and down. Walking up with Mercy and Gabby and Kaj, before they had licenses. Biking down with them at ridiculous speeds while drunk. Hiking up after watching Babe Ruth League summer baseball and acting like idiots about boys in junior high. Finally getting to drive up it, no exertion required.

Going up this hill had always meant complaining, conspiring to avoid it, trying to get a ride. But now it flew by. He stood nearest the road, as if to protect her from something. He didn't seem out of breath but she kept glancing at him, checking to see if he was tiring. Several times, she caught him glancing at her too.

Soon they were at the top of the hill, and where she would have turned to get home, they went straight, toward the building where Faith lived. Of course. He didn't know where she lived, after all. Her phone buzzed in her pocket. Her friends calling, texting. Luke, too. She turned it off with one click while he watched. Then she took his hand, which he covered in his easily. Like he'd been waiting patiently for it. His fingers splicing with hers were softer than she would have guessed.

Sergei's apartment was on the third floor and faced the street. Either he wasn't aware of the elevator or was uninterested in using it. He pushed open the door to the stairs for her and waited until she went through it.

Even after the hill, after all the walking, she was winded by the stairs. She tried to hide it. Even with the Pilates. Embarrassing. They paused at his door while he pulled out his keys. She struggled to get her breath under control.

"Rink is . . ." He continued fiddling with his keys while he searched for the words. "He falls asleep on sofa very much. This is his habit."

Inside, it was dark, but the windows let in the blinding parking lot lights. She could see someone on a sofa in front of a very large television mounted on a wall. There was a table covered in beer bottles and an ashtray. The whole place smelled like Rink's cigarettes.

"Come," Sergei whispered.

She followed him, looking down as if she was ashamed,

listening to the clicks of his black shoes on the kitchen linoleum and then silent on the hallway carpet.

"Here is bath," he said. "My room is this." He knocked his palm on the next door. She nodded and slipped inside the bathroom as fast as possible, undoing her zipper and sitting down to pee. She didn't even turn on the light.

She sat on the toilet, wondering if he could hear her pee, her hands clasped over the web of her undies and her skirt at her knees. Then she was shaking for a minute. She waited until she stopped and grew calmer.

She washed her hands and returned to Sergei's room.

He had turned on no lights but she knew what would happen. He was sitting on his bed. She saw his black peacoat curved over the back of the chair at his desk. The parking lot lights through the window above the bed sparked up and glinted off his hair, his silver watch, three empty blank bottles on his desk in a row, like a nerdy kid would line up pencils. He unlaced his shoes and slipped them off.

"Come," he said.

She laughed at how funny he was when he talked. So formal. He asked her what it was, but she didn't want to make him feel bad. She stood in front of him while he looked at her. Unlaced the tops of her boots and stepped from them. The carpet was springy beneath her feet and the backs of her ankles felt blistery. He took her hand and rubbed her palm with his thumb. It felt sexy in a way she wouldn't have expected.

"All of this may not be good," he said. He sounded concerned and sad. Different from how he was on the way here.

"What do you mean?" She felt shy. Her body felt wrong. How available she had made herself and now he was saying no. She pulled back her hand.

"You cannot belong to me."

"I can't belong to anyone, Sergei," she said, joking. "We live in modern times."

He smiled. Shook his head. Reached for her, his hands on her hips. His thumbs pointing toward each other across the flat of her skirt. She wondered if he wished he could circle her waist with his hands. *Find another girl*, she thought. *That'll never be me....*

"Modern times, yes? You think the world is so different now?"

"I'm not a coat or a watch," she said. "A dog. A car."

She meant to be light, but it still stuck there, between them, like the unknown word of her nature. Her silent phone heavy in her skirt pocket.

He slid his fingers over the zipper on the side of her skirt. She didn't wonder if he'd been with lots of girls like Luke had. It was obvious at his age, what he knew.

"Tonight, I think of home," he said. "I wish to go back. Do you?"

"No," she said. Though that didn't make sense. He frowned for a moment.

"I mean, yes. I mean, I'm here, Sergei," she said. "I am happy to be right here."

"This is good," he said. Then he stood and kissed her for what felt like days and weeks and years. Finally. Finally his cautious concern was gone. They wouldn't be interrupted this time.

He smelled so strongly like the hangover remedy. She slipped her hands around his neck, and felt the smooth place along his hairline. Touched his collar, his shoulders, his chest. She ran her hands around the belt he wore, lifted toward him on her toes.

"You are just like I dream," he said as she pulled his shirt out of his jeans, feeling the bristle of hair on his belly, reaching into his pockets like a thief until she found the little circular tin.

"You are from a dream, I think?" he continued. "Not from here. Not from America." While she held the hangover remedy in her palms, he reached up and lifted off his shirt and T-shirt beneath it. Tossed them on the floor like he was sick of them.

"I am from here, though," she said. "So I'm tricking you." She wondered for a moment if he didn't know the word "trick" and started reaching for a synonym.

But he said, "That is all right. I am happy with the trick of you."

He took the hangover remedy from her.

"This? You want this from me?"

"I like how it smells. What is it made of?"

He didn't answer, just dropped it on the carpet and kissed her. He pulled the tie of her shirt until it slipped open and off. He touched her breasts softly over her bra, feeling the lace like it was Braille. Unhooking her bra, gripping her waist, her hips. Unzipping her skirt and pushing it down until she was there in her undies in front of him. All of her. Sweaty from the walk, Achilles tendons wet with blisters, makeup melting off, stubble growing in or not, here she was. Ready. Nobody to stop it. No one, not even Rink, asleep on the couch.

She reached up to touch the scar along his temple. He spent some time on her breasts, bending in an awkward way that was familiar. Tall guys always had this problem. Guys were all the same, in some things.

While he kissed her breasts, felt them, breathed all over her skin, she undid his belt and jeans. It took a while and then he stood to step out of them. He wore the narrowest cut of briefs she'd ever seen a guy wear in real life. Like something a gay guy who was also a runway model would wear. Before she could even laugh though, he tugged her on top of him as he sat down on the bed.

She could feel how hard he was beneath her and now it was perfectly clear for the first time, how all of this fit together. The point of it. Of sex, but also maybe everything too. To touch what you wanted to touch the most. A hand coasting so smooth over your beautiful legs. Nobody but the two of you. Alone in your own room. How that could be just enough. Just what you needed.

The room was dark, but she knew where his body was, where the bed was, where her hands stopped and started. It felt like having another sense. Night vision. Spatial orientation. She could feel him beneath her. Real and hard and alive.

He had condoms, he said, between kisses.

Mmm, hmmm, she said, her hands gripping his arm muscles. He had no tattoos. She would have guessed he had many.

"You are wanting me, yes?"

Again she laughed. "Are you are wanting *me*, Sergei?"

"Obvious, Rianne. This is obvious." He looked down, grabbed his boner through his tiny boxer-briefs. She was shocked to see him do that. Most of the time, guys were so weird about erections. They had them, they pushed them on you. But she'd never seen a guy grab it and speak about it directly. Not even Luke, who she'd known the longest, did that.

Also, unlike Luke, Sergei kept his condoms in the bathroom. Was that because he was an adult, or did all Russians see sex so clinically? A medical issue? He made her want to ask a million questions she didn't know how to word properly. He went to collect the condoms and she lay back on his bed, marveling at how narrow it was. Marveling at how easily he moved. How he walked, nearly naked, even as Rink slept nearby.

He returned with an entire box of condoms in his hand, like it was a toy. A box of LEGOs. A puzzle. She laughed again.

"What can it be now, Rianne?" He added something in Russian.

"Nothing."

"Take off your . . ." He said something else in Russian. He pointed at her underwear. "Yes. Those. Let us be fair."

She laughed and then he took his off, too. It took a second to register that he wasn't circumcised. It made sense though. Another weird thing. Like his shoes, his tucked-in shirt, his tiny underwear. And so she said it: you're not circumcised. Do they not do that in Russia?

But he was confused. He didn't know the word.

"Please explain. Are you not wanting?"

"No," she said. "I am still wanting."

"Then what is problem?"

"Nothing, it's okay. Let me think."

She lay back on the bed and watched him put on the condom. He lay over her and waited for an answer.

"It is when you are a baby, and only for boys. They cut off a part of the skin. Off the top of the . . . the penis," she said. She was such an idiot! Him with his actual penis almost inside of her and she couldn't say the word.

"Yes. I understand," he nodded. "But of course I do not have this."

"Do they not do this in Russia?"

"This is only for Jews. I am not Jew. Are you religious, Rianne?"

"No."

"My mother was Christian. My father, not."

"Why are we talking about religion right now?"

He smiled down at her. "This is a good question, *pochemuchka*. I have no good answer for you."

He kissed her a minute more. Tickled her ribs under her breasts. Slid his hand up her thighs, and spread them. With his fingers, he made her come again, just like the night in Faith's apartment. He looked her in the eye the entire time. At least she guessed he did. Her eyes shut involuntarily at the critical point.

Afterward, she was dying to ask him, though she felt shy saying the words again.

"Do you . . ." She paused. Breathed. Cleared her throat. "You always do that? With everyone?"

"It is better for . . ." He stopped, searched for the words, then gave up. "It is better, that way. That way, first."

She flopped her arms from around his shoulders to the pillow above her head.

"Okay," she said. "I believe you. You are very good at that."

"You are a very good girl," he replied. Then he pushed himself into her. No more talking.

Reaching back to brace her palms on the wall above the bed, she thought, *this is how adults do it. Real adults. They make the sounds he is making and they don't worry anymore about anything at all. This is what they want, so they get it. This is what I want. What he wants too.*

They did it lots of ways. Her on top. Him from behind. It wasn't just sex, either. He licked her down there, right on her cha, which felt nice enough, though all she could think about was stubble. At one point, he even took a break! Removed the condom and left the room—again fully naked—and came back with a bottle of vodka from the freezer. Poured two shots— both of them naked now—so they could toast each other: her, halting and shy; him, entirely in Russian. After they drank, he got another condom from the box and asked her to put it on him and she did. She didn't do anything but follow, follow, follow.

Finally, while she was watching him beneath her, his hands on her hips, he groaned and closed his eyes. It had been happening for so long—he had made her come again with his hand—that when it was finally done, she was surprised.

Lights from the parking lot streaked over them and caught the silver dad-watch he wore. He kissed her: lips, nose, all over her face. Asked her if she'd like some water.

"Yes," she said. "Yes, please."

"Please," he repeated. Like she was unique for using the word. He said something in Russian as he kissed her forehead and then, before she could ask him what he said, he added, "My little sun. You can have whatever you like."

Then he pulled off the condom, twisted it around his fingers into a knot. She pulled up the blankets and watched everything he did. Everything about him. How long his arms and legs were. How his dick bounced when he stood and put on his underwear, then halfway buttoned up his jeans. She watched his bare back go through the door. Silent and swift, not even turning on a light. She couldn't move. She felt heavy and sore as if she'd just finished a day of preseason training. There would never be any preseason training for her again. That was one thing she envied Luke; he was disciplined about his body.

He was gone forever. She flexed her feet and stretched out her back. Made fists and cracked her knuckles. On this narrow bed, her whole body felt beaten and perfect. The menthol and mint scent of the hangover remedy clouded the sheets. She was almost asleep when he came back.

"Water," he said. She drank a big sip. How lovely, to be served this way.

"What time is it?"

He looked at his watch. "It is almost midnight. My pardon, sorry to make you wait. But Rink wakes up. He has questions. I tell him you are here."

"Shit." She began panicking. "I have to leave soon. Did Rink hear us? Oh god."

"You are not to worry." He took the glass and set it beside the clear blank bottles of vodka on his desk. He stretched his neck to one side, then yawned.

"Are you tired?" she asked.

"Yes. But you are also tired," he replied. "Your voice tells me."

"I will tell you too: I'm tired, Sergei."

"You will fix my English," he said. "I am willing."

"How long did you study English?"

"Since I have ten years. Six? I cannot recall. For so many years."

"That's a long time," she said. "Does everyone take that much English in Russia?"

"No. Not in all schools. The people with the money get the English."

He sighed and she began looking for her clothes on the floor.

"Don't leave now," he said. "Stay. One more of these minutes. We will fix my English. Or other language if you like. Russian. I can teach you. Are you studying other languages?"

"Spanish," she said. "But I suck at Spanish."

"You suck at Spanish," he repeated. "No. I know this idiom. I

210

think no. You cannot *suck*."

She laughed. "You have no idea."

He dropped his jeans on the floor and lay beside her. Somehow, they fit on his narrow bed. His lips on her shoulder, his hands on her hips, her arms scrunching the quilt over her chest, his chest solid against her spine. One of his calves slipped over hers. Smooth and easy.

"I have many ideas for you, Rianne," he said.

"How many?"

"Many. Too many. So many. All of the 'manys.'"

Many, several, much.

MYRIAD. *army, diary, dim, rim, air* . . .

"Yes," she said. She shut her eyes and shivered under his warm hands. Agreed with his bad English. "I have all of them too."

TWELVE

HE CALLED HER a cab and stood out on the front step with her, barefoot and in just a T-shirt. He'd offered her his peacoat but she didn't need it. It was chilly out, but he didn't shiver, either. She imagined how well suited to winter they were.

As they waited, she became fidgety. Rianne had never taken a cab; she had no idea how it worked. And she only had four dollars in her purse.

"I pay already; not to worry," he said. He kissed her neck and cheeks while they waited. Like he was getting all of his money's worth.

"Sergei . . ."

"Can you return to see me?"

"When?"

"Tomorrow."

"I don't know," she said. "It depends on if my parents are angry."

"Pfft," he said, kissing her ear. "Parents are always angry."

She knew he was right; it had been that way since forever. At least with her mom. And maybe she wouldn't be in trouble. She hadn't tested her mom on the "you can do whatever" proclamation she'd made after New Year's. Maybe that had been Lucy Hettrick's plan all along, a kind of reverse psychology. That it had worked made her want to stay with Sergei all night, and she almost changed her mind, but then the cab pulled up.

He waved to the driver, who nodded back. Then she got into the cab and told the driver her address. As the driver pulled out of the parking lot, she felt almost sick to be leaving him. Leaving the life he got to have.

"You know that dude?" the driver said. She was an older lady with a pile of frizzy red hair.

"Yeah. Do you?"

"He's the bouncer at the Pumphouse. I pick up lots of drunks over there."

"Oh."

She didn't know what the etiquette was for cabs. She felt strange and queenly sitting in the backseat all on her own, but she didn't feel like telling this woman all her business. So she stuffed two sticks of mint gum in her mouth to kill the alcohol fumes and turned back to her phone, updating the contact list for Sergei's number, which they had exchanged. She listed him only by *S*. Which felt sneaky and clever, until she realized she didn't know his last name.

Also, there were so many missed calls and texts. Her father.

Luke. Gabby. Mercy. Faith. Kaj. Even Kip. It made her tired to consider all she had to explain. Until she realized she didn't have to explain it. Why did everything that happened to you have to belong to everyone else? Luke she had to share, even with people like Gabby, who then went to bitch her face off at him. What the hell did Gabby care, anyway? Why did Gabby need to pull him up short on why he was wrong for Rianne? Gabby was leaving. She could pretend Luke didn't exist. That Rianne didn't exist, either.

Sergei was all hers. Every bit about him.

"How old are you, anyway, honey?" the driver asked, when they were almost to her house.

"Eighteen," she said. It came out bitchy-sounding, and she worried she was about to get a lecture. She sat up, pressed her thighs together. Though she peed before leaving, she still felt sticky between her legs. *Stubbly. Stubborn.* Were those words related? *Prickly. Sticky.* The cab turned down her street and she saw Luke's truck in front of her house.

MENDACIOUS.

"Looks like you've got people waiting up for you," the driver said as she pulled into the driveway. "At least you've got people looking out for you, girl."

Fuck you, she thought. Luke was underneath the outside light on her front step, leaning against the doorframe.

But what she said was, "You sure I don't have to pay you?"

"He took care of it with dispatch when he called," the driver said. "Always does. You have a good night now."

She slammed the door harder than she meant. *Always does.* Did Sergei send lots of girls off in cabs? There was no way she could be jealous about this. She wasn't jealous of Luke being with half of their grade. With Channa, Ana, Erica, and Anika. Luke had never said one thing about who she'd been with, either. But maybe she didn't care about Luke the same way? How could something feel so perfect, so correct one minute—her in Sergei's narrow bed—and not be good in the next?

Luke steadied himself on his crutches. She felt completely obvious. She could still smell Sergei's hangover remedy on her hands. Her hair.

"Thank me now, girly," Luke said. "You turning off your phone was fucked-up. But I saved your dad from calling the cops."

"What did you tell him?"

"Just what happened. I got pulled over, Cuddy's house got a door-knock and a warning, nothing big. But I told them that you were freaked out and ran."

"Told who?"

"Your parents."

"You didn't tell them about why your hand's all busted up?"

He held up his knuckles, which were scraped from hitting Aidan. He'd hit his friend with a fucked-up leg and crutches and prevailed. Luke was strong and kind of badass, but she just felt sorry for him now. Sorry for herself too.

"Your dad's cool, Rianne," Luke said. "Can't blame him for

being worried about his daughter. Why'd you shut off your phone?"

Rianne wanted to push inside, past him, but he blocked the door with his body.

"Is he home?"

"He's out looking for you. I told him where Cuddy lives. But he'll be on his way back; I texted him when the cab pulled up. I can't believe you shelled out cash for a cab. You coulda called me. Fuck, Rianne. You coulda called *him*."

She shrugged. "I didn't know if you were okay or what. My mom's inside?"

"Yeah. I think she went to bed. She's kind of checked out, isn't she? I think I interrupted them, by the way. I thought they were divorced?"

"They are."

"Well, they don't look that *divorced* to me. I think I embarrassed your mom. Where the fuck did you and Mercy end up?"

Rianne wished her father would just decide where he was going to stay already. He kept coming back to Wereford, a weekend here, a couple days there, while his orders for his next duty station got figured out. Helping pack things, making blueberry pancakes. Making Lucy Hettrick laugh. He was annoyingly helpful on these visits.

Explaining as vaguely as possible about how she got Mercy to Faith, Rianne sat down on the creaky metal porch swing that her mother had put out back in April, when the good weather warmed up. It was slightly wet from rain, making her thighs and butt feel even stickier. Guiltier.

"Why'd you turn your phone off?"

"I didn't want it to make noise. We were fucking freaked out, Luke."

"You could have muted it."

"I was saving the battery."

He hopped with his crutches, swung around, and slowly sat beside her. "Call me next time," he said. "Don't waste your money."

"I just thought . . ."

"I know, I know. Just, remember: next time. Okay?"

She nodded. She hated how nice he was being.

"What's the matter, Ri?" he asked. "Are you okay? Did something bad happen?"

"No. I'm just . . . I'm tired."

"Your dad was telling me how your mom still wants you to move out."

"Yeah. June first."

"He says she doesn't mean it."

"She gets an offer on the house, she's going to take it," Rianne said. "Her Realtor wants her to fix some dumb thing in the bathroom. And then she's getting an apartment."

"With your dad?"

"Jesus, Luke," she said. "I don't know. Quit asking me all these goddamn questions."

"Do you want to go inside?"

She didn't answer. If they went inside, he'd want to sit on the couch, and maybe touch her. And then he would know. He'd have to know. He wasn't an idiot. She didn't think she could fake wanting to touch him now.

"Hey." He leaned toward her. "Hey, Rianne. Listen to me. Listen, look at me. Okay?"

She looked up. His face so earnest and kind. As open and loving as Sally the puppy's face.

"I told your dad this too, though I wasn't gonna say anything about it until later. But I hadn't really thought about how your mom said you needed to move out after we graduate. I just figured she'd back off. Moms do that, you know. Anyway, you and me. And Sally? We could get a place together. Of our own. This fall, maybe? After summer's over I should have enough saved up."

She couldn't believe he was saying this. Her face was scraped up from the whisker burn of Sergei—and not just her face, but her cha too! *His face between her legs*, she thought, and her stomach trembled. Now Luke was saying they should live together. With his puppy as their pretend baby.

"That . . . Luke, god. Seriously?"

"What? It's a good plan. I'm gonna help my grandpa out in the office this summer, and my grandma's got some work for me at the clinic too. So I'll be raking in the bank. You've got money saved up too, right?"

"Not much."

"How much?"

"Like, I don't know. A thousand dollars or so?"

One thousand two hundred and twenty-four. She knew the savings balance by heart, each time she dumped in a new paltry Planet Tan check.

"That's a good start," he said.

"It doesn't help me with where to live in June, Luke."

"Why you never ask for any help on this kinda shit blows my mind, Rianne," he said, running his hands through his hair like he wanted to tear it out. "You act like you're on your own. And then you don't do shit to let people help you."

She wanted to say, *because people don't do shit to help me, that's why.* But then he'd argue back. And there was no arguing now. Already he'd ruined the good feeling she'd had with Sergei, in his room. Though realistically, the cab driver had started the whole ruining process.

"Just live with me. At my house. Until we get a place. My mom won't care; she loves you. So do my grandparents. And I told your dad this. He acted like he wasn't sure, but he didn't seem mad or offended."

She said she'd think about it. But, really, how dumb could he be? Did he think a girl's father would be happy to see her move into the basement of her boyfriend's parents' house? Probably her mom wouldn't care. Lucy Hettrick would expect that kind of loser move from her youngest daughter but Dean Wynne had been all over the goddamn world. He might like Luke, respect him in that man-to-man swagger bullshit way, but that didn't mean he wanted to see his daughter settle like that.

"Kaj broke up with Kip tonight," he said. "Did you know that?"

"No!" She was shocked. Not because it had happened. But because Kaj had actually done it. And so soon. Before prom, even.

"Yeah. They were in the drive-thru of fucking McDonald's! Did you know she was going to do that?"

"Well, not in the drive-thru of McDonald's," Rianne said. "But she'd said she was thinking about it. I didn't think she'd do it until she left for school."

"Why didn't she just wait?" Luke yelled. Like this was Rianne's personal fault.

She asked him, quietly, so he'd stop yelling, what exactly happened.

"He was kind of drunk and they got into a fight. Usual bullshit. You know Kip can be kind of an idiot. But whatever it was, she just fucking dumped him about it. Told him they could still be friends. As if that's possible! Then she drove him home and dropped him off like nothing. He's a fucking mess."

"Wow."

"Yeah. But that's, you know. Not surprising. They've been together since Jesus was a baby. Neither of them has ever done anything apart. Of course, after a while, you'd want to go out and tear it up. See what else is out there."

"I guess."

"We don't have that problem, at least," Luke said. "We're smart. We got all that shit out of our systems." He grinned, like

220

he was pleased that, effectively, they'd been such sluts. Or she'd been a slut. They didn't call guys like him anything special.

"It makes sense we get a place together, the more I think about it, girly. We're kind of breakup proof at this point, you and me."

He looked so sincere. Open. Like Sally on her back, begging for a belly rub. She couldn't think of an idea that was more idiotic than moving in with him. But she just repeated that she'd think about it. She repeated that she was tired, that she was sorry, and he grabbed her hand. She hoped he wouldn't want to do more. And finally her dad's truck pulled up in the driveway, the headlights blinding them.

"Call me tomorrow, girly," he said. Standing up, kissing her on the mouth really quick, then setting his crutches in place to head down the path, stopping to say hello to her dad. Every day he moved faster on the crutches, needed them less. He'd been following his physical therapy exercises like religion, though she knew how frustrating they were, and how pissed he got at being limited. But he never would show it. Since the accident, he always moved like someone—his trainer, his coach—was watching. Like he had something to prove constantly. Luke moved like he'd always gotten what he wanted in the end. Like he'd never lost anything in his life that really mattered.

Breakfast the next morning is when it all came out. At least it came after she had a shower. Though she hated washing away the scent of Sergei. The ghost of him touching her slid down the drain, and the idea that he might leave at any time made her feel sick.

Her father stood at the kitchen counter, making French toast and sausage. He drank coffee and listened to the news on the radio he kept in the kitchen now. Her mother lurked behind them on her chaise lounge.

"What's up?" Rianne asked, trying to seem natural.

He turned down the radio.

"So. Interesting night we all had, huh?" her dad said. He was wearing one of his million ARMY tees with one of his millions of dad jeans. Light blue denim, so dorky.

She sat down at the counter, shrugged.

"Were you so drunk you couldn't just call?"

"I was barely drunk. And it wasn't me I was worried about. You know Mercy's dad's a cop."

Her dad set down the spatula and poured her a glass of orange juice. "Still. These are things you could just call and tell us. We understand spoken English."

"I could tell *you*, maybe. I doubt Mom cares." She picked up her juice and started to drink. Then he smacked the counter, and she jumped back.

"Goddammit," he said. "You're acting like a child. You want to be all grown-up. But you're being a brat."

Slowly, she set down her juice glass. She could feel her mother behind her, just as still.

"I'm eighteen, Dad. I think I can legally be a brat if I want to."

"I don't think your father's talking about legality, Rianne," her mother said softly. She came over and sat in the stool next to her.

"Well, okay," Rianne said, holding in her trembling stomach. "Here we all are. I might as well get it over with. Yes, I went to a party. Yes, I drank some beer. Yes, the cops came. Yes, me and Mercy ran to avoid that. Then I brought her to her sister's. Then I took a cab home."

"Sounds like it was worth it. All that *fun*," her dad said, frowning down at the frying pan.

Rianne flashed back to the earlier part of the night, when she had such high hopes for it being okay. Her cute outfit, her shaved legs. When it had seemed like maybe Gabby and her friends would get along, have a good time again. When she herself could be good.

"You know, it might have been fun. It's been fun before. Other times I didn't get caught. It has nothing to do with either of you, really. But I get the message. You want me out. Fine. I'll get out. Can I stay here long enough to graduate?"

"Will you even graduate, though?" her mother asked. "I got an email from your English teacher that you were missing work."

Rianne rolled her eyes. "I handed all that crap in. Most of it. The last part is almost done. I'll hand it in Monday."

"You get it done and you show me," her father said. Tough talk again from Mr. Spatula.

"It's just a paper," she said. "All I have to do is print it out."

"Then print it out and show me."

"Fine." She stood up.

"Wait," her mother said.

"God." Rianne sighed, dropping back down.

"I need to have a conversation. A discussion. Something where we're really talking. Not just me saying a bunch of stuff and you tolerating it. Is that possible, Rianne? Can we do that?"

She shrugged.

Her mother laid her palms flat on the counter. Rianne stared at the slightness of her mother's fingers. The thin silver band on her pointer finger. The wrinkles and veins.

"I lay in bed last night while your father talked to Luke," her mother said. "Neither of us had reason to think anything was amiss until Luke showed up looking for you. Obviously, he's a good kid, with a sense of responsibility. Which is wonderful. Maybe just what you need; a guy looking out for you like that."

Rianne felt a twinge. Her mother being positive? About anyone or anything in relation to her?

"Luke is a nice kid, that's for sure," her father added.

"But still, I'm lying there, thinking about you. All the things I've said to you. All the things I've wanted for you. All the stuff about you making your own choices. I always compare. My choices, next to yours. Next to Renata's. Next to your father's. Next to your aunt Emma's. Even my own mother's choices; a woman who lived in Wereford her whole life and will now never leave it."

Rianne looked at her father. Who was looking at her mother. Who was looking down at her frayed slipper that was crossed over her knee.

"The point is," Lucy Hettrick said, as if she could sense her ex and her daughter were waiting for it, "I just want the best for you. From you. It's no secret that I don't understand you. Your dad does a little better. But I want so much! For both my girls. I just don't know how to say that in a way that doesn't piss everyone off."

"It doesn't seem to piss Renata off."

"No," her mother agreed. "It works on Renata."

"Your mother is trying, Rianne," her father said. "She's trying to see things your way. My way."

There was something in Rianne's throat that made it hard to talk. She felt tears threatening, building up, sliding down her nose. She sniffed. Gulped. Thought about how she hadn't even made any sort of plan since her mother's big pronouncement. She was that bad, really.

Because you've always been the baby, Renata would have said. Always said, complaining to their mother, when Rianne did something and didn't get punished or assigned chores:

She's the baby. And the baby never has to do anything.

"I don't want you to move into Luke's house because I made an ultimatum. Your father telling me that you were considering that last night just set my teeth on edge."

"I don't want to move in with Luke, Mom."

"Even if you do," she said. "Please don't make it because I'm selling the house. Make the decision something active, something you want. Not just something you're doing because of what I've decided or where your father's going to be.

Rianne said to her father, "Are you moving back to Wereford or something?"

Her father turned off the burner.

"Tell her, Dean," her mother said. "Enough with the evasive bullshit."

In her father's expression, Rianne could see a knot of anger toward her mom. Like in the past it might have been him storming out. Or shouting.

But he just tipped his head to the side. Scratched his neck, his dad-watch shining in the light of the kitchen window making her instantly remember Sergei. Naked. How good that felt. How good that was.

How bad. Sergei was twenty-five years old. It wasn't *that* much older. But it *sounded* so much older than eighteen. It sounded worse than it was. And what if he put girls like her in cabs all the time? What if this was the end?

"I want to be with your mother," her dad said. " After I get my orders and I finish out the last billet, we're getting our own place. But we've got a little while until that can happen."

"Not too long," her mother said. And smiled.

"Yes," her father agreed. Smiled back.

Rianne felt sick and she couldn't stop the tears any longer. She reached for the roll of paper towels on the counter. Blew her nose.

"I don't want to get between you," her father continued. "But things have changed for me. And your mother. And maybe, this will change things for you too? I don't see why it has to be one way or the other."

"Then why, someone please explain, why in the hell you're selling our house?" Rianne said. "Why, if you're going to get back together, would you sell a place that has space for both of you?"

Her mother patted Rianne's knee in a way that was completely foreign. And made her cry more.

Rianne wiped more tears with the backs of her hands.

Her mother exhaled, looked at Dean Wynne.

"It's largely a financial decision," he said.

"Emotional too, though."

"Yes," her father said, looking at her mom. "We would want a place that belongs to both of us. That's why it can't be your grandmother's house, either."

That last reason sounded exactly like her mother's logic. At least something was constant in this. Rianne cleared her throat. Her father poured her some more orange juice. Rianne drank some and coughed. Her mom reached to pat her back.

"Honey?" her father said. "What is it?"

It. What was it? *Just one thing*, she thought. *Only one thing out of all this insanity?*

"What if I did move in with Luke? What would you do?"

Her mother looked at her tenderly, full of pity. "If that's what you decided, if you've got something set up, that's perfectly okay. It's just, your father reminded me of what happens when you cut your kids loose too quickly."

"My parents were ninety-nine percent of the reason I enlisted," he said. "I sometimes wonder if things would be different if I hadn't."

"You wouldn't have met Mom, though."

"No," he said. "But I knew almost nothing back then, honey. It wasn't a great choice."

"You've done okay with it."

"He has," her mom said. "Luke is a nice boy, but moving in with him? With his family? That might put some stress on you both that you don't need. It might actually make it harder for you in the long run. And we think he's a good match for you, honestly."

Jesus. First they were like, *We like Luke.* Then? *Don't move in with Luke.* And finally, *Marry Luke, though.*

She put her head in her hands and just let it go. The crying. The tears. The runny nose. Her mother smoothed her hair. "It's okay, honey," she said. "Just . . . it's okay. It's a lot to think about."

"You don't have to decide now," her dad added. She heard him move from the other side of the counter. His big warm hand on her back. Her mother handing her another paper towel. Both their bodies crouching around her, the bar stools squeaking beneath them. She wondered what Renata would say if she could see this. She would think it was pathetic.

But Renata couldn't say anything. Renata didn't have to know. She decided instantly, thinking of Renata and the snotty comments she would make, that she wouldn't live with Luke. Or anyone else. She'd pack up her truck and move. First place she could find in Minneapolis. No job, no nothing. Just go and put down the money and make it work.

Sergei. She wanted him. She wanted sex with him. But he was

leaving. It didn't matter where she ended up, really.

"You gotta stretch a little here, honey," her dad said, his voice getting low and choked. "But let's just try to be there for each other, huh?" Was he crying now too? God.

"Yes," her mother said. "With everything so up in the air right now, that's the best we can hope to do."

Both of them formed a ring around her. Her mother wasn't teary-eyed, but her dad was. Her mother patted his cheek. Rianne swallowed tears and hot spit that tasted like orange juice. She exhaled. It felt relieving to cry. To make a decision: she would get her own apartment, all on her own. She looked at her parents, who were looking back at her like she was some new precious creature just born. Something perfect they had made, that they were just seeing for the very first time. Something they might give a name to. Something they might call good.

THIRTEEN

"I THINK TO understand your parents, I need better English, yes?" Sergei asked. He pulled the sheet and blanket over them. Dipped in to kiss her once more. Lazy. Leisurely.

AMBIGUITY: *big, bag, tug, guy . . .*

She had told him the whole story. Her father and mother reuniting. Her decision to find a place of her own. She wasn't sure if he understood it all, though he seemed like he did. She hoped that he wouldn't see her as something stuck here too, like how she saw Mercy. Something he could move past and leave. The only part she left out was Luke's offer and how she had cried. To Sergei, she had to appear better. More grown-up. Lying naked beside him in his bed, that felt possible.

"Yes," she said. She touched his face. Eyebrows. The spikes of his hair that had shook loose during sex. He put lots of gel in it, she had discovered. It was crunchy and sticky. He worked to keep it tidy. The back of his neck was freshly shaved.

"When do you graduate?"

"After I do internship. You know this word?"

She nodded. It was funny how he thought the most basic words were exotic.

"I will complete this somewhere else. Not here. I must research this. Or maybe I complete in Russia. Now, I go to Chicago," he said. "Rink will go to Russia in July. His sister has a baby."

She thought guiltily of Luke's new nephew. Not yet born. How excited Luke was about it.

"What will you do in Chicago?"

"I have a cousin there. He has a bar. I work for him before. He has let me stay with him. I prefer not to go to there but . . ."

"Why don't you want to work for him?"

"I must stop that work. Working with fists. Hands." He made a dismissive noise with his mouth.

"Oh."

"Bars: I am done with the bars. Nothing good coming out of such a place."

She rolled away from him, felt him notch his arms around her, pull her to his bare chest. "Sergei," she said.

He said something in Russian. "Tell me," he added. His voice rumbled through her body, low and strange.

"What are you calling me?"

"Sweet names. Is good, not to worry. Difficulty in translation."

"Fine. I will trust you. But—explain this to me. You make

231

your own vodka. And now you say nothing good comes out of a bar."

"Both of these are true sentences."

"But ... who would drink your vodka, Sergei, if there were no bars? And making vodka? You do that with your hands."

He squeezed around her belly, as if to agree with her. She tensed. She still wasn't used to being touched there so eagerly. Especially while she was sober. And not in the relative quiet of the middle of the afternoon on Wednesday, just the distant sounds from the street from the closed window. It was the first time they'd been together since the night of Cuddy's; Luke had physical therapy on Wednesdays and Rianne switched work shifts with Kaj. She'd broken land speed records driving up to his apartment, her eyes open for Faith while she ran through the parking lot. He was waiting on the front stoop, clutching his keys. He'd stripped her out of almost all her clothes before they made it back to his bed.

He continued running his hands up and down her body. Over her hips and thighs, breasts, collarbone, belly button. Feeling all her parts like he was trying to remember them for a test.

"Sergei ..."

"I say the story now," he said. "Would it please you to listen?"

"Yes."

"Yes. Good. I will say. I make in my cousin's dacha out beyond Chicago," he said. "Not true dacha. But far from others. Secret. A beautiful house. Not true dacha."

"Dachas aren't beautiful?"

"Dachas, no. Simple. They are for pleasing times, not being proud. The distilling machinery I build? Gone. He puts this in the trash. It is not beautiful like the house. My cousin's wife complains."

"Why did he have to throw it in the trash? Couldn't he give it to you?"

"I have no places for it." He gestured around them. "This is only place. I leave soon."

She thought about what the word *soon* might mean to him. Only a few weeks? She let herself be squeezed by him. Her hands over his. Only a few days they'd have in her new place. Maybe she could persuade him to stay. But how?

"And it is against your law. My cousin must keep business, his license. So that is over. No more hands for that." He ran his palms over her breasts as if to show her.

"It is not important," he continued. "I am well in school," he said. "I am all the A+, my *pochemuchka*."

"Really?"

"Yes," he said. Kissing her neck. Reaching down between her legs. She rolled on her back so he could have better access. "In school, I am very good. Is necessary for visa. I am trying now. Being better in my studies than when I am younger. I am learning all the subjects."

"What's your favorite subject, then?"

He kissed her belly. His hand was soft inside her, slow. She was enjoying both things now. Touching. Talking.

"I like maths. Also botany." He pronounced it "boa-tinny."

"You mean 'botany'?"

He nodded, looked her in the eye. "Yes. Botany." He repeated it a couple times. "Thank you."

She felt his dick, already hard on her thigh.

"I also like geographics. No . . . Wait. *Geography*." He sighed as she gripped his dick. She felt absolutely wonderful.

"I like geography too. I think about that a lot. All the places in the world. My dad has gone to so many of them. He's in the army."

"Your father is soldier?"

"Yes. Not like you think. He works in intelligence. You understand?"

"Yes. He is a spy. You are daughter of spy." He smiled.

"Not really, Sergei. But . . ." She paused while the feeling inside her intensified. God, he was so good.

"Your mother is beautiful. Like you. I know this, without seeing her."

She shut her eyes. Concentrated on how she felt. On his words. She didn't look at all like her mother. Being called beautiful was so nice it was embarrassing. She breathed in, imagining what they must look like. If they were in a movie. If a bird could fly up to his window and see them now. His hair sticking up, his pale skin and blue veins, the bits of light hair around his chest. Her own body, open and exposed, no sheet to cover it. She wanted to believe she really did look beautiful in this light.

"He is retiring," she said, trying to control herself. "This means . . . uh . . . ending his time? Not working the job anymore? He hasn't lived here with us for many years. He goes everywhere, while my mom and I live here." Sergei kissed her and she was relieved to stop talking. Her own speech was getting as strange and affected as his and she worried he'd think she was making fun of him.

"You wish to go many places, Rianne?"

"Yes."

"Come with me to Chicago then. Yes? I will take you."

"I don't know. I don't have enough money."

"Is not your worry. This is good part of my father and his money. He and I do not get on well. We do not have a nice relation. But he has his money, and I have some of it. I can see places." He positioned himself right at her cha. He could sink in, bare, so easy.

She cleared her throat. "Have you been on all the continents?"

"Sorry?"

"Continents," she repeated. "North America, South America, Europe, Asia."

"Ah, yes." He nodded. "I see." He thought a minute.

She thought for a moment about the word. CONTINENT. It was a noun; it was also an adjective, signifying self-restraint. Control over the self, over bodily functions.

"I have been to all continents," he said finally. "Wait. Not Antarctica."

"What's Australia like?"

"This is why I like you," he said. Smiled down at her, his palms combing and spreading her hair out on either side of her head. "You are so .. *lyboznatelnaya.*"

"What are you doing to do my hair?"

"Playing."

"And what does *lyb* . . . what does that one word mean?"

He ran a finger over her lips. She watched the muscle of his other arm holding himself up. She wished she had a quarter of his muscle. Luke's were even bigger. It wasn't fair.

"I like your mouth," he said. "There is perfect . . ." He struggled again for the word. "How it is to look. The way it is made."

"Shape?"

"Yes." He smiled.

"Why don't you like bars, Sergei? For real?"

He laughed. He kissed her a few more times before answering. "No surprise. Everyone wants the same thing. Get drunk. Fight. Fuck."

"Will you be done fucking me too, someday?" she asked. "Like with Faith's roommate?"

He looked confused.

"Allie?" she prompted.

"Ah, Allie . . . ," he said, making a face. "She. She is not *lyboznatelnaya.* I wish I remember English. But for you, I am not bored. You, I will take anywhere I go." He kissed her again, pressed himself against her cha. Bare. Nothing between them. Though it felt so dangerous, it also felt so good.

Until her phone rang. They both leaned over to the floor.

Luke's face popped up on the screen, the phone itself shaking with each ring. Sergei backed off of her.

"What was that word for me again?" she asked, hitting the mute button on the phone and flipping it over so she couldn't see Luke's face.

"I need condom," he said, standing up. He looked grim about it. Determined.

"Was it 'whore'?" she said to the ceiling, while he rummaged around the floor.

"No."

"'Prostitute'?" she continued as he put the condom on.

"No, no," he said. He laid his body over her again. A spoke of his blond hair fell over his forehead.

"What does it mean?" she said.

Again, he thought for a moment.

"We go to village where my dacha is. You and I. Because you are *lyboznatelnaya*, when I take you there—and I can, if you want—you say, '*Sergei, what is this, what is that?*' That is *lyubopitstvo*. Questions about everything."

"Curiosity?" she said.

"Yes!" He groaned with relief. Then pressed himself into her, so hard and quick she flinched. Still he kept talking.

"*Lyubopitstvo.* Curiosity. My *pochemuchka. Solnishko.* You will fix me. My English. All of me. Rianne, my beauty." He said more in Russian but she no longer was listening. She was looking up at him. She had no more words to say.

This time, she didn't come. She appreciated Sergei's kind, odd words, but she knew she was being bad again. All she could think of was Luke's face on her phone.

Afterward, he sat on the bed, watching her dress. His head tilted to one side, his frowning mouth to the other, one elbow on his knee. She zipped her skirt and pulled her T-shirt over her head. Her phone rang again. Luke's face, his laughing open mouth, blond curls around his blue hat. She quickly side-buttoned the call, but the phone kept vibrating in her hands. Sergei's frown continued. He stood, put on his jeans. Turned from her to find a clean T-shirt. She stood holding the phone and feeling shy.

"Him," he said, when he turned around. Again, the grim look. His hands in fists as he put his wallet in his pocket. Buttoned up a fresh shirt, this one a dark blue that was almost black. "I cannot see this. I have a jealousy. No more calling of you by him."

"Sergei . . ."

"It is not pleasing to me to see that. His face on your phone." The phone rang again. Luke. This time she turned the whole thing off. Felt her face get hot with guilt.

"Tonight, my little sun. You will fix that for me." He looked at her one last time before leaving the room.

The senior barbecue was at Cattail Park. Even though it was a no-alcohol event, sanctioned by the school, with all the teachers and parents there, grilling, running carnival games and raffles, and handing out T-shirts, it was fun and all the seniors went. The juniors manned booths for photos and cotton candy and there were a million vendors there, handing out coupons and stickers and other junk that the almost-graduated group might need. Water bottles from the army recruiter, key chains from the Murtch-Hutchinson chicken plant, the soybean co-op looking for summer workers, the haircut place on Leroux handing out coupons. Even Gwen had a Planet Tan booth. As if new graduates needed a fake bake more than they needed a job.

It was hot and sticky out. Cloudy with the sun peeking out here and there. Rianne came with Kaj and Mercy. Kaj was a disaster. Kip was calling her constantly. Leaving messages. Crying. Texting. Yelling. Coming over to her house. Her father had threatened to call the cops.

"Can we do this as quick as possible?" Kaj asked, putting on sunglasses as they walked from where Mercy had parked her car. "My parents are sort of losing their minds about me even being at school by Kip. My brother called the other night and basically told me everything they've been thinking but won't tell me. That they've been waiting, all these years, for me to get rid of Kip. They thought being patient about me being with a non-Hmong guy would make it end. And now he's basically being their nightmare."

"Do they want you to be with a Hmong guy, then?" Rianne asked, suddenly curious. Dr. Vang seemed so hip. He collected very expensive bicycles and did road races. His wife wore a FitBit and did yoga. They had never seemed like old-fashioned people.

"It depends on who you talk to," she said. "My brother is like, don't be stupid, they want you to marry one of us. But if I was to ask them straight out, I doubt they'd say that."

"Did you ask them straight out?" Rianne asked.

"No, are you kidding? I already feel like I'm in trouble enough for picking Kip to start with. I can barely stand to talk about the weather with them lately. My mother is always looking out the window like she expects the cops to be standing there. Or worse."

"It'll be okay," Mercy said, linking arms with Kaj. Mercy, being cheerful again.

"I didn't see Kip's minivan anywhere," Rianne added.

"His mom's minivan, you mean," Kaj corrected. "Which smells like nasty hot lunch. I hate that fucking car."

"Why does it smell like nasty hot lunch?" Rianne asked.

Kaj shook her head. "His gross little brother and sister throw their shit everywhere."

"I want to get one of those corn dog things," Mercy said. "And cotton candy. And we have to do the photo booth."

"We should see if Gabby wants to do the photo booth," Kaj said, glancing at Rianne.

"Whatever you guys want," Rianne said.

"We don't have to," Mercy said quickly, linking her other arm in Rianne's. "But I think it would be nice."

Rianne let herself be led through the barbecue this way, attached to Mercy and Kaj, walking slower than she'd like. Mercy had driven them, had insisted they attend. Mercy was being strangely positive, so Rianne knew they had to go along with it. She had told Mercy's mom she wasn't sure all the Pilates and ice cream runs were helping.

"It takes time," Mrs. Kovash told Rianne as she waited for

Mercy one night to get ready to go for a walk. "Nobody figures everything out all at once."

But Rianne thought you could. Renata had. So had Kaj and Gabby. And Luke too. He'd practically had it figured out since birth.

She hadn't been able to "fix it" with Luke. It was like Luke knew what was coming and had decided to be extra sweet. Luke made fajitas with her mom and dad, Luke showed her some apartment listings that his grandfather's friend owned, Luke told Lucy that he'd help Rianne get her stuff sorted in her room. He was in the best of moods because he got a walking cast and could ditch his crutches. He was making plans like crazy to condition himself back into shape. Riding his bike was the latest thing he was planning, though at this point he couldn't do it. Running was out but he craved speed, he said. He dragged Rianne's old mountain bike out of her garage the day before and pumped up the tires.

"You know, I can drive my dad's truck now," she said.

"What's the fun in that?" he said. "We ride bikes, we can get drunk somewhere, ride home together."

"Luke, you can't even pedal yet. And isn't biking while drunk illegal?"

"Who's gonna stop us?"

"Ride home where? To your house? Or mine?"

"Jesus," he had said, leaning her bike against the garage wall. "I just want to have fun. You've got to be all technical about shit. Come on, girly." He scowled at her but then kissed her cheek. He

241

was like Sally, biting at her sleeve, then licking her. Never able to stay mad.

Now Rianne scanned the crowd for him, for his blond head, his slight dip when he walked. She didn't see him, though she saw Gabby and Claire Andale come out of the photo booth with Aidan Golden. Gabby smiled at them and waved. She yelled, "Hey, you guys!" But she didn't stop to talk. It was worse than being rejected, Rianne thought.

"What the fuck ever," Kaj said. "So much for us being friends again."

"Maybe she actually likes Aidan," Mercy said. "Like, for real? They're going to prom."

"Oh, fuck Aidan Golden!" Kaj said. "Fuck him and his gross hairy fucking arms!"

They all laughed, so Kaj kept going. "And hairy toes! He sits by me in physics and wears these flip-flops and his toes are hairy. And his toenails are all yellow. Bald eagles have nicer pedicures than that dude."

"It's not like he can shave his toes, Kaj," Mercy said.

"Why not?" Kaj said. "I certainly wouldn't stop him."

"You're leaving in three months," Rianne reminded her. "Who even cares."

"Good point, Ri," Kaj said.

They walked toward the grill area to get the meal tickets and food. All the teachers handing out the hot dogs and chips and whatever wore whistles and fake Mardi Gras beads and other weird shit: giant sombreros, glittery eyelashes and face paint, assault helmets, suspenders, shutter shades. It was all meant to be happy, but it felt so babyish. It would have embarrassed her for Sergei to see it.

As they were sitting down to eat, Luke came up. He kissed Rianne's cheek and dropped his truck keys on the picnic table. He wore shorts and his walking cast and a Wereford hockey T-shirt. He looked sweaty and healthy and sunny as usual. Sally squirmed under his bicep.

"Hello, ladies," he said. Pure cheesiness.

"Hello, douchewad," Kaj said, picking at the watermelon in her fruit salad. It was tasteless and pink. Rianne hadn't even taken any. But then Kaj saw Sally. "Oh my god! What a cutie!"

"He's so sweet!" Mercy said.

"She," Luke said. "Her name's Sally."

Luke probably knew that Kaj couldn't resist a puppy. Maybe that was the plan too. Because while Kaj was loving up Sally, Kip came over and sat down. Everyone got kind of tense and Sally jumped from Kaj to inspect and lick Kip. It occurred to Rianne that Luke had done this on purpose. First him and the puppy, then Kip. They all knew Kaj would do anything to avoid making a scene.

"I didn't know your guy was back, Mercy," Luke said, loudly. Sally whimpered in his lap, trying to crawl up to the table where the food was. Luke's sunglasses were pulled down around his neck, which reminded Rianne of her dad.

"What?"

"He's at the church booth thing? That nutjob church that's always handing out Bibles."

"Caleb?"

"Yeah." Rianne could feel Luke's hand nudging her leg under the table.

But Mercy was already up and gone, her corn dog half-eaten on her paper plate.

"Do you think she'll want that?" Luke asked. "Or can I give it to my dog?"

Kaj rolled her eyes.

Kip stood, announced he was getting some food, and did anyone want anything. No one said anything.

"Is he okay?" Kaj asked Luke, after Kip was out of range.

"No."

"He's acting okay right now," Kaj said.

"Because I told him to act fucking decent, that's why," Luke said, ruffling Sally's neck while she chewed on Mercy's corn dog.

"Good," Kaj said. "Thank you. I'm glad someone can get him to quit freaking out."

Luke ducked her compliment. "I told him to fucking chill. That you needed some space and time."

Kaj stared at Luke like he was from Mars. "Aren't you the relationship expert now," she said, her lips twisting up while she wiped her mouth with a Taco John's napkin. Her taco-in-a-bag sat abandoned and a bee starting buzzing around it.

Luke was quiet. Rianne could feel his opinion hovering in the air. She turned and scanned the crowd. Caleb was back? Why?

"I'm just looking out for the both of you," he said. "No big deal."

Now Rianne could feel Kaj's opinion hovering. But she didn't say anything because Kip returned, holding his plate of food.

"I can hold Sally while you get yours, dude," Kip said.

Luke shook his head. "I don't want to eat that shit."

"You're on a full protein-power diet now?" Kip joked. Kaj stared at her ex like he was a speck of dirt in something she previously might have eaten.

"No point in filling up with crap," Luke said. "Body's got enough to deal with right now." He squeezed Rianne's knee under the table. Kip started eating. Kaj looked at her fingernails.

Rianne wanted to ask Luke: *If you don't want to eat crap, what are you doing here then?*

Then Mercy was back with Caleb. They were holding hands and looking a little stunned. Caleb's hair was trimmed down to nothing but fuzz and he looked thinner. Mercy was transformed from her usual couch tumor self they'd known all these weeks to a bouncing girl with a smile that wouldn't break. Kaj complimented Caleb's hair while Kip and Luke stared. Caleb rubbed the top of his fuzzy head and laughed. Rianne noticed he wore a WWJD bracelet and a hospital patient band.

"Hey, we're gonna run up to my house for a little bit," Mercy said.

"Right now?" Kaj said.

"I just want to show Caleb something," Mercy said, still bouncing, still gripping his forearm.

"Don't be long."

"The barbecue's over at nine," Kaj warned. Her eyes locked onto Mercy. Rianne could see her wanting to shout *and you're my ride*. But Mercy didn't seem to care; she bounced away, tugging Caleb along through the crowd.

Luke looked amused. "What's the whole deal there?"

Rianne started to explain and Kip interrupted her. "How did you not know this shit, dude? It's all Kaj could talk about for like a month."

Kaj popped up an eyebrow at Kip. Who then just dipped back into his taco-in-a-bag.

"Rianne never said anything," Luke said.

"You don't pay attention half the time, dude," Kip said.

"Go get me one of those taco things," Luke said.

"Fuck you, get it yourself," Kip replied, his mouth full of taco.

"You need a meal ticket to get one." Kaj sighed. "You just might have to get up and do it yourself, Mr. Pinsky."

"Can you hold Sally?" Luke asked Kaj.

"Why?"

"Cause I want Rianne to come with me."

"Why?"

"Quit asking why, Jesus," Luke said, dumping Sally and her leash on Kaj's lap. Kaj picked up the dog, but she was more restrained this time around. When they left, Kip was laughing.

"See?" Luke said as they walked over to the food area. "It's just a blip."

"Them?"

"Yeah."

"I don't know," Rianne said.

Luke grabbed her hand. "Don't be negative," he said. "You never know for sure what people'll do."

She watched him sweet-talk the school secretary lady, the one who was usually a huge bleeding bitch about late passes, and then get his own taco-in-a-bag, spooning salsa and cheese into it while joking with all the parents. Several teachers and parents asked him about his leg, how his recovery was going. He dug his plastic spoon into the bag of Doritos and munched while he chatted about the gory details of the pins and the strength of his bones, the surgery he'd have to have later to remove them, the medical note he'd need if he was going to get through security in the airport. "Doctors say I'm done growing, which is why it's healing so quick," he told them, which was something she'd heard him say—and his mother and grandmother—many times.

Rianne stood beside him, gripping his hand and feeling shy. Wondering how to fix this. Fix Luke. There was nothing wrong with him. Even his leg would soon be fixed.

She had no story to tell him, either. Only her decision to get her own place but nothing she'd done about it yet. At least Kaj and Gabby had college. Too bad no one ever sold college that way—as a place to go, not just another big heap of tests and work and grades. As far as Luke was concerned, she could slide right into his basement bedroom and camp out forever. Gabby and Kaj would be gone, no matter what Kip did. And Mercy? Who knew. Whether Rianne moved didn't even matter anymore. Now her parents loved each other. Now they loved her too. Nobody cared if she went anywhere.

FOURTEEN

THE NIGHT BEFORE prom, Caleb went back into the hospital. Checked in voluntarily. Mercy, bouncing since the senior barbecue, was now completed flattened. That next morning, Rianne picked up Kaj, who had made a bowl of cookie dough especially for the occasion and they drove over to the Kovashes' with the bowl on Kaj's lap.

"Don't!" Kaj said, flicking away Rianne's fingers from the bowl as she drove. "Eyes on the road!"

Mrs. Kovash was still in her nurse scrubs when they came inside.

"You know where to find her, girls," she said.

"Is Caleb okay?"

Mrs. Kovash sighed, shook her head. "I can't tell you anything more."

"Maybe his parents will keep him in there, this time?" Kaj asked.

Mrs. Kovash grabbed three spoons from the silverware drawer and stabbed them into the cookie dough bowl. "It's going to get worse before it gets better."

They passed Kaj's half-finished black and white and red dress on the dressmaker pattern in the living room. Kaj refused to look at it. Mrs. Kovash wouldn't take any money for it. After they'd got along at the senior barbecue, Kip had thought everything was back on. He'd started writing Kaj letters and leaving them everywhere. Her locker. The Vangs' mailbox. The windshield of her car. All of them said the same things, a million different ways, about how much he loved her and how great she was. One day Gabby found one and read it out loud in psychology. Kaj ditched out that day in tears.

The week hadn't been easy for anyone. An offer came in on the house and her mother had accepted it. Her father was back in Colorado, making everything quiet again. She and her mother weren't at war, but the house was empty and sad. Boxes piling up in the garage. Every room slowly being emptied of anything not essential.

Rianne had looked at three apartments, two in Wereford and one in Dalby. They were all on the top end of her price range, except one, which was above the Pizza Palace. Rianne could barely stand to be in that one for the smell of it. The guy who showed it to her kept staring at her too long while she looked around. When she told her mom about it, she half expected her to say something. Do something or give her some money, help her out. But Lucy Hettrick just gave her a hug and said how proud she was of her daughter growing up and then left the room to refill her glass of wine.

In the basement, Mercy was rolled up like a burrito in her quilt. The TV was on a show about people who hoard things and the screen was showing a garage door rolled up to reveal a massive pile of junk.

"Oh my god," Kaj said, handing Rianne the cookie dough and grabbing the remote. "How is this shit helping!" She flicked the channels, finding only more depressing shit: a crime scene with a bloody floor, a courtroom drama about a rapist, a mob of Kardashians trying on clothes.

"Mercy, sit up," Rianne said.

"No."

"Come on," Rianne said. "Kaj made cookie dough. With walnuts, just like you like it!"

"Fucking walnuts," Kaj added, flicking from baseball to a show about survival in the rain forest. "Who puts walnuts in cookie dough?"

"My mom, for one," Mercy said. "And Faith."

"Then eat it," Rianne said. "Come on. Shove over and let me have some room."

Slowly, Mercy sat up. The quilt fell around her and they saw she was in pajamas and her hair was so greasy it didn't look blond anymore. Rianne lifted a spoon of cookie dough toward her, like she was a baby.

"Jesus, there is literally nothing you can watch that's not horrible," Kaj said, flopping on the floor in disgust. "Give me one of those spoons."

"I thought you didn't like walnuts," Mercy said, licking the spoon as Rianne smiled and reloaded it.

"Cookie dough's cookie dough," Kaj said grimly, eating a spoonful of dough while she worked through the grid of channels on the Kovashes' television.

"Your mom wouldn't say anything about Caleb," Rianne said. "What's going on?"

Mercy took the spoon from Rianne, dug out a big slab.

"He's definitely got more than demonic infestation," Mercy said. "I think his parents are finally getting that."

"'Demonic infestation'—are you fucking kidding?" Rianne asked.

"Speaking of, I'm going to assume no one wants to watch old episodes of *Supernatural*," Kaj said, clicking away on the floor.

"Not if it's season seven," Mercy said. "That was such a total flusher."

"So, what are they saying is wrong with him?" Rianne asked.

"They don't know," she said. "They have to see how he responds to certain medications. It's going to be a while. They have to get him stable first. I think it's schizophrenia, personally. I mean, he's hearing voices, Rianne. Telling him all this shit."

"Like, to hurt people? Or himself?"

"Only himself," she said, and then she gulped. Put down the spoon. Rianne could see she was trying not to cry.

"Oh, Mercy," Kaj said, turning from the TV to sit beside Mercy and hug her.

"That's why he checked himself in," she continued, tears rolling. "Before it was just weird stuff. Telling him what to wear. Or what to say. Telling him things to watch for. He didn't want to talk about it, because sometimes the things he would hear were good. They helped him."

"Jesus," Rianne said.

"So, I don't know," she said. "I've just got to be patient. Wait and see."

"Fair enough," Kaj said. "But there's no rule you have to wait and see lying on this couch for days on end."

"Seriously," Rianne said.

Mercy slumped back, pushed away the cookie dough bowl.

"But I love him," she said. "You don't even know what that's like."

"Mercy, come on!" Rianne said.

"You don't," Mercy said. "Kaj doesn't either. Rianne only likes chasing after shit, having fun. Kaj just got stuck with Kip. I *love* Caleb. I want to spend the rest of my life with him. He understands me. He loves me."

"You're freaking me out here," Kaj said.

"He is so so good to me, you guys. You don't even know."

"Yeah, yeah," Rianne said. "He goes down on you. He's so loving."

"Fuck off! You act like it's nothing."

"No, listen to me," Rianne said. "You can't lie in the basement growing mold all over you while it's beautiful weather out, we're almost done with school, and you've got so much to look forward to."

"It rained yesterday."

"For like an hour! Then it was beautiful! I went for a run!" She didn't mention that the run had ended at Sergei's house and that she'd walked home in a daze, feeling high and delirious as she watched the stars come out. But she wasn't the depressed person here.

"Rianne, really? *You're* going to lecture me?"

"No," she said. "I'm going to tell you why you need to keep living. You can't just stop. Look, Kaj gets harassed every day by Kip. He won't stop calling, he wants her to pay for his prom tux rental—"

"Seriously?"

"—and you don't see her lying on the couch like a lump! She blocked his number, she had her dad call Mr. Jelinek . . ."

"She should have my dad talk to him."

"See? That's a good idea! Yes!"

"And I'm packing all my shit," Kaj said. "College. I'm going to college. Where you should be going, too. Both of you."

"Not me," Rianne said. "I can't fucking stand any more homework."

"Mercy should, though," Kaj grumbled, sliding back to the floor to keep searching for something to watch. "*Fast and the Furious*?"

"I hate those fucking movies," Mercy said.

"The original is the best one," Kaj said, but clicked to another option.

Rianne took one last spoonful of cookie dough. "My point is, you're going to be moving in with Faith. Do you have your stuff packed?"

"No."

"Why not?"

"Because Faith wants to move to Seattle now," Mercy said.

"Oh, for fuck's sake," Kaj said. "What is with that? Who wants to live there? It like rains three hundred days out of the year."

"Her roommate, Allie, is going, I guess."

"I can't handle that shit right now," Mercy said. "I can't handle anything. I need my own house, my own room. I need my mom."

Kaj glanced at Rianne, like *who needs their mom still?*

Rianne shrugged. Maybe normal people did. Maybe she and Kaj weren't normal. They were heartless girls who didn't know what love was, who didn't want to stay with their mothers.

Kaj finally flipped to a channel showing an old James Bond movie.

"No!" Mercy said. "I hate the old-timey Bond."

"Find a cartoon," Rianne said, watching the grid on the screen.

"Tom Hardy's in this one." Kaj pointed to the screen.

"He's wearing a fucking thing on his face, you can't even see him," Rianne said.

"God, you guys get HBO too? How about *Cathouse?*" Kaj suggested.

"That show makes me never want to have sex again," Mercy said.

Kaj flipped up another screen. "There! Put it on that!" Rianne said.

The Little Mermaid. The part where Ariel was singing and slowly losing her voice.

"Okay," Kaj said, clicking the remote so that Ariel filled the whole screen as she walked ashore to Prince Eric. "Can we all live with this one?"

When Rianne came in for her shift at Planet Tan, Gwen had good news. There was a studio in her building opening up.

Gwen explained the situation while she bedazzled the product display shelves with little stickers that looked like a mixture of rhinestones and suns.

"The guy below me died," she said. "Actually died!"

"In the apartment?" Rianne asked, setting down her backpack under the appointment desk.

"No, he was in a car accident," she said. "It's not like I'd tell you to move into a place where there was a corpse, sweetie," she said.

"How much is it?"

"I don't know, but after we close, I'll bring you over and introduce you to the landlord. He's working on my kitchen sink so it's no big thing."

"What's wrong with your kitchen sink?"

"Oh, who the fuck knows," she said.

After her shift, she followed Gwen back to her apartment,

which was over by the smoothie shop Mrs. Vang owned.

"It's a garden-level situation," Gwen said, while she unlocked her mailbox and collected a raft of bills. "But that just means it'll probably be cheap."

Rianne nodded. She was excited. She followed Gwen up the stairs and into her apartment, where a guy in a dirty shirt was lying on her kitchen floor. Gwen's apartment was cute. She had a matching red and purple love seat and chair, a flat-screen TV in a bright red cabinet, framed art and photos everywhere. It smelled like grapes and peaches. Like the lotion Gwen always was slathering on her hands at work. There was a wine rack on the wall, a shelf of cookbooks, a pile of magazines on the kitchen table.

The dirty guy had awful teeth but at least he didn't look at Rianne's boobs. He was too busy looking at Gwen's. And Gwen was laughing like she didn't mind. Rianne waited, wanting them to do their flirting some other time. She wanted to see the place.

She didn't know "garden level" was a nicer way of saying "the basement." There were only window wells for natural light. And it wasn't very big. Just one room, with a bathroom off the side, a tiny lane for the kitchen.

The dead guy's stuff wasn't lying around, but it wasn't entirely gone. A futon mattress was rolled up like a big dusty pastry. Boxes were half-filled and stacked everywhere. There was a Bob Marley poster with one edge curling up on the wall beside the big pipe that ran all the way across the ceiling.

"Utilities aren't included," the dirty guy said, while turning on a light above the kitchen sink. "And I can't really offer it up yet, because we have to do inspections and some other maintenance first. But Gwen said you'd be a good renter."

"When will it be ready?"

"Dunno. Maybe August. Sooner, if you're willing to put some sweat into it. I might be able to knock off some rent, if the owner allows it."

At least it didn't smell bad. Faintly like pot. But nothing else.

"Can I paint the walls?" Rianne asked. She was looking at a big rust spot by the window well.

"We'll paint it for you," the dirty guy said. "Unless you want to do it yourself. That'd be subject to my inspection, of course. You ever rented before?"

"No," she said. "I'm graduating next week."

"I can vouch for her," Gwen said, squeezing Rianne toward her, her long fingernails snapping against Rianne's shoulder. "If you need an employer reference."

"So if I do some work for you, I could get into it earlier."

The dirty guy shrugged. "Let me figure a few things out. We'll see."

Later that week, she met with the dirty guy, whose name was Benji, and he gave her a bunch of tools and told her to start pulling down the drywall right where the rusty stain was. To her surprise, it came off surprisingly easy and had a weird rotting smell that was almost pleasant. She filled two giant contractor bags full of the debris before she had to go pick up Luke from his physical therapy session at the clinic.

As she listened to him talk about his progress, she realized she had become so good at not telling people things. Nothing about Sergei. Nothing about the apartment. Not even to her friends. She'd asked Gwen not to mention it to Kaj, even. He reached for her hand across the seat and told her she looked hot as fuck and said he didn't think anyone was around at his house right now.

"My grandparents are at Fleet Farm in Dalby," he said. "And you know how my grandma likes to make a whole day out of that."

She laughed; Grandma Pinsky's idea of heaven was dried fruit and bulk dog chews and mitten warmers and chicken wire fencing as far as the eye could see.

"I can't," she said. "My mom needs to borrow the truck to move some stuff to storage."

"Maybe after that?"

"Yeah," she said. "Maybe."

With no homework to do and just days from being free from high school, she found herself getting sick of everything. Mainly, packing and making lists. Digging through the crap under her bed. Her red lacquered jewelry box on her dresser and all the little bits she'd collected. Her friends' tiny school photos, her passport. Eli's necklace bead, Devin Trauger's busted one hitter he'd forgotten to ask back from her, one of the Gabe magnets of him in a baseball uniform. It bugged her that she didn't have anything from Aidan Golden. Unless you counted Hat Trick

Girl. But that had been printed under her name in the senior showcase of the yearbook.

She put on two sports bras and some workout clothes. It was hot and beautiful and she could hear birds from the open window in her room. She texted Sergei and told him she'd be over.

yes my beauty he texted back.

Rianne didn't run the whole way. It was hotter than she guessed and at almost five thirty, the sun was at its peak. But halfway there, she thought of how much she wanted to see him. She was keeping the apartment from Sergei, too. Once the walls were rebuilt, and taped and mudded, a process Benji mentioned, which sounded exotic, then they could paint and she could move in. But even with her working for as many hours as she could fit in, between work and school and Luke and Sergei, she still wasn't sure how long it would take.

Part of her knew it wouldn't matter. Sergei had said he was leaving. She had avoided bringing it up, though he had said June fifteenth and that was just days away.

He was standing on the stoop, in his same pressed shirt and shoes and Levi's.

"Look at this," he said, reaching for her. "You are health."

She wiped her forehead, tried not to flinch at his hands on her sweaty shoulders.

"Aren't you hot? Don't you ever wear shorts?"

"Why do you ask me this?" he asked back.

She shook her head, let him hold her. Even though she was sweaty, it felt good to be near him. And she could tell he felt the same way, because he pressed her through the door and up to his apartment, stripping off his clothes and hers with great speed.

This time, it happened in the living room, which was strangely clean. The coffee table was empty, no bottles or ashtray full of butts. Nothing but the flat-screen television on the wall and the sofa.

When it was done, he brought her a glass of water. Stretched while she sat drinking it.

"You are so beautiful," she said. "How do you . . . do you ever work out? Exercise?"

He smiled down at her. "No," he said. "I am not health. I am . . . luck."

He wanted to make food for her. Breakfast foods—toast, eggs, bacon. She was starving after running so after she went to the bathroom to pee and rinse off in his shower, she stood watching him.

"Is Rink gone?"

"Yes," he said. "He leaves sooner than he plans."

"He left all his stuff?"

Sergei slid the cooked eggs on a plate for her. "He cannot take it on airplane. I will leave it too."

She ate the food while he washed the dishes. She liked watching him move around the small kitchen, whistling through his teeth, barefoot in only his jeans. The coffeemaker, the toaster, he would just abandon them. The piles of mail and papers on the counter, same thing. She thought of her house, the boxes stacking up in corners. Her mother strapping tape over them and labeling each with a black Sharpie (BOOKS, RENATA, FINANCIAL FILES), then loading them in her dad's truck to various destinations: Goodwill, the storage place in Dalby, the post office.

She nodded and he smiled, which made her unreasonably happy. He took her back to his room and opened the laptop on his desk.

"I show you this," he said.

It was open to an airline site.

"I leave these days. First Chicago, then Moscow. Chicago, I am there a few days. A week? Then Moscow until . . . whenever. I get this ticket, I get one for you as well. Come with me?"

"For how long?"

He shrugged. "Some weeks. Maybe longer."

"I don't have enough money for it," she said.

"You do not pay for things, my *pochemuchka*, so not to worry. You only need passport and clothes."

"But, what about my job?"

"Is not a matter. Let us just go, yes?" He pushed her against the desk, kissed her for a minute.

"What will we do in Moscow?" she asked. "Will I meet your brothers?"

"We will do all that you want. I will show you everything."

"Will I need warm clothes?" Automatically her brain sprang back to all the sweaters she had packed in the boxes for her mother.

"Maybe, is not a thing. I buy you what you need. There is nothing you cannot buy in Moscow. We can go to my dacha too.

There you will need only swimming suit."

She bent her head beneath his chin, looking at the little blond hairs around his collarbone. His hands slid down her back, over her ass.

"Maybe not even swimming suit," he said, his voice getting both deeper and quieter. "We can be naked there. Like animals in dirt." He kissed along her neck for a few minutes.

"I want to spend my own money, Sergei," she offered. "Can we leave after I get my last check?"

"*Tsk.* If you like. Is not a matter. Keep your money, my beauty. Just say to me you will come. It will please me greatly if you come."

"I don't know," she said. "I mean, I'm not sure how to explain it."

"To your parents? No explanation. You are eighteen. You just take passport and go."

"And after that? We come back here?"

"After that, we have a saying. It goes, 'After that, cat soup.'"

"What?"

"Difficulty in translation. It means, whatever. Who knows what we'll do."

"Yes, but still. There's so much going on. I need a little more time."

Luke's words to Kaj echoed in her head. She needed a little *space and time.*

He leaned away, held her by the shoulders. It was like he could tell she was thinking about Luke.

"You have not fixed it with him yet," he said. His eyes were on hers and she couldn't break away. The sunlight in the window spiked through a passing cloud and lit up the fine stubble around his neck. But the way he didn't blink from her made her realize that this was serious. He was serious, about all of it. About leaving, about Luke.

"I haven't," she said. "But I will."

"When?"

"Tonight."

"Good. Then it will be finished. I buy tickets when you get me passport. I need that, yes? You have current one?"

"Yes."

"Good. You bring. I fix."

There was more to say, more to do. But she let him undress her again, anyway.

FIFTEEN

HE WAS OWED it in person, Rianne thought, as she rinsed off in Sergei's shower. He had joined her at first, but got out when his phone rang in his pants pocket on the bathroom floor.

"Is my brother, I must answer," he said, sliding the curtain away from her and grabbing a towel.

She would miss Sergei's shower. It smelled like him. Like soap she would never buy—Irish Spring—and the hangover remedy and the strange cologne that Rink had left in the medicine chest. She wished she had a shower scrub or some body oil, a loofah to scrub the backs of her thighs. Some reason to stay under the hot water longer and avoid breaking up with Luke. Which she knew she couldn't wait to do any longer. She didn't love him, and it wasn't his fault.

If she'd never loved Luke, was it really breaking up with him?

She wasn't sure if she loved Sergei, though. Maybe Mercy was right and she didn't know what love was. She knew that she thought about Sergei constantly. Wondered about everything he did, every little gesture, every tilt of his head, every shrug of his shoulder. It all fascinated her and she couldn't look away.

But maybe, that was how love happened, then. It wasn't a decision, but more like a disease. A fever that burned you up, was how some people described it. It didn't burn her. It made her feel like everything was brighter, though. The whole world, her whole body, him.

Wrapped in one of his heavy white towels, she carefully squeezed water from her ponytail and wiped smears of makeup off in front of his mirror.

In his medicine chest, there was nothing beyond Rink's cologne, a tub of crappy yellowy hair gel, and a razor and some shave cream. He didn't even have any lotion. The little glass shelves were clean, though, and so was the sink and counter. There was a fluffy bath mat under her feet and the tile was swept tidy. Did Sergei have someone clean his apartment? Or had Rink cleaned before he left? She imagined living here herself for a moment. That her products would sit on the shelf beside his, her hair dryer and straightener on the counter. That underneath the sink would go her tampons and body lotions and the bucket of nail polish she'd been toting to sleepovers at her friends' houses for years. The bathroom in her new apartment had no sink yet; Benji had pulled it out to get a new one, he said.

Her lips were red and whisker-burned; Sergei didn't even have Vaseline. Even Luke had a thing of Vaseline in his bathroom.

But that was in a house with women in it. Luke's bathroom also had a candle on the back of his toilet and little decorated soaps that looked like daisies in a pink polka-dotted dish. Since Tana and Lance had moved into the cabin on Gullwing Lake, he'd inherited the little ceramic *If you sprinkle when you tinkle* plaque too. Which he'd probably bring with him when he moved out. Though she noticed the fuzzy pink toilet covers and rugs hadn't made the cut.

"Rianne! Your phone!"

Startled, she came out of the bathroom into the living room. Sergei was standing there in his jeans again, holding both his phone, with his brother's voice crackling out of it, and hers, with Luke's face in the blue hat smiling steadily.

"Now," he said in a low whisper, his face grim. From his phone came a dim voice in Russian. "You tell him now."

"No! I can't! Not on the phone!"

He said something into his phone in Russian, and the name "Dima" and then he clicked off. While also hitting the "talk" button on hers.

"Yes, hello," he said, the photo of Luke's face smashed against his own.

She stood in her towel, about to vomit in fear. She heard Luke's voice squawk from it.

"No, you have correct number. Rianne is here. She is with me," he said. There was a pause while he listened. Then, "I am Sergei. You are knowing me. Rianne can speak now."

She didn't want to take the phone but Sergei had put it in her hand. Luke's voice shouted, "Rianne? Are you there? Are you okay? Rianne!"

"I'm here," she said.

"What the fuck is going on? Why's some Russian dude answering your fucking phone?"

"Luke, can I call you back in a few minutes?"

"No, what the fuck already? Are you with that guy? Your mom has your truck but she doesn't know where you are."

"Are you at my house?"

"Yeah, I just stopped over, because I was dropping stuff off for the guys at the goddamn elementary school. Where the fuck are you?"

Sergei sat on the back of the sofa, his hands gripping the edge of it, his face blank.

"I'll be home in a little bit," she said. Her voice was crackly and unnatural.

"Where are you? Something's not right. What's going on?"

She was silent. She could hear her own breathing amped up to a million. She could hear everything. Even the ticking of the clock on the wall. Or was that Sergei's watch?

"Are you . . . what the fuck are you doing with that guy, Rianne?"

"Luke, I have to break up with you. Okay? But I don't . . ."

"What the fuck? Are you fucking serious? Is this . . . is Kaj with you?"

"No! Kaj isn't here."

"Where are you?"

"We have to do this in person, Luke. This isn't . . . it's not fair . . ."

Now his end was silent.

"You're fucking right it's not fair," he said. "You're a fucking liar, for one thing. And if you're fucking that goddamn Russian cocksucker, I swear to god, Rianne, I will lose my shit. I will straight up kill that motherfucker."

Sergei stood up. Hands at his sides. She stared at him like he was going to go after her, not Luke. She stepped back; Sergei stepped forward.

"Luke, let me just talk to you, okay?"

"You *are* fucking talking to me," he said. "It's this thing called a phone? We're both using it! So just talk already. Are you fucking that Russian dude or what? You have been?"

"Luke, can we . . ."

"I can't believe this. You're fucking *that* guy?" He laughed for a minute. "Jesus Christ. Say you're not. Say you're not, and it's all good. Dump me all you want, Rianne, but please tell me you're not fucking that dude."

Sergei stared at her. There were tears everywhere. Out of her nose, dripping down her mouth, onto her neck, onto Sergei's fluffy towel.

"Fucking say it, Rianne!"

She remained silent.

"You are then," he said. His voice softer now. "You're fucking some guy who's probably a goddamn criminal. Who doesn't know shit about you. I can't fucking believe you."

"Luke."

"No, don't say my name. Don't even talk."

"Luke, it's not what you think."

He laughed. "Oh, really, Rianne? Are you gonna say, 'it doesn't mean anything, it's just like Aidan Golden and all the other guys you've fucked'? Except this dude is, what? Ten years older? And, what'd you pick him for? Because he's the last dude in Wereford who hasn't seen you naked? I mean, except Kip. Or are you gonna tell me you've fucked Kip now too? Jesus."

She sniffled. Wiped her nose.

"Oh, spare me. You're crying now? You're the one crying? This is fucking excellent work, girly. Just excellent. Perfect, really. You're gonna cry because you're a goddamn cheating whore bitch and expect me to feel sorry for you? You keep waiting for that. Have fun while you do."

"Luke, I didn't mean it to go like this. I didn't mean . . ."

"Who gives a damn what you mean, Rianne. It is what it is. Fuck off and don't ever talk to me again."

He clicked off and she stood there, dripping. Tears down her neck, water from her ponytail, snot from her nose. Sergei took her phone and put it in his pocket. Then, with his sleeve, he wiped her eyes and under her nose.

"See?" he said. "Now you have fixed it."

She walked all the way home. The sun was only going down, even though it was nearly nine o'clock. There was no energy left to run. Her thighs were sore, her back aching. She called Kaj and Mercy, but neither answered.

Alone, in the quiet, it was funny how she had never seen Wereford like this. How she could hear it and see it and feel it. And smell it! All the fragrances of this little crappy town, whirling in the summer air. Soybean processing and burnt meat on the grill. Exhaust and tacos. Stale beer from crushed cans in recycling bins set out on the curb for the morning pickup. The night had a glow too that was almost a smell. A cool smell, sapping the heat of the day. Something that smelled of trees and birds and bees making pollen runs from petal to petal. Something that had an undernote of rusty garden-hose water and chalk from the softball fields that marked the baselines and home plate. Something that was full of yeast and corn and sin and sex and blown-out tires on the highway and little kids screaming they didn't want to come inside and take a bath.

When she got home, her mother was gone. A note, scribbled on the back of one of Renata's sheet music piles on the table, said she would be back soon.

She peeled off her workout clothes. Found an old Wereford volleyball tank top and yoga pants and crawled into bed. She lay there, the quiet feeling of the walk home stacking inside her. The window of her room was open and she could hear the chittery sound of night bugs. Crickets.

She heard her mother pull up. The familiar sound of her truck's engine. Her mother's light steps, the sound of keys landing on the table, the kitchen sink running. Her mother having a drink of water. Her mother softly walking upstairs, undressing, sinking into the bed, snapping off the light.

Her mother's hitched almost-snore.

Sunday morning, her mother did it all reverse. Got out of bed, showered, dressed.

"I'm going to Grandma's," she said softly, approaching Rianne's bed.

"Do I have to come? I don't feel well," Rianne replied.

"It's not a visit," her mother said. "Just dropping off some paperwork. Go back to sleep." She touched a palm to Rianne's forehead. "You feel a little warm. Looks like you've got everything almost packed up."

"Yeah."

"Go back to sleep," she said again, and left the room. Rianne stared up at the blank roll of corkboard before drifting back off.

She woke to faint knocking. Then her phone buzzed with a text from Luke: *I'm here come talk to me please*

She put on a bra, went to the door. It wasn't raining, but the day was gray and misty. He looked horrible. He wore basketball shorts and a shitty muscle tee, the kind with the big gaps under the armpits, that said "Y'ALL NEED JESUS" on it. He'd found it in a church parking lot he was snowblowing and liked to wear it as a joke. His eyes were red and sad.

She couldn't talk. Her mouth felt pasted shut with guilt and morning breath. But it didn't stop him from rushing to her in a big hug. Holding her so tight she thought she might pop. She heard him make a gulping sound that was way too close to crying.

"Goddammit, girly," he said. "Goddammit."

She couldn't touch him back. She was afraid even to touch the back of his neck, to run her hand over his cheek, would make him explode. He repeated "goddammit" a few more times and gulped again, with sniffling added to the whole thing, and she stood against him, crushed.

Then he pulled back. Finally looked at her. Her mouth frowned again, braced for her own tears.

"This wasn't Kaj's idea," he said. "I know that. I talked to her."

"Did you tell her everything?"

"That's on you," he said. She wondered why he didn't say it was on Sergei. But the squint in his eyes told her a moment later. Of course he wouldn't say it was another guy. Another *man*, actually. He couldn't be Luke Pinsky and say his girl had gone off and fucked someone like that.

He wiped his eyes, rubbed his nose on his wrist. She could still see grass-grit under his fingernails, caught in the hair on his hands.

"You gonna be with that dude, now, then?"

She shrugged. It felt like twisting the knife telling him yes.

"He's not even staying here, Rianne," he said. "He's going back to Russia. All them guys do."

"I'm sorry, Luke."

His mouth settled into a knot, then a line, then a smile. He turned, headed to his truck. "God," he said as he walked down the driveway. "And to think? Everyone told me to stay away from you. Everyone said you were no good."

Graduation was fine. Terrible. Dumb. It rained so they had to have the commencement ceremony in the gym. Gabby still didn't talk to anyone. She posed for pictures with Claire Andale and held Aidan Golden's hand. Rianne had heard she was actually going out with him. That she liked him, even if he was going to college in Wyoming somewhere.

Luke avoided her eyes. Kip avoided her eyes. Kaj and Mercy posed for pictures with her. And then, instead of going out to Gullwing Lake to see the traditional fireworks they set off at the campgrounds, they all went to Kaj's house for a barbecue, with the parents and everything. It was still raining and the grass was wet and soupy, but they all pretended it was fine, stood under a little carport off the side of the house, crammed into the screen porch. Mai Vang did a big spread of delicious everything, including papaya salad and fruit smoothies and grilled kabob things. Her parents mingled with the Kovashes and the Vangs, her father, back from his new billet in Colorado, was full of loud laughing and handshaking and eating everything he piled on his paper plate. Her mother hung back beside him, shy and quiet, but smiling.

Kaj had invited tons of family, but she and Mercy and Rianne stood in a huddle in the kitchen, trying not to own up to how miserable and mediocre the end of high school had turned out to be. Though they couldn't say they missed her, their historic foursome was down to three with no Gabby. There was no Caleb, because of the hospital. No Kip, because Kaj had dumped him. No Luke, because everyone knew they broke up.

"Devin Trauger told me it was because you cheated," Kaj said. "Is that shit even true?"

Rianne downed her smoothie, wiped berry off her lip.

"Come on!" Mercy said. "You have to tell!"

"What if it is?" Rianne said.

"Well, who with?" Kaj asked. "Please tell me it was Aidan Golden," she said, crossing her fingers and looking skyward like she was begging for a miracle. "Please please please!"

Rianne paused, knowing she would tell and knowing it would feel both good and bad to do so. "It was that one Russian guy," she said.

"The one guy who looked like a troll? The short Dracula guy?"

"No! That's his roommate. No, the tall blond. The bouncer at the Pumphouse. The one who made the vodka."

"Him?" Kaj had practically spat out her food. "That freak with the shiny shoes?"

Rianne couldn't help giggling. Sergei's shoes were sort of ridiculous.

"When did that happen?"

"A while ago," Rianne said. Which wasn't totally a lie.

"And Luke's that fucking pissed about that?" Kaj again. "Him? Luke fucking Pinsky?"

"Kaj . . . ," Mercy started.

Rianne waved it off. Spooned another pile of papaya salad into her mouth. Finished her smoothie. Thought of Luke's family, the weird tense glances they gave her at graduation. How she had to pull her dad back from going over to talk to them, pinching his wrist and whispering, "Dad, you can't, we broke up," and Dean Wynne had looked at her skeptically.

"Well, that was crappy timing, Rianne," Dean Wynne said. "Could have at least had one last good summer together."

Rianne thought about Luke looking past her, over her shoulders, beyond her. Not even a hint of the guy who'd wanted her to move in with him. Who loved her. Who gave her a ring with a purple stone that was now buried in the bottom of her red lacquered jewelry box.

"It doesn't even matter anymore, you guys," she said, tossing her paper plate and plastic fork into the trash under the sink. "I mean, really. Come on. Everything's starting over again. It's all brand-new."

SIXTEEN

"YOU CAN'T LIVE here," her father said.

"Oh my god," her mother said.

"It's not done yet," Rianne said. "And this has to be some kind of an accident. It did not look like this yesterday. Benji the land-lord guy said . . ."

"Are you kidding? The plaster's shot. That wiring looks like it's a hundred goddamn years old. And this?" He didn't have to elaborate. The floor was not a floor but a puddle. The grounds crew hadn't moved a gutter back in place when they came to mow, flooding the window well in Rianne's apartment, soaking the plaster until it crumbled to the studs. She didn't want to ask if it was Luke's family's business that did the landscaping.

Of course, this was the day her dad was back for graduation. June second. She had promised her mom that she would show them her new place. Benji had put in new drywall and they were supposed to start painting in a few days. Soon, he told her. Pretty soon, we'll get the paperwork.

Rianne walked over to the dehumidifier that Benji had her run when she was doing demo on the walls and flicked it on. "That thing helps," she said. "It'll dry things out."

"Honey, did you pay anything for this place?" her mother asked.

"Lucy, look at this shit! It's a fucking flooded hole!"

She held in her arms her red lacquered jewelry box. Her dresser was in the back of her dad's truck, along with her bed and the unrolled corkboard from above it. She had hoped Benji would let her store things here until they could paint. Then she would put the corkboard up. Pin up new pictures. New memories.

"Dean, keep your voice down."

"Keep my voice down! This place probably has black fucking mold. This Benji dude is probably some slumlord running a scam on her! This is no place to live, Rianne."

"Did you sign any papers, honey?" her mother asked, her hand light on Rianne's arm.

"Who cares even if she did!" Her father was red-faced; his bare forearms kept snapping out, pointing at the sad apartment. "You couldn't be legally bound to live in a place like this."

She set the jewelry box against her hip, adjusting her bra strap under her backpack. This was unreal. This couldn't be happening. She had come so goddamn close to figuring this out. Her own place, at a low price.

"You cannot live here, honey," her father said. "I refuse to allow it. I refuse to let you have my truck if you insist on this. I cannot condone it. I will not."

He sounded like something from the Bible. So serious and old. Her mother stood beside her father and her face looked pained and sorry.

"Do you want us to talk to the landlord, Rianne?" her mother said.

"I don't know where he is," she mumbled. "And I don't want Dad to talk to him right now."

"Oh, I plan on talking to him," Dean Wynne said, making a face one last time at the disastrous apartment and heading to the hallway. "I have a whole bunch of things to say about this bullshit." She followed him, and her mother followed her.

"Dad, please!" Rianne raced to kept stride with him, the jewelry box clutched in her arms clacking with its treasure. "Don't say anything! He was just being nice!"

"Grown men aren't nice to girls your age about shit like this," Dean Wynne said. His face had the same wrinkled-up look she often saw on her mother's. Once they reached the street where the trucks were parked, her mother looked relieved to be outside. She pulled Dean Wynne toward her little car and they had a conversation that was tense and involved Dean nodding but still looking pissed. Rianne stood beside the tarp her father had secured over her stuff in the flatbed of his truck. In the front seat was her volleyball duffel, packed to bursting with summer clothes and her makeup and shower stuff. She had thought, stupidly, that she might just stay in the place tonight. At least store her stuff here. It was exactly one day after the deadline her mother gave her back on New Year's Day, which was an achievement in itself, though obviously not the perfection Renata would have achieved.

Now it was clear how dumb the idea was. All the hours of pulling down the old wall, of cleaning and sweeping and helping Benji, hauling the contractor bags, scrubbing the toilet, dreaming about her own place? Gone. For nothing.

Her mother approached her, her hand gripping her purse strap, her face serene and calm. "Honey, I'm really proud of you. This was all a very good thing. Good intentions, for sure. But, let's try to figure out a better situation. You have no idea what kind of problems this might bring."

Rianne felt herself want to cry. She saw herself let them have it, saw herself give up. Saw them drive all the way home, passing all the familiar places: roundabout, Planet Tan, Liquor Barrel, the high school, the Goodwill on the highway where her mother was emptying out her house. Saw all her boxes go into some storage pod, or stacked back in the garage. Saw them sweat to move the bed and box spring back up the stairs to her empty room. Saw her whole life going in reverse, until everything she had done was undone, Sergei, Luke, Aidan, Gabe, Devin, the hat trick guys, Eli. All the money she'd earned gone, the truck she drove now driven by the previous owner, and then driving backward to the factory that made it, which probably wasn't even in the United States, for all she knew.

And then Renata would be there, playing tennis and teasing

her, and her father's vacations would erase into fun they'd never had. All her friends unmade, invisible to her, and her school reports turned to zeros, all her yearbooks unstacking until there was nothing but her elementary school photos, her first year of kindergarten, the drive from the airport to live here without Dean Wynne.

She said okay. She said she was sorry. Her mother nodded and patted her cheek and said they'd meet her back at home, that they'd have some lunch. That they'd talk. She got in her father's truck and drove straight to Sergei's apartment. He didn't answer right away and she stood there, feeling like she might cry again. She wouldn't cry in front of him. She wouldn't. She had cried in front of Luke that one day, for such a stupid thing. She wouldn't cry in front of Sergei. She called him and he didn't answer. She texted him. Waited. She stood under the front awning until the rain stopped. She was sweating and could feel the heat of the day rising. She had to work today at three, covering Kaj's shifts while she was in Iowa visiting some relatives.

She called him again. Praying that he'd pick up. His voice mail was a few words in Russian. She didn't leave a message. She texted. The mailman came, and she stepped out of the way so he could fill up the boxes in the entryway. She watched him sort each slot, folding magazines and promotional flyers. She saw the Planet Tan logo on one of them. Summer was a slow time for tanning, especially when the weather was nice. Though it looked like maybe the rain was going to let up and clear off.

The mailman huffed past her, noise from his earbuds

crackling as he walked away. She was getting hungry; the scent of Taco John's whirled in the air, not entirely appetizing, but also reminding her that she had skipped breakfast. What she was doing here wasn't clear. It made her embarrassed that she did things for guys, not for herself. The apartment was supposed to be about her own life, but really she wanted to have her own space for Sergei. And now he was gone. Not answering her calls. What did he have to do, anyway? She had no idea. All she knew of what he'd been doing lately was that he was having sex with her.

Her phone buzzed with a text and she went into the entryway to read it where there was no glare.

Luke.

want to see you, just for a little bit

She texted back: *why?*

nothing serious. Just have to tell you something

She was about to reply when Sergei was behind her.

"Rianne? You are here?"

"Yes," she said, shoving her phone in her back pocket.

He kissed her, gripped her ponytail.

"I go to liquor store." He held a paper bag with a bottle inside it and pushed back the paper to show her: Johnnie Walker Red.

"I called you. Like ten times?"

He pulled out a phone from his pocket. "I get new one," he said. "Old one has bad battery."

"Did you walk to the phone place?"

"Yes. Is in same place as Liquor Barrel. And suntan place where you work."

She felt her phone buzz in her pocket. She hoped Luke wouldn't call.

"Are you ready to go now? When is your ticket for?"

"I have to buy. You haven't told me yet."

"Can we go tonight?"

He kissed the side of her mouth, tugged on her ponytail. "I like this."

"My hair? Or my idea?"

"Both of these things."

"So, can we?"

"Tonight, no. Tomorrow, yes. Let me pack, my beauty. I have most of what I require in my hands. But I may need some clothes, yes?" He squeezed her around the waist.

She leaned against his chest, breathed in and out for a minute. He ran his hands up and down her back. She was sweaty from moving. She was always sweaty around him. She wanted to go inside and get clean. Strip everything off in his shower and give up. Let the rain rot all her furniture under the tarp of her dad's truck.

"Let us go, yes?"

"I've got to . . ." She pointed toward the truck. "More things to move."

"For your mother."

"Yes."

"Give me passport, can you? Then I make reservation."

She collected the passport out of the red lacquered jewelry box and rushed back to deliver it.

"You are my beauty," he said to her, kissing her one last time. "Always ready. Like a little puppy."

She nodded, he smiled back. But she still felt that unbearable gulping feeling like she needed to cry.

She pretended everything was fine and slowly drove home. Everything seemed to slow down. Everything seemed to sizzle inside her body. She was leaving tomorrow. She was leaving. Sergei had her passport. He had money. She parked her father's truck in the driveway, saw a text from Sergei: *car tmrw at 9*

She texted it to him, her body still feeling liquid and bubbly. Was she going to be sick? She felt like she was about to be caught at something.

Her father stood out in the yard and stared at her while she jumped out of the cab. She hovered beside the truck, wondering what to do with everything in the back.

"I'll take care of that, sweetheart," he said as she jumped out of the cab. He took her hand. "Go inside. Your mother made some lunch."

Her mother made turkey and cheddar sandwiches on kaiser rolls and a salad with grapes and berries and pineapple. She had the only plate on the table and she sat and ate alone while her mother fussed in the kitchen: filling the dishwasher, putting away the mayo and mustard, twisting the tie on the bag of rolls, wiping the counter with wide, decisive arcs. She looked at the kitchen with its empty walls, her mother's living room with nothing but the chaise lounge in it now. For some reason, she felt sad about the corkboard. She had hated emptying it and had felt beholden to filling it back up. The pictures from magazines weren't valuable but she had felt terrible throwing them away. The pictures of her friends she had stuffed in a box with school papers and folders. You can look at them someday later, she told herself. Her friends all had pictures everywhere online, anyway. Print pictures were special but they weren't the only record anymore. Mercy thought she was nuts for making a point to print them out on photo paper, which was expensive as hell. She didn't have a camera anymore, beyond the one in her phone, which had a scratched lens.

Maybe Sergei would buy her a new camera. Or a new phone. That seemed to be his answer for most of life's problems. No wonder everyone wanted to be rich. It wasn't that being rich meant your life was so luxurious. It only meant that things weren't as big of a hassle all the time.

Her last night at her mom's house was so normal in some ways. Except for that she just helped her dad drag the mattress and box spring into Renata's piano room, which was now empty except for some boxes and a rolled-up area rug.

Except for the fact that it was the last one and only she knew it. Her parents warily helped stack her other belongings into the garage, not getting real specific about the next destination of these items. Her mother was being protective and gentle now, but Rianne knew this could easily change and Lucy Hettrick might call her back into the living room and bark out new proclamations about what Rianne needed to do with her life next. This was happening to her father, bit by bit.

After dinner, her parents decided to see a movie and invited her but she said she had plans. Her mother holding her father's hand while slipping her flip-flops on in the front hallway made her stomach pinch again. Her mother wore a summer dress and a hoodie and the seam of gray down the center part in her hair was so bright, so tidy, that it looked intentional. Like her mother was saying, *Yes, I am old, I don't give a fuck, this is my hair and this hoodie is the same one I wear to yoga class and this is the man I divorced but now who I smile at so happily when he returns every few weeks that you'd never be able to guess that I once hated him so much that I removed him, so forcefully and completely, from my life, from my daughters' lives. But I don't care about that, and what you think. I'm going to the movies with him now, in this tiny little town where I grew up. And soon he'll be back here for good.*

She spent the night looking through bathroom drawers for travel-size tubes of shampoo and conditioner, lotion and toothpaste. After packing up everything she thought she might need—swimsuit, extra tampons, a blank journal she'd received as a graduation gift from her aunt Emma—she threw a quilt over the bare mattress and lay down. She was exhausted. There were texts on her phone from Kaj, who had sent her a picture of some girl in a bikini made out of slices of pizza for a joke, and Mercy, who was coming over to pick up some workout clothes Rianne had borrowed.

And two more texts from Luke:

you want me to be patient, fine

im the most patient mfer youll ever meet, girly

She liked knowing he was patient. He was waiting for an answer. Of course he would be. It made her feel rich, letting him stand by for a reply.

She was asleep before her parents even came back from the movie.

"You are ready?" Sergei was standing over her where she sat waiting out front of his apartment, sitting on the curb changing into her sandals. She wore her black sundress from graduation so she'd look nice at the airport but with her running shoes so the walk over here wouldn't give her blisters. The strap of her duffel bag made a red mark on her neck, which he touched lightly with his fingers.

"Yes," she said, standing now, hitching her handbag on her shoulder.

"You are only woman in world who is ready so quickly." He smiled.

"I hope you're worth it."

"I am not. But I will be the trick of you. These are the only things?"

"Yes."

"I cannot even carry anything for you. You are too good, my beauty."

"What do you mean?" she asked. "That I am too good?"

He smiled.

"Exactly what I said."

"No, but why did you say that?"

"*Pochemuchka*, you do not learn. It is better to don't ask all the questions. It is better to believe what a person tells you."

She didn't know what to say to that, so she asked if he had the tickets. "We check in at airport," he said. He reached into his messenger bag for her passport and handed it over, then put on some sunglasses.

"You have said your good-byes?" he asked, scanning for their ride. He had said he'd called a car, and she didn't know if he meant a taxi or something else.

She nodded, not wanting to think of it. Mercy had dropped by briefly last night and Rianne had listened to her talk about Caleb, never once mentioning her plans, knowing Mercy would freak out about it. She would send Mercy a postcard once she had arrived and tell her all the cool stuff and then Mercy would see it was fine.

But she hadn't said anything to her parents at all. They had gone for breakfast without her, and planned a day of errands and other move-related stuff. She had waved to them from her bed in Renata's piano room, unable to even acknowledge their leaving. She expected to be in the air by the time they might wonder where she was.

Then a black sedan with tinted windows pulled into the parking lot.

Sergei stood tall and reached for her hand, just as she reached for her duffel.

"Driver gets it," he said, pulling her aside.

And then the driver jumped from the front, a man in sunglasses and a suit, with a gold name tag pinned to his lapel, popped the trunk as he rushed to open the backseat door. He introduced himself but she was so embarrassed at how fancy it was, that she didn't say anything. Sergei took her handbag and gestured for her to get in the car, then handed his messenger bag to the driver and got in beside her.

He belted himself in. "You as well," he said, gesturing to her seat belt.

She clicked it on. She stared forward as Sergei checked his phone. She could hear the driver putting their bags into the trunk and then seconds later he was back in the front seat, fiddling with dials and making a note into his iPad.

"Minneapolis-Saint Paul Airport, terminal one, correct?" the driver asked. She noticed he had very curly hair that bunched up around his ears, which stuck out quite noticeably, and were pierced, with little silver hoops. She wondered why a man with such big ears would choose to call more attention to them with jewelry.

"Yes," Sergei said. "But let us wait a minute before we go."

"Knock when you're ready," the driver said, and he rolled up the privacy window so he was now hidden to them behind tinted glass as well.

"Why are we waiting? Is something wrong?"

"Is Russian custom," he said. "Strange tradition, yes. But we always do, before a journey. You sit and wait some minutes before you leave."

"What for?"

"Is to keep bad luck from following you when you travel. The evil spirits."

"What?"

"Shh. We must be silent. Just a moment. Then we go."

She put his hand over hers. The sun was blaring bright now, but the tinted windows made everything feel so cool and calm. Sergei's hair was white in the glare, the hair on the back of his hands golden.

"For our good luck," he said, finally, knocking on the privacy glass. He squeezed her knee and kept holding her hand tight in his, both of their hands a lopsided fist resting on the tight expanse of her dress across her thighs. "Let us go now, you and I?" he added. He kissed her, then he pulled out his phone to check a text.

The driver started the car and it slowly pulled out of the parking lot. Even the deliberate, careful way the car moved felt luxurious, wealthy. She rubbed her thumb over Sergei's hand on her lap, skimmed a finger over his knuckles, briefly nudging the links of his watch. She felt scared and a little turned on and very fancy. Very mature.

She watched the houses and lawns pass by. The elementary school where Luke mowed the lawn. The park where she and her friends hung out and played volleyball and watched boys play summer league. Other places, ones they weren't going by, also slipped across the screen of her mind. The church where Caleb's family went, the smoothie shop Kaj's mom ran, the strip mall of businesses that everyone zipped and unzipped through all week, every week: Planet Tan, Liquor Barrel, Tobacco World. The Jimmy John's where Jeff Melk got arrested. Cuddy's. The Pumphouse. Taco John's, Pizza Palace, Herberger's, the movie theater, the Goodwill where everyone got Halloween costumes.

Their hands in her lap meant she wasn't alone and that she didn't need to stay here. The passport in her bag too. The man beside her, now speaking on his phone in Russian—to his cousin? to one of his brothers?—had no intention of turning back.

As they pulled onto the highway, all the morning's clouds were burned off and there was nothing ahead of them but sunlight, sunshine streaming all around the interior of the backseat until she could imagine her skin warming and browning, Sergei's unknown words filling up the gaps in her brain, clogging the screen of her mind where all the other vocabulary had uselessly bided its time until graduation. Sergei was still speaking to the invisible person on the other end of the line, perhaps telling them all about who she was, where they were going, why they were headed there. She squinted and Sergei handed her his sunglasses, a heavy pair of Ray-Bans that she knew had to be real. Expensive. Costing probably more than the rent of her abandoned shithole of an apartment. Costing more than maybe anything she had ever bought. She put them on and he squeezed her knee again and they kept heading north, right into the light, and the whole time she felt blinded, felt beautiful, the sun drenching her face in what was to come.

ACKNOWLEDGMENTS

As always, several people helped me in writing this book and deserve mentioning.

Michael Bourret, you are such a nice person and I am so lucky to have you. You make it so I can concentrate on the writing above all other details and it is such a relief.

Thank you to Alyssa Miele for her editorial insight and Erin Fitzsimmons for her beautiful cover.

I received technical assistance from Swen-Marie Germann, former high school teammate and dream athlete, who gave advice on volleyball; Stephan Eirik Clark and Kaia Lawton, who helped with various Russian names, words, and sayings; and May Lee-Yang, who offered me great perspective on the character of Kaj Vang.

Special thanks to Kaia Lawton, again, for being an early reader who helped me imagine Sergei into existence.

Thank you to Brandon Terrell, Shaina Olmanson, Stan Sveen, and Beth Spencewood for reading early chapters and providing feedback.

Christa Desir listened to me spin many versions of this story on our daily telephone dog walks (as well as cleaning up my lousy grammar). My henchwomen Martha Brockenbrough and Elana K. Arnold also bolstered me in countless ways on the virtues of unlikable characters.

In my head, there are always the girls I grew up with, and the stories of our sleazy, thrill-seeking youth. Amy, Becky, Cheresa, Danielle, Kristin, Hallie, and Makeba: thank you for being some of my best teenage memories.

Finally, to my editor, Alexandra Cooper, who worked endlessly to defend my writing tics, which she repetitively and flatteringly insists are really just "voice." Thank you for never shying away from the uncomfortable and difficult topics that I enjoy writing about, which was so important this time, because I was afraid to write about being a girl, especially the girl I once was. You never made me feel ashamed about creating the story of Rianne Hettrick-Wynne, but rather you encouraged and aided me in bringing her out into the world, where we can all see her for what she is and for what she might yet become. I cannot thank you enough.